RETURN OF THE STAR

A JACK SAGE WESTERN - BOOK 3

DONALD L. ROBERTSON

COPYRIGHT

Return of The Star

Copyright © 2023 Donald L. Robertson
CM Publishing

All rights reserved. No part of this publication may be reproduced, distributed or transmitted in any form or by any means, including photocopying, recording, or other electronic or mechanical methods, without the prior written permission of the publisher, except in the case of brief quotations embodied in critical reviews and certain other noncommercial uses permitted by copyright law.

Publisher's Note: This is a work of fiction. Names, characters, and incidents are a product of the author's imagination. Locales and public names are sometimes used for atmospheric purposes. Any resemblance to actual people, living or dead, or to businesses, companies, or events, is completely coincidental. For information contact:

Books@DonaldLRobertson.com

Return Of The Star

ISBN: 979-8-9855100-6-5

❦ Created with Vellum

1

March 12, 1872

Jack's three horses and mule were lined up downstream, drinking. He knelt, with one hand lifting the cold, glass-clear water from Live Oak Creek. It was delicious. His submerged canteen gurgled, filling in the creek.

He took another drink from the stream and suddenly raised his head. The faint report of shots echoed through the hills. Jack Sage was familiar with gunshots, and it took only an instant to recognize them for what they were. He drank the last handful he had scooped from the creek, grabbed his canteen, and, as he stood, slapped the stopper back in, dropping the strap over his saddle horn. The full canteen slapped against Thunder and the big gray head turned to stare at Jack.

He was a beautiful gray, his color smooth from head to tail. Muscles rippled strong beneath his lustrous coat. Jack had bought him and Pepper, a striking chestnut, from Truman Shelby, a man well known for raising superior horses. They had to be strong to carry Jack Sage's two hundred pounds of muscle spread across his massive frame. Almost four inches over six feet tall, the man provided an imposing sight, but he needed a large and powerful animal to carry him. When he purchased Pepper and Thunder, he had also bought Dusty, but Dusty and Buster, a fourteen-year-old wrangler, had formed an immediate bond. Jack gave the boy the horse because he didn't want to break either's heart.

The shots were faint, but looking in the direction of the sound, through the dark green of the pecan and live oak trees, his wide-set gray eyes picked out black smoke lifting above the rocky ridge. It was faint at first but quickly grew thicker. He led Pepper and the other two animals, Stonewall his mule and Smokey the grulla, to a grassy spot along the creek and tied them with slipknots, just in case something happened to him.

Once the animals were secured, Jack Sage swung into the saddle and turned Thunder toward the relentless pound of gunfire and thickening smoke. He broke out of the tall trees along the creek at a dead run and guided Thunder up a rocky hillside. Thunder topped out on the long plateau and raced through the tall grass, dodging around prickly pear and small cedars.

Jack Sage leaned forward over Thunder's neck. He slipped the leather thongs from his holsters and checked his 1866 Winchester, loose and ready in the scabbard. Nearing the plateau's edge, he slowed Thunder and guided him behind a large cedar. The smoke, rising from just ahead of them, was thick and black. He halted his horse behind the cedar and leaped from the saddle, leaving Thunder ground hitched.

Easing around the right side of the tree, its biting scent strong in his nostrils, he brought the rifle to his shoulder. There were eight men, mounted and firing at the house. Occasionally, a rifle would fire from one of the windows, with little effect. The rate of fire from the men made it difficult for anyone inside to expose themselves long enough to fire accurately.

The house was typical of German construction in this part of Texas, made with the rocks of the area and large timbers. It was a solid structure. The barn was built in the same manner, belching flames from the roof. With the alternating thick timbers and rock of the walls, the roof would burn, but the sides would probably have little damage.

Jack heard a horse scream from inside the barn. *Animals are in the barn,* Jack thought. He brought his rifle up to his shoulder, aimed for only a second, the front sight firm on an outlaw's chest. Jack squeezed the trigger and switched to another target.

In his peripheral vision, he saw the first man jerk and slump in the saddle, but he was already working the lever, his front sight settling on another outlaw.

Before he could fire, someone burst from the house, running for the barn. *Stupid,* Jack thought, *the horse's scream must have brought them out.* Jack had picked his next target and was beginning to squeeze the trigger when he saw one of the horsemen turn to race toward the running person. He switched his sight to the pursuer and pulled the trigger.

The instant he fired, he knew he had missed. *Too big a hurry,* he thought. *Slow down.* The rider was reaching, stretching far out of the saddle to grab a young girl, her skirts flapping against her churning legs as she ran through the dusty yard. Jack fired again. This time he didn't miss. His target had leaned to the right. The impact of the bullet carried him the remainder of the way out of his saddle. He rolled across the ground and was still.

The girl disappeared into the burning barn. Jack breathed a sigh of relief. The gun, from inside the house, fired again, and one of the outlaws jerked from the impact. The remainder of the men turned and raced their horses out of the yard. Jack threw one more shot at them. He watched his target jerk, but the man stayed in his saddle.

Jack worked the lever of his rifle and brought it down from his shoulder, relief filling him that the kid in the barn was alright, when a horse and rider burst out of the barn. The child was gripped tight in the rider's grasp. Jack swung his rifle back to his shoulder and tracked the man until he disappeared, chasing after the other outlaws. There was no shot. If he tried to fire, he might hit the child. The only option was to wait. He immediately saw the door burst open, and a woman charged out the front door, rifle in hand, wailing. He leaped back to Thunder, swung into the saddle, and quickly made his way down the rocky hillside toward the house and burning barn.

The woman must have heard him, for she swung around, bringing her rifle up to bear on Jack. He raised both hands and kept Thunder walking slowly toward her. As he drew closer, he could see she was wounded. Either a bullet or a splinter had grazed her head. Her blonde hair was matted with the red of blood.

He called out to her, "Don't shoot, ma'am. I'm not with that bunch."

In a high, desperate voice, she cried, "How can I know that?"

"Ma'am, two of those men lying in your yard are carrying my bullets. You're just gonna have to trust me."

She waited a moment longer, the long rifle trained on Jack's chest, and then she let her arms drop, the rifle across her thighs.

"Gotta get to the barn and get those animals out!" Jack shouted. He urged a reluctant Thunder toward the fire and smoke. Reaching the barn, he leaped off and dashed inside. Flames were roaring from the roof, sucking both burning and charred straw and hay upward in a hurricane of wind. A milk cow near the back was lowing frantically. There were two plow horses in separate stalls. The first, untied, was rearing and smashing at the stall gate with his hoofs. Jack ran to the first gate, yanked it open, and raced to the next one. The horse charging for the open barn door just missed the woman running behind Jack.

The big horse in the second stall was tied to a post. He frantically shook his head and pulled, the rope tied too short for him to rear. Jack dashed in, yanked the slipknot, jumping clear of the big animal. Feeling its freedom, the horse spun, flung itself out of the stall, and raced for the open barn door through which its companion had disappeared.

Jack saw the woman open the stall where the milk cow was tied. She ran in and copied Jack's movements, releasing the slipknot. Over the crackling and roar of the flames, Jack could hear her calm voice trying to soothe the cow's fear. Though the animal's eyes were wide, she came to the woman, who took the rope and calmly led her toward the barn door.

Passing Jack, the woman yelled above the noise of the flames, "These are the only three in the barn. Everything else is safe. Let's get out of here."

Jack nodded. He had no desire to spend any more time than necessary in a burning barn. He followed the woman out. Behind them, a roofing joist collapsed and crashed to the floor, sending sparks flying in all directions. Jack jumped, looking up and back at the blue sky he could see where part of the roof had been. When he turned back, he saw the woman jerk to a stop and stiffen. Automatically he drew his Remington and stepped outside.

The fella who had been chasing the girl was sitting up, one hand holding his shoulder and the other holding a big .44-caliber Colt. He was pale, but the muzzle of the revolver was steady, pointed directly at Jack's midsection. Jack Sage didn't hesitate. He lunged away from the woman, drawing the man's shots toward him, while at the same time pulling the Remington's trigger.

His move surprised the man. The outlaw's reaction was slow, and the .36-caliber lead ball plowed into his heart before he could pull the trigger. The muzzle of the outlaw's Colt dropped and was resting in the dirt when he fired. There was a blast, a cloud of dust, and it was over. His hand relaxed from around the revolver, and he toppled to the ground, dead.

Jack approached the dead man, the Remington covering him. "Sorry, ma'am. I know better. I should have checked him before going into the barn."

"I'm glad you didn't, mister. If you had, Klara might be dead."

"Klara?"

"Our milk cow. I've owned her since I was a girl. I'd hate to lose her."

The cow had wandered out of the yard and was chewing a mouthful of grass.

Then the woman realized what she had said, and broke into tears. "But I did lose my sweet Marlene. What am I going to do? What will I tell Wilhelm? I didn't protect my Marlene."

Jack checked the other man who lay prone on the ground, the first he had shot from the hillside. After ensuring the man was dead, he turned back to the lady.

Two children dashed from inside the house to stand next to their mother. A boy who looked to be around eight, and a little girl who could be no older than five. The boy stood close to his mother, but independent, while the little girl held tight to the woman's dress.

Jack glanced at Thunder, who had found the watering trough and was helping himself. He looked back at the woman. "You've been hurt, ma'am."

She touched her head. The flow of blood had almost stopped, oozing only a little. "I shall be fine, sir. I want to thank you. I do not know what might have happened if you hadn't come along. My name is Deborah Schmidt, and these are my other two children, Elke and Dirk. My husband, Wilhelm, should be returning soon. He went to town. If they can see the smoke from Fredericksburg, he will certainly be quick about it. I'm afraid he is going to be upset with me for losing my Marlene."

"Mrs. Schmidt, I sure don't know what went on in your house, but from what I could see, it looked to me like she wanted to save the animals. Almost immediately after the horse screamed, she came dashing out. You were busy trying to fight off those outlaws. You couldn't suspect she would dash out like that."

Mrs. Schmidt took a handkerchief from one of the pockets of

the blue apron she wore and blew her nose. "Yes, I should have known. She is as attached to Klara as I am, maybe more."

"Ma'am, you hit one of those marauders."

She looked up, blue eyes wide with surprise. "I hit him?"

"You sure did. I saw him slump over in the saddle."

"Oh." She looked down and, without thinking, pulled her children closer. Her face came up again. "What is your name, sir?"

"I'm Jack Sage, ma'am."

"Thank you for rescuing us, Mr. Sage."

Jack's response was drowned out in the sound of galloping horses and a wagon racing so fast it sounded as if it would rattle itself apart at any moment. Horsemen pulled up. Their guns covered Jack.

The leader of the group looked around the yard, at the now smoldering barn, and the four people in the yard. "Holster your guns, boys. This ain't no outlaw we got here. Get buckets and see if you can get that fire out. Looks like it's pretty much burned itself out, but see if there's any gear remaining that can be saved."

The men with him leaped from their mounts and ran to the watering trough, where several buckets sat. Each grabbed one, filled it, and headed inside. The ranger watched them for a moment and turned his attention back to Mrs. Schmidt.

He touched his hat. "Mrs. Schmidt, you've been hurt. You need help."

"No, Captain Heath, not for me, but I do need help for my Marlene. The outlaws took her."

The wagon was behind the riders. As soon as it pulled into the yard, the driver, a man of taller than average height, yanked the horses to a stop and leaped out. He dashed to Deborah Schmidt's side. The children ran to him and each grabbed a leg as he took his wife in his arms. "You're hurt. Your head is bleeding. Let's go inside, and I can see to it."

She pushed back from her husband and shook her head, then dropped it in shame. "I lost our Marlene."

The man's face turned pale, his eyes flew wide, and he stared at his wife. "She's dead?"

She shook her head violently. "Oh, no, Wilhelm. She's not dead. She was taken by those bad men. They took her and rode away."

Wilhelm grabbed his wife by the shoulders, color returning to his face. He placed a finger under her chin and gently raised it until she was looking into his eyes. "Debbie, we'll get her back. She'll be alright. You'll see."

Mrs. Schmidt looked deep into the eyes of her husband. Tears flowed down her cheeks. "Oh, Wilhelm, do you think so? Do you think it's possible we will get our Marlene back? And if we do, what condition will she be in? What kind of terrible things will those awful men do to our little girl?"

"I'm hoping they'll do nothing, but honey, we can't control that. We can only hope and pray for her."

Captain Heath had dismounted. "Mrs. Schmidt, I don't think they'll harm her other than scaring her mighty bad, but it's almighty important we find her. I've had reports of other children south of here being grabbed. It's a gang who sells these young folks. We've got to find her before they meet up with their contacts. It's my understanding these children are taken to the west coast and loaded on ships. But let me tell you, it's a long way between here and the west coast. We're gonna find 'em. We'll bring your daughter back."

Jack listened to the exchange and thought, *I sure wouldn't be making those kinds of promises. In fact, I'd say the heck with that barn, and I'd be on my way after that bunch right now. Time is wasting.*

Deborah Schmidt looked up at her husband, grasped his arm and turned him toward Jack. "Wilhelm, they would have gotten all of us if it hadn't been for this man. He saved us. He also saved Klara and the horses."

Wilhelm thrust out his hand. "Thank you. I am Wilhelm Schmidt. Most people call me Will."

Jack took the man's hand. It was firm and calloused from hard work. "Jack Sage, Will. Pleased to meet you. I only helped a bit. I got here in time to see your wife shoot one of those vermin. She made it pretty hard on them."

Will, eyes wide again, looked down at his wife. "You shot one of them?"

In a low voice filled with hate and anger, she said, "I wish I had shot them all. If I had, our Marlene would still be here."

The ranger captain interrupted. "Mr. Sage, can I have a word with you?" He turned to the Schmidts. "I need to talk to Mr. Sage. Why don't you go inside and take care of Mrs. Schmidt's wound. We'll come in when we're through."

"Sure," Wilhelm said, reached down, and picked up Elke. The little girl threw her arms around her papa's neck and squeezed. Dirk crowded closer to Will's leg. The man dropped a hand to his son's head and stroked it as they walked inside.

Jack waited for the captain to speak.

"You said you're Jack Sage?"

Jack nodded.

"Are you the Jack Sage of Laredo, Cherry Creek, and Oklahoma?"

Jack placed both hands on his hips and leaned back, feeling the stretch in his spine and listening to the vertebrae pop. "I've been to all those places."

The captain nodded. "Good. How'd you like to join the Texas Rangers?"

Jack shook his head. "Not today. I'm headed west. I've never seen California, and I've a hankering to go."

Captain Heath looked down at the ground. "Look, Mr. Sage, I really need your help. We can only trail this bunch for a ways. Then I've got to cut back north. There's some Comanches off the reservation in Oklahoma, and they're playing hob with our settlers. I've got a day, two at the most, but if we don't have any luck by then, I'll have to head out with my company. If you sign up, you can stay on their trail."

Jack stared at the ranger captain. "That's a sorry way to treat these folks."

The captain's face turned hard. "Those folk's up north care about their families just as much as these do. I can only do my best. Now I asked you a question. Do you want to help or not? I'll swear you in and give you captain's pay, same as me, one hundred dollars a month. You provide your horses, ammunition, and weapons. We'll cover your food."

Jack laughed. "What a great deal. You must be starving to death."

A corner of the captain's mouth turned up in a wry grin. "I thought about gettin' married, but I couldn't afford it. Figured at least the state of Texas would bury me when I get shot."

Jack nodded. "Who wouldn't want a free burial? When are you pulling out?"

"Soon."

"Alright. I'll ride with you. I don't promise I'll join up, but I'll go along for now."

"That'll have to do, for now. Let's ride."

Jack shook his head. "Hold on, I've got some horses and a mule tied back a ways. I didn't want to bring them into a fight."

Heath checked his men, who were still busy bringing equipment and supplies from the barn. "Why don't we swing by and get your animals and then work back and pick up the trail."

Jack stepped toward the house. "Good. I want to see if I can get a piece of clothing and a photograph of Marlene. If I get close on the trail, I may be able to round up some hounds, and there's always the possibility we may need to identify her body."

The captain winced at the thought of finding her dead, and the two men strode toward the front door.

2

Jack removed his hat and lowered his head prior to entering the door of the Schmidts' home. To the right was a large sitting room with a stone fireplace that took up most of the end wall. Several comfortable-looking chairs and a large, padded settee built to accommodate several people were situated near the fireplace.

To the left was a roomy kitchen and dining room. The solid, well-built table seated at least ten people, and this was where the Schmidt family was gathered. Will was wiping the blood from his wife's face while the children looked on with concerned curiosity.

"Come on in," Will said, "and leave the door open." He motioned for the two of them to sit at the table.

Jack spoke first. "Thanks, we'll stand. Time is important. Do you have a picture of Marlene and maybe an unwashed piece of clothing?" He saw the puzzlement on Deborah's face and quickly explained, "We need clothing with her scent on it. There's a possibility we might have the chance to use dogs to follow them." He knew the dogs would probably be used to locate her body, but there was no need to bring that gruesome thought to these parents' minds.

"Oh, yes. Just a moment." Deborah jumped up and ran to a back room.

As she was leaving the room, Jack said, "Mrs. Schmidt, if you could also pack a change of clothes for her. Marlene might need it when we find her."

Her voice brightened. "Oh, thank you. Of course she'll be needing clean clothes."

Moments later she returned with a pair of dirty pants, a picture of their daughter, and a change of clothing for her. She also brought a newspaper from the sitting room and laid it on the table.

She first folded and laid the small pair of pants in the center part of the paper and wrapped it around the clothing. She stepped to the kitchen counter, reached for a lower shelf, and brought out a ball of twine. With this, she tied the paper and set the package aside. She did the same with two more sheets of the newspaper, wrapping and tying the clean clothes and finally handing the two packages to Jack.

"Thank you, ma'am." Jack took the two packages gently from the distraught woman and asked her again, "Do you have that picture?"

"Oh, yes." Visibly exasperated with herself, she drew a photograph from a pocket in her apron and held it out to Jack. It was of a pretty ten-year-old blonde. A wide smile showed even teeth, and her eyes in the photograph almost twinkled.

After examining the photo, Jack looked into the tear-filled eyes of her mother. "She's a beautiful girl."

Deborah said, "She has blue eyes."

Wilhelm spoke up. "She looks just like her mama did at that age."

Deborah smiled at her husband. "She is such a sweet girl and always helpful. It seems she knows what is needed and immediately starts doing it. Work doesn't frighten her. It's like today. She heard our horses and dashed right out into that gunfire to save them."

"She's strong, too," Wilhelm added. "She even helps me in the barn and with the trees." He looked up at Jack, fighting the tears that were filling his eyes. "Please bring her back, Mr. Sage. We can't lose her. Promise me you'll bring her back."

Jack felt he could almost see the tortured soul of Wilhelm. "We'll do our very best, Mr. Schmidt." Jack felt a deep, intense anger. What kind of men would take children from their families and condemn them to such a horrible life? He made a silent promise. *Wilhelm, I will find the people who have done this to your daughter, and I will put an end to their devilry. These people will no longer steal children. I swear.* He cleared his throat. "If we're going to find Marlene, we must be on our way." He turned to the ranger. "Don't you agree, Captain?"

"Yes, we must."

Wilhelm stood and shook the captain's hand and took Jack's big hand in both of his. "Thank you, Mr. Sage, for saving my family. Now, please bring Marlene back to us."

Jack nodded to the man and turned to Deborah, whose tears were gone, and her face was calm.

She thrust her warm hand in his. "I don't know why, Mr. Sage, but I feel a bond with you. I believe you will bring our daughter back to us. I know you have appeared at this time to save us. Go with God."

Jack was silent. He nodded to her and, with the captain following, turned and stepped through the door. As he reached the sunlight, he heard the noise of racing wagons. Through the trees, wagon after wagon appeared, men, couples, and families. There must have been ten or twelve wagons.

Captain Heath stepped to Jack's side. "Family and friends. Both Wilhelm and Deborah grew up in Fredericksburg. Like us, those folks saw the smoke from town. It took them a little longer.

They had to get timber, tools, and other supplies, but I guarantee they'll have that barn rebuilt before the day is out."

Jack watched them pouring into the yard. "Not a bad place to live. Now, shall we get on the trail?"

JACK PULLED the cinch tight on Smokey, fastened it, and dropped the stirrup. After the hard run on Thunder, he elected to give him a rest. He reached up and scratched the grulla behind his ear. The horse rotated his head to make sure the hand reached the right spot. Jack chuckled. This horse and Stonewall had been with him for quite a while.

He glanced at the rangers watering their horses in the creek, and caught the eye of Captain Heath, who had been watching him.

When Heath saw the stirrup drop, he turned to his men. "Mount up. Cart, up here with me and Mr. Sage."

An older man with big hands and wide shoulders swung up onto a nice-looking lineback dun and turned him toward the captain. Jack watched the man approach. He had noticed him in the band of rangers, a quiet man in a sea of agitation. Steady green eyes had assessed Jack. Several of the rangers were talking excitedly when they pulled up at the Schmidts' home, but the quiet man had been off his horse and headed for the barn before Heath had issued his first order. Jack liked the look of him.

"Cart," Heath said, "this is Jack Sage. He'll be with us while we're chasing the bandits." He turned to Jack. "This is Taylor Cartwright. He goes by Cart. He's our tracker and probably the best in Texas."

Cart ignored the compliment, leaned forward and extended his hand. "Pleased to meet you, Mr. Sage. Looks like your ma didn't spare the vittles."

Jack grinned at the smaller man. "Call me Jack." Then his face grew serious. "We've got our work laid out for us."

Cart nodded. "That we do. We'll pick up the trail easy enough, but they'll have horses waiting somewhere ahead. This first leg, we've got to be careful not to push too hard, or they'll kill the girl and scatter."

Captain Heath nodded. "Yeah, they grabbed two girls outside of Austin. A chase was mounted pretty quick. Those animals must've felt cornered. They killed both of the girls and escaped into the hills. That's one reason we haven't pushed them hard here. We don't want to lose this one."

Jack turned to Cart. "The captain here seems to think you're a good tracker."

Cart shrugged his shoulders. "I get by. Learned my skill in the mountains, trapping beaver back when they was worth something. Been doin' it for quite a while."

Jack watched the man closely as he spoke. There was no pride in the man's eyes. They were steady and honest. He'd do. "What say we get on their trail?"

Cart nodded. "Yep. This is a good time. They should be relaxed now that they're away from your rifle. I'm sure having two men dropped will give them pause."

"Four," Jack said.

Cart's eyebrows rose in a question.

"Mrs. Schmidt hit one who stayed in the saddle, and so did I. Those two should slow them down."

"Good to know. Once they figger they ain't bein' follered, they'll probably pull up to take care of their men." Cart turned to the captain. "We might want to take it a mite easy, at least to start out."

Heath nodded. "Good idea."

Jack swung into the saddle.

Captain Heath eased his horse next to him and reached into his vest pocket. "Here, you'll be needing this. I dug it out of my saddlebags while you were switching horses." He pulled a ranger's captain badge from his pocket and tossed it to Jack.

He caught it and glanced at it before dropping it into his vest pocket. He started to remind the captain of his reservation back at the house but chose to forego the comment. He was going to accept the offer. He knew it, so it might as well be now. Jack gave the captain a nod. The three of them rode forward, the company waiting to follow. Jack looked over each man as he rode past. All looked to be good men. Most were young, but in this country, age didn't necessarily determine seasoning. Probably all of these men had been in gunfights before, and most of them had the experience of enforcing the law alone.

One of the men caught Jack's attention. He held his eyes with a stare that bordered on defiance. He was a big fella. Strong looking and hard. He was wearing gloves, so Jack couldn't assess the scars on his hands, if there were any. He'd bet there were. He put the thought out of his mind. He was wearing a badge again, and he had to admit, it felt good, although he hated the reason.

As they neared where the outlaws had raced away, Cart eased out ahead of the company, keeping an eye on the ground. They had ridden only a short distance when Cart turned his horse west and pointed at the ground. He had found their tracks.

Heath turned to Jack. "This might put them a couple of hours ahead of us, but they're going to have to stop and take care of the wounded men. That'll eat up their time."

Jack frowned. "If they're prone to killing the kids when pursuit gets too close, we sure don't want to ride up on them. What do you think about a couple of men riding ahead? Two might get an opportunity."

"I'm guessing the couple of men you're thinking of sending are you and Cart."

Jack watched Cart tracking. "You guess right. If you hold the rest of the company back, maybe we can surprise them and rescue the girl before they know what hit them."

Heath rode on in silence while Jack considered the alternatives. He went over them carefully. They could circle around and get in front of the outlaws, but they were far enough ahead it would be impossible to get around them today, and there was no telling what direction they would head out tomorrow. They could just charge into the gang. The outlaws' numbers had been reduced by four. They were at half-strength. There was no doubt the ranger company could overpower them, but would the girl survive? Jack pulled out her picture and gazed at it. *The girl,* he thought. *It makes it so much easier to think of her only as a captive, but that's impossible now. I have her picture. I know about her. I've got to save her and get her back with her parents.*

He returned the picture to his inside vest pocket. No, he and Cart slipping in, maybe tonight, was the best idea. Eyebrows raised, he glanced over to the captain.

Heath nodded. "Go ahead. As jumpy as this bunch is, I don't want to take the chance of spooking them. I'd hate to have to live with knowing it was my fault those folks would never see their daughter again."

"Thanks. You mind looking after my animals? I'll pick them up when I get back."

"Be glad to."

Jack tossed the three lead ropes to Heath, who immediately turned and motioned for one of the rangers to come up. It was the big fella. The man rode up, and Captain Heath tossed him the lead ropes. "Take care of these animals until Ranger Sage gets back."

The handsome young man's thick lips curled in a sneer. "I ain't takin' care of nobody's jackass."

Jack turned his head and locked his eyes on the young fella. He returned Jack's stare, hard and mean. Before Jack could say anything, the captain spoke up.

"You'll take care of whomever and whatever I tell you to. Do you understand me, Hud?"

There was a long period of silence before the ranger said, "Sure, Captain."

He started dropping back and gave Stonewall's lead rope a hard jerk. The mule's ears lay back, and he dug his feet into the ground.

Jack stopped Smokey in his tracks. "Listen to me, boy." Jack could see the ranger turn red at the use of *boy*. "I'm going ahead with Cart to try to save that little girl. I don't care a turkey track about whether or not you like taking care of my animals. But if you mistreat them, when I get back, I'll beat you with an inch of your life. You understand *me*?"

The boy spit. "You know where you can go, old man."

Jack had work to do. He had the girl to think about. He didn't want to be distracted by this prideful upstart. He turned to Heath. "When I get back, I'll take care of this. But my animals can't protect themselves from the likes of him. I'm not only holding him responsible, I'm holding you responsible. Is that clear?"

The captain's face turned red. "Are you threatening me?"

"Do you want me involved in this chase?" Jack could see Heath's chest expand and hear him release an audible blast of air.

"I'll make sure your animals are taken care of. Trust me." Heath then turned and gave Hud a cold look.

The young ranger held the captain's glare for only a moment. "I'll take good care of these animals until he gets back." He tossed his head toward Jack. "But then I'm teaching him you don't mess with a Texas Ranger."

The captain nodded once to Jack, who turned, spotted Cart disappearing in the cedars ahead, and urged Smokey into a fast walk.

JACK AND CART had followed the trail into some deep canyon country and had to be careful at each ridge to ensure they weren't seen. The trail had been easy to follow. It was obvious the outlaws weren't worried about pursuit, but a stray glance over their shoulder might catch a silhouette on a ridgeline or a glint from a rifle.

Cart leaned close to Jack. "This country is filled with caves. It's made up of sandstone. Wind and rain can cut into the rock until you've got a great hiding place. We have to be doubly careful. Not only can we be spotted on a ridgeline, we could ride within twenty feet of a cave mouth and not see them."

Cart stopped talking to gaze at the country ahead. They let the horses pick their way down a rocky hillside. Reaching the bottom, Cart turned to Jack again. "The one thing in our favor is that I know this country like the route to my outhouse. I've been all over it. I'm not sayin' I know it all, but I pretty much know it better than most folks except maybe the Injuns."

They rode slowly, trying to keep the sound of the horses' hooves to a minimum. The day was dying. The brilliant sun had turned a deep red as it drifted beneath rocky rims. A cloudless sky had first turned the color of fine-spun gold, then red and eventually purple. Now darkness was settling over the hill country. Cart dismounted, and Jack followed.

The tracker leaned close. "They cain't be far. There are two shallow cutouts up ahead, where the wind has worn the sandstone walls of the hills. One is across a canyon that's impossible for us to navigate at night, even with the moon we'll have later. I'm bettin', though, with the wounded men, they didn't make it that far. They'll stop at the first one."

Jack nodded. Cart started forward, leading his dun, and Jack followed suit. *Hopefully,* he thought, *we'll end this tonight and get Marlene home to her parents safely. If not, I'll follow them all the way to California because I'm going to save that girl.*

They continued in silence. All that was heard was the soft footsteps of the walking horses. From the distant hills came the yip of coyotes, followed by more barking and long, high-pitched howls. They made Jack chuckle silently. He always found it funny how two or three coyotes could sound like a dozen. Their howls filled the night, accompanying Jack and Cart as they moved slowly over the rocky ground.

Then there was a deeper, longer, more threatening howl, followed by another. Wolves. The coyotes shut up, and the night was left to the wolves. The deep howls lasted only a minute or so more, and then there was a thick, desolate silence that pervaded the night.

The horses were edgy now. The coyote howls hadn't bothered them, but those of the wolves had gotten their attention. Jack could feel the tension in Smokey. It was a deep ancestral thing, handed down from generation to generation. Wolves meant death, to man and beast. Not so much now with the advent of firearms, but those feelings were still there.

Cart halted.

Jack could see over the man. The winking of a fire was visible in the distance. Cart motioned for Jack to come forward. He eased Smokey next to Cart's dun and leaned close to the smaller man's ear. "That's them, right?"

Cart nodded. "Yep. But it's bad news. It looks like they already made it across the canyon. If that's the case, there's no way we can get to them tonight. They'd hear us long before we got there, and we'd probably break our necks trying to cross through those rocks."

Jack shook his head. He had really hoped he would be able to rescue this girl before she had to spend a night with those men.

"But that ain't all the bad news." He paused, looking around, obviously straining to hear every little sound of the night. "You heard those coyotes?"

Jack nodded.

"Notice how they shut up when the wolves started?"

Jack waited.

"That's because the coyote is one of the smartest animals

around, and he knows you don't mess with the wolves, especially when you've got a pack of 'em." Cart looked around again. "And, brother, we've got a pack of 'em tonight. We need to leave the horses and slip to the edge of the canyon so we can take a look, but if we leave the horses, the wolves might get 'em."

Jack considered Cart's explanation of the problems. "Cart, I've got an idea. Why don't you stay with the horses. I'll take my binoculars and slip ahead. Maybe I can at least get a good look at the camp."

"Good idea. I'll take the horses down to the bottom of this draw and build a fire. It won't be visible from where the outlaws are located, but it'll help keep the wolves away, and the company might see it. That'll make it easier for them."

Jack was already slipping the binoculars from his saddlebags. He also opened a sack and pulled out four horse biscuits. He took one and gave three to Cart. "Here, give one to each horse. The extra one's for you."

"For me?"

"Yeah, just try it. I'm bettin' you'll eat the whole thing." Jack moved carefully into the darkness. He could hear Cart slowly making his way down the ridge with the horses.

Jack worked his way slowly through the rocks. His foot slipped, and his shin crashed against a jagged boulder. It hurt like crazy, but thanks to his boot top, the blow didn't break the skin. He took two more steps, and the wolves howled again.

They were closer.

3

Jack slowly worked his way through the night. The outlaws' campfire had grown brighter. With his naked eye, he could make out men moving around the fire. A shallow cave protected them from the wind. It was more like Cart had called it, a cutout in the sandstone wall. A small tent was erected inside the mouth of the cutout, facing the fire. He suspected that was where they were keeping Marlene. *I'm hoping,* he thought, *she's not tied up, and they'll bring her out to the fire. That'll give me a chance to see how she's doing.*

There was a faint light in the east. It wouldn't be long before the moon would be rising. The light would help, especially in getting back to Cart and the rangers, if they had made it. Both shins were sore where they'd taken a beating from multiple falls. He was happy no bones had been broken, so far. A little moonlight would be a great boon. He continued to work his way forward.

Finally the moon rose high enough to give him enough light to provide fairly secure foot placement in the loose rocks. He increased his speed. He was concentrating on moving as fast as possible when he glanced toward the fire. Marlene was out and visible.

Jack yanked the binoculars to his eyes, and the girl leaped into view. He felt he could almost reach out and touch her. He could clearly see her face. She had been crying. He could tell by the puffy eyes, but overall, she looked pretty good. It didn't look as if she had been struck or abused. She was moving around the camp normally. She even served coffee to several of the men.

Good girl, Jack thought. *Make them like you and feel protective toward you.* He saw her smile at one of the men. The man returned a friendly smile, nothing inappropriate in his look or his gestures.

Jack moved the glasses from Marlene to each of the men. There were five. Two of them were propped against their saddles, and he could see blood on their shirts. One had a wound near his shoulder. The other, not so lucky, had blood on his chest. *Five. Five men. There should be six.* He examined the camp and where the horses were tied. The moon now gave him enough light to make out the shadows of the horses, but he still only saw five men.

He watched Marlene take a canteen to one of the men who had been shot. She knelt down and held it to his mouth, helping him. Jack could see the man say something to her and raise his hand. He patted her on the arm. She patted his shoulder, stood, and went to the other wounded man, giving him a drink.

At least she's safe for now, Jack thought. At that moment the man Jack had been missing came out of the tent. He was well dressed and seemed to be in command. When he spoke, the men listened. Jack concentrated on the man's face and shoulders, imagining him on a horse. He was the outlaw who rode out of the burning barn with Marlene. Jack thought about raising his rifle and ending the man right now, but there were two reasons not to shoot. The most important was Marlene. The others would immediately kill her and escape. The second reason was that he had brought his Winchester not his Spencer. It was too far across the canyon for accurate fire with the Winchester.

Frustrated, he continued to watch. Marlene was allowed to eat, and evidently there was a place for her to go to the bathroom, for she walked out of sight, and no one followed. A few minutes later she returned. Jack could see the boss man say something to her, and she shook her head. He pointed to the tent, and she shook her head again.

Jack, his binoculars trained on the drama taking place across the canyon, felt the helplessness of a man unable to come to the aid of a child. He watched, the deep boiling anger filling his every pore as he saw the man lift his hand and slap the sweet little girl who only moments before had been helping their wounded.

The blow drove her to the ground, where she turned tear-stained cheeks up to the man. Jack could read the short one-word statement spit from her lips, "No!" Jack's jaw was clinched so hard his facial muscles began to ache, but he didn't notice.

The man bent over and grabbed Marlene by her left arm, took three steps, dragging her across the rocks, and threw her into the tent. He turned and looked directly into the binoculars.

Jack knew the man couldn't see him, but he had a perfect view of the cruel face. It was printed forever in his mind. He softly voiced a promise. "I'll find you, and when I do, I promise you, you will never raise your hand to another child."

The man said something to one of the other men. He was the first one Marlene had taken coffee to. The man shrugged and started to pull his revolver from its holster. He stopped, looked toward the boss, who was talking, and shoved the weapon back. He then reached behind the holster to the long Bowie knife he carried on his hip and withdrew it from the scabbard. The man with the chest wound held up his hands as if to protect himself. Jack could hear the man, across the canyon, yelling no at his assailant.

It played out quickly. The attacker bent over the wounded

man, grabbed his hair, yanking his head back, and with a quick slash drew the Bowie knife across the wounded man's throat. Jack could see the blood spurt.

The attacker wiped his knife on the dead man's lower leg, the only place that wasn't bloody, straightened, and slid his knife back into the sheath. He turned, made his way back to where he had been sitting, refilled his coffee cup, and seated himself. Jack watched the killer adjust his back against his saddle and take a sip of coffee, no more concerned than if he had castrated a calf.

The binoculars held steady on the man's face. This was another face Jack wanted to remember. Screams had begun from the tent when the dead man's throat was slashed and continued until stopping abruptly. He could only figure that Marlene had seen what was happening, and the boss had stopped her screaming by slapping her again.

The moon climbed into the night sky, and the fire in the camp burned low. There was no more movement. Jack eased himself off the ground, his right leg stiff. There was nothing he could do here. He knew Marlene was with the men. His logical mind told him he would be better off getting some sleep so he'd be fresh in the morning. As much as he wanted to stay, he knew his time would be wasted, and come daylight, the outlaws would be able to see him. He didn't want them discovering him or any of the pursuers, so he made his way back toward Cart's camp.

Working his way along the ridge was easier with the moonlight. He was able to prevent the slips and falls that had occurred earlier. However, he hadn't realized how far he had traveled. When he had been moving toward the light of the outlaws' fire, he had been so focused the time seemed to fly by. He must have traveled at least two miles, maybe more.

At last he reached a point he could make out the light from their campfire. He was tired. The stress of the travel, slipping through the dark, and then having to watch Marlene without being able to do anything had taken a toll on him. He also realized how hungry he was.

He closed the distance until reaching a point where he could hear subdued voices. The other rangers must have reached the camp. His years of experience had taught him caution, and he slowly advanced on the camp until he could recognize Cart, Heath, and several other of the rangers' voices. Jack called softly, "Coming in."

"Come ahead," Cart replied, equally as soft.

Jack saw his gear near the fire, headed straight for it, and pulled his cup from the saddlebags. He stepped to the pot and poured himself a cup of the steaming black coffee, taking a long sip. It was hot, bitter, and just what he needed.

Captain Heath was leaning against his saddle, a plate of beans in his hands. "Well?"

"She's there, alright. Seems to be in pretty good shape, but there's no way we can reach her."

"None at all," Cart said. "They're across a rocky canyon. We'd sound like an army trying to get across that mess of rocks and cactus. Plus there'd be more than one horse's leg broken in the process."

All the rangers had been listening intently. Hud spoke up, his tone hard and belligerent. "I vote we attack tonight. We can't leave that little girl in the hands of those six men."

There were several murmurs of agreement.

Jack stared at the big man across the flames of the fire. "Five."

Hud stared back. "You said there were six, were you wrong, or did one die?"

"I was right, and one was murdered. One of his partners slit his throat with his Bowie knife."

"What do you mean?"

Jack was tired, and his shins ached. He'd just had to watch a young girl brutalized and was helpless to do anything about it. His patience was running thin. "I didn't stutter, Hud."

The big ranger was on his feet. "Don't get smart with me, old man. You're messing with a Texas Ranger."

Jack saw several of the rangers roll their eyes while others shook their heads.

Cart said, "Young feller, if you know what's good for you, you'll sit down and close that pie hole of yours."

Hud turned on Cart. "I'll take care of you, too."

Cart didn't answer him. He turned to Heath. "Cap'n, you wanta keep this young feller in your company? As big as he is, if he makes a move toward me, I'll leave his remains for those wolves to take care of."

Heath, who was sitting next to Jack, looked across the fire at the standing Hud. "Sit down, Hud. We'll have a fight soon enough. Save that energy for the outlaws."

"But, Captain—"

"Don't but me, Hud. Sit down and shut up."

The young ranger glared at Cart and then Jack but returned to his saddle and sat.

Captain Heath turned to Jack. "What happened?"

Jack opened his saddlebags and pulled out a slab of jerky. One of the other rangers filled a plate with beans, dropped a spoon in the plate, and handed it to Jack.

Jack nodded his thanks and began his story, telling everything from first spotting the camp, the tent, Marlene, and the killing of the wounded outlaw.

Several of the rangers were shaking their heads. One let out a long, low whistle.

Heath spoke for them all. "I'd love to get my hands on that bunch. The nearest tree wouldn't be punishment enough." He turned to Cart. "You know this country. Is there a way we can circle around them, maybe cut them off before they get away from us?"

"There sure is, Cap'n. We need to be in the saddle at first light. We can swing north, then cut west, and beat them to where they cross the Little Devils River. We'll have to ride hard, but with the number of men we have, we can set up a fine ambush. They'll never know what hit 'em."

"Good. We need to make sure they don't have a chance to kill the girl. If they're completely cut off, I don't think they will."

"Maybe," Jack said. "The leader of this bunch is a cool customer. I wouldn't begin to try to forecast what he may or may not try to do. I think the main thing with an ambush is to kill them all before they know we're there, before they have a chance to harm the girl."

Heath stared at Jack. "You mean don't give them a chance to surrender?"

"That's exactly what I mean. You've ambushed Indians, haven't you?"

"Yes."

"Do you give them a warning?"

One of the rangers laughed. "You give a Comanche or an Apache a warning and he'll have yore scalp hanging on his belt before you can blink twice."

"So what's the problem? Treat them the same way you would a Comanche."

Heath shook his head. "But these are white men."

It was hard for Jack to keep the disgust from his voice. "These men have already killed at least two little girls, maybe more we don't know about. I just saw the leader slap Marlene and drag her across rocky ground. Shortly after that, he ordered the murder of one of his own men by having his throat slit, and you want to treat them like gentlemen? I promise you, if you don't kill every one of those men, one of them will kill Marlene before we can get to her."

The captain's eyes were fixed on Jack. "You believe that?"

"I know that, but I've said my piece. You'll do what you want. I'm hungry." Jack turned to his beans and jerky, ignoring the captain and the rest of the rangers.

Heath looked like he was about to say something else, but decided against it and turned to his men. "Alright, men. Let's get some sleep. Sergeant Stevens, set up a guard. We want to be moving at daylight."

Jack finished his beans and jerky, cleaned the spoon and plate in the sand, and handed it back to the ranger who gave it to him. He stood and headed for the makeshift corral. He wanted to check on his animals, especially Stonewall. Cart joined him.

Reaching the horses, Cart said, "You're right. If it were me, those fellers would never get a chance to clear leather. We've got too many soldier boys in this bunch who think it's always the right thing to give the other feller a sporting chance. I learned a long time ago, whilst up in them tall mountains, the chance you give away may be your last."

"Thanks, Cart. I wish the captain felt the way you do. I'm afraid his attitude may cost a little girl her life, but it's out of my hands. I'm going to check up on my stock and get some sleep. The chips will fall wherever they may."

The tracker gave an emphatic nod. "Yessiree, they surely will." He turned and headed back to his bedroll.

Jack patted and scratched each of his animals as he came to them. He gave Smokey a quick rubdown and moved to Stonewall. The mule looked fine. In the firelight, Jack could see no welts or bruises. "Good boy. Looks like that Hud treated you alright. You're a fine mule, better than most horses."

Stonewall nuzzled Jack for a biscuit, but they were in his saddlebags by the fire. "Not tonight, boy, maybe tomorrow."

The mule turned and rubbed his head against Smokey's neck. Those two had been friends since Jack had gotten Stonewall. It made sense that mules liked horses. Their mamas were horses. Jack gave each a last pat and headed back to the fire. He made a quick bed and stretched out under his blanket. His last thought of Marlene drifted through his mind. *Tomorrow will be a busy day.*

MORNING CAME EARLY. They were up and ready to go before daylight. Jack checked his weapons as soon as he woke. He felt the same cold determination he always felt before going into battle. He had noticed it first when he was aboard ship as a boy, and it carried over to the Legion and then to the U.S. Army.

He never had the nervous, stomach-turning excitement or apprehension of his companions. He had watched other soldiers throw up with fear or anticipation. He respected them for having those feelings and continuing into the teeth of battle. For him, he found the only difference was his mind seemed more alert. It worked faster, more precisely. This morning was no different. He was ready. He wanted to get moving, cut the outlaws off, kill them, and rescue Marlene. Then they'd take her home, and the Schmidts would be together again.

But Jack knew it never worked like that. Planning was good. It was necessary to hone the brain and prepare it for any contingency. But when the first shot was fired, the plan went out the window because the enemy never performed as forecast. They would be better or worse than expected. They would go left when they were expected to go right. They would attack when expected to retreat. They would kill the girl and escape when expected to surrender. He knew it. He just wished Captain Heath also knew and believed it.

"Mount up," Heath called.

Jack had saddled Pepper this morning. The big red chestnut was not like him. Jack was calm and cool. Pepper was powerful and excited. The horse could feel the excitement in the air and reflected it.

Jack felt the shudders travel through the heavy muscles beneath him. He leaned forward and patted Pepper's neck and spoke softly in his ear. "Calm down, boy. You'll do fine. There'll be plenty of excitement for everyone. Just relax."

Jack rode forward, pulling up next to Heath. "Captain."

Heath looked at Jack. "Mr. Sage, are you ready?"

"Believe me, Captain, I'm ready for whatever may come along."

Heath waved Cart forward. "Move us out. Let's get to the ambush spot before the outlaws."

Cart gave a casual wave that passed as a salute and rode forward.

Heath and Jack started forward with the remainder of the company falling in behind. They had ridden no more than a hundred yards when a rider burst over a ridge to the east, riding hard. Heath halted the company and waited. He turned to Jack. "That's Bo Saunders, a ranger from Austin. I wonder what he wants."

The ranger yanked his lathered horse to a halt. "I'm glad I found you, Captain. I have a message from headquarters."

"Go ahead, Bo."

The ranger handed him a document and stated, "You are to proceed north immediately. The Comanches have raided and killed several families. Your orders are to apprehend, detain, and if possible move the Comanches back to the reservation."

Heath took a deep breath and turned to Jack. "I told you this could happen."

4

Jack felt it difficult to keep the frustration from his voice. He knew he couldn't carry this ambush out alone. He needed at least two additional men. "Are you going to conduct this ambush first?"

Heath looked at him like he was crazy. "These orders say immediately. They don't say when I get good and ready. You understand the necessity for following orders?"

"Yes, Captain, I understand, but if you could give me only two men, I feel sure I can carry this off. All we have to do is keep those outlaws from getting close enough to harm Marlene. Three good shots could guarantee it, and then we'll take out the farthest from her."

"No dice, Mr. Sage. These orders don't give me discretion to leave part of my force. It's up to me to proceed immediately with the full force of my company. I'm sorry. I wish headquarters had waited another day, but there's nothing I can do to change my orders." He turned to Bo Saunders. "That is right, isn't it, Bo?"

"Yes, sir, that's for shootin' sure. The major wants you moving yesterday, and he wants you to do it with all your people."

With the arrival of the courier, Cart had returned to hear the message. He spoke up. "Cap'n, you could let me go with Mr. Sage. As soon as we take care of the situation, I'll hightail it after you. I'll probably catch you before you ever get near the Red River or even the Canadian."

Heath contemplated the suggestion for a moment, then shook his head. "I appreciate you volunteering, Cart, but I can't spare anyone, especially you. We'll need you to track those Comanches." He turned to Jack. "Mr. Sage, you shall retain your commission, but I am unable to leave anyone with you. It will be up to you to find and rescue Marlene Schmidt. Our place is chasing Comanches."

Dumbfounded, Jack watched Heath give orders to ride north. The rangers turned and rode out. Several of them looked at Jack and shook their heads in frustration. Hud grinned at Jack and made a point of passing close enough to be heard. "If it's all up to you, Sage, that little girl is a goner." He leaned closer. "If'n I ever meet you again, it'll be yore end too."

Jack said nothing. He held Pepper still and watched the rangers ride away. They soon disappeared behind the ridge covered in cedar, rock, and prickly pear.

He was numb. He had no idea where to go now. Maybe he could ride north for a ways and then turn west, and maybe he'd find the Little Devils River crossing. *Maybe,* he thought. *Maybe never won a battle.*

But Jack was not a man to get mired in indecision. He rode north. He had ridden only a short distance when he saw a rider galloping toward him from the direction the rangers had taken. It was Cart. Drawing close, he yanked his dun to a stop and bailed out of the saddle, dropping to the ground over a flat sandy area. His big gloved hands cleaned the area of limbs and debris.

"I ain't got but a second here. The captain said I could draw you up a map. Maybe this'll help."

Jack watched as Cart started sketching and explaining distances and hills, small peaks and creeks. The man laid out a detailed map and circled an area he described as a small valley on the Little Devils River. "This is where they'll probably cross. Everything, hills, valleys, they all kinda open onto this area. It's about forty miles from here, but with the three horses, you'll be there long before the outlaws'll make it. There's a bluff a couple of hundred yards west of the river. The sun'll be behind you, and they'll be looking directly into it. It's a great place to set up." The tracker stopped drawing and stared at his map. "But as far as rescuing the girl?" Cart shook his head again, stood, and looked up at Jack.

"I think it would've been a cinch with the company, and even three men, but Jack, by yourself, I don't think you've got a snowball's chance." He glanced at the sun. "I'd best be on my way. The captain made me promise I'd come right back. He knows how much I want to go with you." Cart placed his left foot into the stirrup and swung up onto the dun. "One other thing. Watch out for Hud. You ever run into him, be ready to kill him. He's made up his mind you've belittled him, and he'll have nothing less than stomping you into the ground."

Jack grinned. "He didn't seem too happy with you."

Cart snorted. "Shoot, he knows I'll kill him if he comes at me. He'll never get a chance to put those big hands on me." Cart raised his hand in a wave and turned Sandy north. "Adios." The horse leaped away, and Jack watched his only ally disappear behind a thicket of cedars.

He examined the map until he had it memorized, and walked the horses through Cart's drawing, wiping it out. He turned Pepper north and set out at a gallop. It would be a hard ride for them all.

JACK EXAMINED the river with his binoculars for the third time. It was late in the afternoon. He crosschecked his position again to make sure this was the spot Cart had mapped out. It had to be. Beneath the bluff he was on, and less than two hundred yards from his position, was the Little Devils River. An easy crossing showing the tracks of many users, animal and man, horse and wagons. This had to be the place, and there was still no sign of the outlaws and Marlene. Had he chosen wrong? Was this the wrong bluff? Had he misread the map or misread one or more of the markers? He could be miles from where Cart had said. He might not even be looking at the Little Devils River.

Knock it off, he thought. *This is the place. The river, the sparse tree line, the twin knolls, this is the crossing. I traveled so fast, I've arrived way ahead of them. It's just a matter of time.*

He waited. He glanced back at the animals. They were all tired, especially Stonewall. He'd carried his load the full distance. Jack had switched horses, making it easier on them, but they too were also tired. When they had crossed the Little Devils earlier, he let the animals stand and drink in the river. They didn't want to leave, but at least they'd slaked their thirst, and were now cropping the bunch grass. They'd be fine. This would be over soon, and he'd have Marlene away from her abductors, and it would be home for her.

This time he had his Spencer in hand and his Winchester on the ground next to him. Alongside the Winchester he had two full tubes of .56-56 Spencer loads from his Blakeslee box. He was ready.

Lying on the bluff overlooking the river, Jack's muscles began to relax. It had been a hard couple of days for him as well. He was getting older, and he didn't recuperate like he had in his twenties. The warm sun felt good on his back and shoulders. He flexed his thick muscles, feeling them pull tight and then relax. He took a deep breath, letting the air out slowly. His eyelids grew heavy. He watched the countryside blur and then disappear.

Jack jerked his eyes open. The outlaws were in the middle of the Little Devils River. The horses were watering. He had completely missed their approach. Luck was with him that they hadn't made it through the crossing and continued west. He might have missed them entirely. He stopped wasting time berating himself, and lifted the binoculars to his eyes. Four men and Marlene. They must have murdered the other wounded man. They wouldn't just leave him behind for possible capture and questioning. The outlaws led a packhorse and two extra riding horses. Marlene rode behind the well-dressed man. His mind raced. *They don't even allow her to ride separately?* Jack had considered this possibility, but had put it aside for being too uncomfortable for both riders. The leader was taking no chances.

Jack eased the rifle to his shoulder and considered his options. *Closer, I'll let them get closer. They'll pass less than fifty yards from this bluff. The other three aren't even watching Marlene. I'll be able to drop them before they get near her.*

He watched the three still in the river. The leader and Marlene pulled farther and farther ahead of the stragglers. The front sight of the Spencer followed the slight bounce of the man's head, up, down, up, down. They drew closer. The others were talking, still in the river. *Maybe,* Jack thought, *this just might work. Stay back*—Jack's thoughts were interrupted by the leader halting his horse and turning in the saddle. He could hear the man clearly.

"Get out of that water, and get up here! How many times do I have to tell you, we stay together. Move it!"

The horsemen spurred their horses and raced toward him.

Jack recognized a military command voice when he heard it. *That fella's served as an officer or NCO somewhere,* Jack thought. *Those men didn't question or delay. They dashed toward him. He definitely has their obedience, probably from fear since he's ordered the murder of at least two of their men, and this could have been the bunch who killed the two girls. He's mean through and through.*

But now, the men were almost to the leader and Marlene.

There was no separation. He wouldn't have time to keep the others from killing the girl if he shot the leader.

Jack kept his rifle to his shoulder, tracking the man as he and the others rode past in a tight group. He could see Marlene's face clearly. The tear tracks stood out plainly, cut through the dust on her cheeks.

He wanted, no, he needed to rescue her. The longer she spent in the clutches of those animals, the more her psyche would be damaged, maybe even for life.

It was obvious to Jack the men had no idea he was anywhere around. He slowly lowered the rifle and watched them pass from view. If it hadn't been for Marlene, he could have killed all four of them, dropped them right there in the river bottom, and let them lie, buzzard and coyote bait. But her well-being came first.

Jack pushed himself up from the ground and, with his reload tubes, two rifles, and the binoculars, dashed to the horses. He stowed the equipment, keeping his Winchester handy. Finished, he swung aboard Thunder, clucked softly, and walked them quietly into the cedars and mesquite.

Suddenly, he realized he was choking the reins as if he had the leader's throat in his hands. His knuckles were white. The tendons and muscles bunched hard like rocks. He took a deep breath, released the tension, and stretched first his right hand and then his left. There had to be a way to rescue the girl. He'd follow them and, tonight, try at their next camp.

The party was traveling a little north of west. Jack stayed well to their north and worked his way through the mesquite- and cedar-filled draws and high grass in the flatter areas. The hillsides were rocky, and in the warmth of the afternoon sun, Jack kept his eyes open for rattlesnakes. The rattlers loved to come out on a flat rock and soak up the warm sun until they grew too hot, slithering deep into their hillside dens.

He continued northwest, only occasionally catching a glimpse of his prey as they held to their original direction. It was growing late in the day when he crossed another creek. If his navigation was right, from Cart's map, this should be Johnson Fork.

He slipped the animals through the trees, though it was difficult with all the dry leaves on the ground and with three horses and a mule. However, they seemed to feel his need for stealth and stepped lightly. Dismounting, he looped the lead ropes over his saddle horn and ground hitched Thunder. Slipping silently from tree to tree, he reached the edge of the creek and peered in each direction, checking the creek bottom for a possible straggler from the outlaw gang. He saw nothing, with the exception of a raccoon and her three youngsters fishing along the water's edge. The four masked faces snapped up, staring at him. They turned and scurried up the creek bank, disappearing in the trees and brush of the opposite side.

Good sign, he thought. *Those little rascals wouldn't have been there if the outlaws were close. I still figure they should be at least a mile south of me, and it's getting late. They should make camp soon.*

Jack found an easy crossing and slipped back for the horses. The water flow coursed in a small clear stream over a narrow portion of the wide, rock-covered crossing. Jack winced at the scrape and clump of the horses' hooves making their way across the rocks. Upon reaching the narrow stream, he stopped, allowing the horses to drink their fill.

They were all tired, including him, and if everything went well tonight, this chase would be over, and they'd all have an easy ride back to the Schmidts' ranch. He kneeled on one knee and scooped up a handful of water, drank quickly, and scooped another. All the time his head was constantly moving, checking every portion of the river for hint of horse or man. He drank until the horses finished, then swung onto Thunder. He led the animals through the narrow stream and up the opposite bank.

They moved out to the edge of the treeline, and he again stopped them while he cleared the exposed area they would be riding through. There was no sign or movement, so he moved out into the grassy flat. Each time he had to ride across open ground, his shoulders and back muscles tensed. It was always possible he might miss something, a flash of clothing, flick of a horse's tail, or glint of a rifle barrel. Any of those could mean the end of Jack Sage. He had been fortunate so far. He'd like to keep the winning streak going. He let out a long breath as he passed into the cover of a mesquite thicket. His shoulders and back relaxed. Safe again.

Dusk drifted across the West Texas countryside, bringing the nocturnal animals out to stretch and prepare for the night. For Jack, it was time to make a cold camp and ready himself for his role tonight of hunter and rescuer.

He had learned his nighttime stealth as a young man in the French Foreign Legion, exercising his skill from the hot, stinking swamps to the Tell Atlas mountains and on to the Sahara. Tonight, he dressed in dark clothing and, with a little water from his canteen, made mud and spread it in streaks across his face. He took no rifle with him, only his Remington revolvers and a large, well-balanced Bowie knife he had acquired from an outlaw who no longer had a need for it.

Jack hated to leave the horses, but he was by himself, and it must be done. The moon, at one-quarter, would be up earlier tonight and would give him the needed light, but not too bright, to accomplish his mission. He fished his moccasins from his saddlebags, slipped them on, and moved south, away from his camp and toward his enemies. *Finally,* he thought, *tonight will be the night. Hang on, Marlene. You'll be home soon.*

The big man glided through the wilderness. His moccasins made little sound. His long strides devoured the distance until he caught the first glint of their campfire.

He dropped to a knee and listened.

The faint sound of metal pots carried over the darkening hills. They were there, unsuspecting. He rose to his feet, slipped to the edge of a cedar, and waited. He wanted it darker when he attacked.

The moon rose, casting a pale light over the Texas prairie. He waited still.

Finally, it was time.

The chase was over.

He felt good.

Jack began moving toward the camp.

Between trees, he could make out two of the men working around the fire. *They must be preparing a meal,* he thought. *With any luck, this will be the last they ever prepare.* He moved closer, looking for the other man and especially Marlene and the leader.

He moved out from behind a cedar that gave him a different angle on the camp, and he saw the tent, still only one. Jack scanned the camp. He could see the horses. They were hobbled. *Bad move, boys,* he thought. Then a third man came into view, adjusting his pants and fastening his gun belt.

One of the men at the fire said, "Everything come out alright?"

The question elicited laughter and an obscene curse from the returning outlaw.

That's three, Jack thought. *I just need to find Marlene and the leader, probably in the tent.* The thought had no sooner registered than the leader stepped from the tent and held the flap open. Marlene walked out. She looked pale in the flickering firelight. Her face was drawn, and her eyes were wide with fear as she looked from the other men to the leader.

One of the men at the fire spoke. "Mr. Haggard, when do you suppose Mr. Sanford will be arriving?"

Haggard spoke up and, placing his hand on Marlene's back, gave her a shove. "Get over there, girl. Go eat." He looked at the men at the fire. "I would think tonight or tomorrow. It just depends on whether or not he ran into trouble."

Haggard, Jack thought, *that's his name, and he's expecting someone else, a Sanford. How many of these animals are there? I've got to act quickly if I'm going to save Marlene.*

"Know how many girls he's bringing?"

"Hopefully three or four. I am extremely sad we had to kill those two down south. They would have brought quite a lot of money."

Jack watched as the man affectionately patted Marlene on the back.

"But this little doll alone will bring as much as the two of them."

Jack felt his blood turn cold with rage at the man speaking so nonchalantly about killing the other two girls. Now was the time. If he was going to get Marlene out of here, he couldn't wait any longer. He marked the location of Marlene and each of the men, stooped, and moved to the edge of the trees, just behind the girl. He pulled the Bowie with his right hand, passed it to his left, and filled his empty hand with one of his .36-caliber Remingtons.

5

The two men preparing supper were just in front of Jack, with the outlaw who had just relieved himself across the fire, facing them. Marlene was to the right of the two men, with Haggard to the right of her.

Normally, Jack would have given the men a warning, an opportunity to surrender, but Marlene's life was at risk.

He stepped from the darkness and into the firelight.

The man on the other side of the fire was talking. "I hope these beans aren't burned as bad as those were last—"

His mouth dropped open at the sight of the huge apparition that had just stepped into the clearing. It was all black and stood at least ten feet tall, a tiny gun in its right hand and a huge knife in its left. In the shadows and flickering firelight, Jack's muddy face appeared misshapen.

Jack could see the man's eyes grow as wide as saucers. The outlaw's jaw dropped open, and he mouthed with little sound, "What, what, what..."

Jack showed him a big grin, his white teeth gleaming in the firelight, and said, "I'm the grim reaper, boys, and your time has come."

The outlaw across the fire came out of his trance and went for his gun. Jack shot him between the eyes. The man was in the process of standing, and his momentum carried him chest first into the flames. Jack turned the Remington on Haggard and shot him in the right shoulder, driving him back and to the ground, away from Marlene.

The two men in front of the ranger were trying to draw, stand, and turn at the same time. None of which worked out for them.

Jack drove the big Bowie into the chest of the man to his left. The power of his thrust drove the knife deep through cartilage and bone and into the outlaw's heart. Jack left the knife in the man's chest and turned his full attention to the last man, who had managed to turn and stand. He was finally pulling the .44 Colt from its holster when Jack shot him in the third button of his shirt. The bullet traveled only five inches before slamming into the outlaw. He fell straight back into the fire, on top of his companion.

Jack turned to Haggard, who had sat up and was holding his shoulder. He stepped past Marlene, who was standing aghast, her blue eyes wide and her mouth hanging open. Stepping by her, Jack patted her arm. "You're alright now, Marlene. I'm a Texas Ranger. Your folks sent me to bring you home. Do you understand?"

He watched as the little girl gave a slow nod.

"Good. I'll be right back." He continued past her to the outlaw. "*Mister* Haggard."

The man held his shoulder and rocked back and forth. "You've broken my shoulder. How could you do it? Don't you know who I am?"

Jack kneeled down until he was almost level with Haggard and shoved his revolver's muzzle against the outlaw's injured shoulder. The man screamed. When he stopped screaming, Jack said, "I don't care who you are. I know what you are. You're the animal who steals little girls and kills them on a whim."

He moved the muzzle of the revolver toward Haggard's shoulder again, and the man jerked away, moaning. "Please, no more. You've got to help me."

Jack yanked Haggard's weapon out of its holster, stood, and turned to Marlene, who was watching. "You're safe, honey. These bad men won't hurt you or anyone else. I promise." He stepped past her again and dragged the bodies of the outlaws from the fire, then beat the flames out that had caught on their clothing. He wasn't concerned about them. He didn't want the little girl to have a memory of the smell of human flesh burning. It was something a person never forgot. Once finished, he turned back to her.

She looked up at Jack. "You're big, mister."

He smiled at her. "I had a momma who fed me well, just like yours. Would you like to go home to her?"

Her eyes brightened, and her blonde hair danced with her nodding head. "Oh, yes, I would, I would." Then she grew sad again. "But these bad men burned our barn, and they caught me before I could rescue sweet Klara."

Jack shook his head. "I've got good news for you. Your mama got Klara out of the barn, the horses too. They're all safe."

The child's mouth split in a brilliant smile. Her eyes wrinkled with happiness. "Oh, that's so good. I'm so happy."

"Good. Are you ready to go home?"

"Oh, yes, I'm ready." She grew serious again. "I'm really ready."

"Good. I'm going to tie up this man, then I'll saddle the horses. Why don't you go pick out a horse for you and this bad man, and I'll be over in just a minute. Is that all right?"

She nodded, turned, and ran toward the horses.

Jack yanked a piggin' string from one of the men's saddles and strode to Haggard. The man held out his left hand. Jack looped the leather rope around the man's wrist and jerked it behind him. Haggard was moaning, but the moans turned to screams when Jack reached around him, grabbed his right wrist, and yanked it back. He tied both hands behind the man's back, pulled Haggard's neckerchief off, and tied it around his mouth.

"I'll be back. Think about the girls you killed while I'm gone."

While Jack was loading the mule's pack, he asked Marlene, "Would you be all right if we left the tent?"

She looked at him for a moment. "I don't know your name."

He smiled. "I'm Jack Sage. You can call me Jack."

She shook her head solemnly. "No, sir. Mama says to always be respectful of your elders. I'll call you Mr. Sage, or I could call you Ranger Sage."

"Honey, you can call me whatever you like."

"I'll call you Ranger Sage because you're so big." She gave him a shy grin. "But you do need to wash your face."

He couldn't help himself. He laughed. Jack had forgotten the mud he had smeared on his face. "I guess I could. How about if I do that when we get back to my camp. Is that all right?"

She grinned. "That's all right, and I don't want that old tent. I want to sleep out under the stars. My papa says that's the way to do it."

Jack had the two horses Marlene had shown him saddled in short order. He also saddled one of the biggest ones and loaded the mule. While he was working with the animals, he gave each one a few ear scratches and promised them some treats.

He picked her up and set her in the saddle. "Your papa's right. Let's get out of here. When we ride by those bad men, you can close your eyes if you want to. I'll tell you when to open them."

She closed her eyes tight.

Jack guided the horses next to Haggard. He stepped down and lifted the wounded man into the saddle. Once in the saddle, Haggard struggled feebly. With his hands tied behind him, it made balancing difficult. Moans and unintelligible words filtered through the neckerchief.

Jack ignored him, picked up the coffee pot, poured it over the fire, and then kicked dirt over the remaining coals. He looked around at the three dead men. From two of them, smoke drifted up from their burned clothing. It brought pictures of battle, living and dead warriors to his mind. He paused for a moment, then shook his head.

He didn't have time to bury these men. Their associates could show up at any time. The most important thing for him to do was to get Marlene out of this carnage and back to her home, and he was anxious to question Haggard. If he could find out who was paying for these girls, perhaps he could put an end to these horrendous kidnappings.

Holding the reins of Haggard's horse and the lead from the mule, Jack led off with Marlene at his side.

Haggard groaned with every step of his horse.

I can't pretend to be very sympathetic with a monster like Haggard, Jack thought. *I've represented the law most of my life, but I can't work up a lot of guilt for killing these men without a trial. This is the west, and sometimes it falls upon us to be judge, jury, and executioner.*

Thirty minutes put them back at Jack's camp, but he didn't think it safe to camp so close to the dead outlaws. From what he had overheard, they were expecting another group to meet them. Would they have more children with them? The outlaws expected them to. After interrogating Haggard, he'd work out a plan.

He wanted to get Marlene home, but the nagging thought of other children being in the same situation rankled him. He couldn't leave them to the fate that had awaited Marlene. He was beginning to see that no matter what decision he made, it could have a bad result. Save Marlene and allow the other children to remain in captivity, or take a chance on rescuing the others and possibly sending Marlene right back into the situation he had rescued her from. They rode on in silence.

Reaching Johnson Fork, he led them across the creek. Haggard had finally quieted down, and Marlene was sleeping in the saddle. Jack rode close to her to catch the little girl if she started to fall, but she had spent much of her growing years in a saddle. She slept soundly and maintained her balance as the horse walked across the Texas Plains.

Jack found an adequate camping spot. The moon was drifting lower, but there would be light for another couple of hours. He unloaded the animals and tied them on decent grass.

Haggard, on the other hand, had almost fallen out of the saddle several times. Jack arranged the camp, made a bed for Marlene, laid her on it, and spread a blanket over the girl. Moonlight slipped through the cottonwood trees, sifting across her golden braids. He felt a tug at his heart. He could only imagine what her parents must be feeling. He turned his head to see Haggard watching him, and anger boiled inside.

Jack stepped away from Marlene, grabbed a canteen, strode over to Haggard, and grabbed him under the left arm. He yanked the outlaw to his feet, wringing a cry of pain from the man. He walked Haggard down the creek bank to the water's edge, spinning him around so the outlaw was looking into a pair of angry, unforgiving eyes.

"You get one chance, Haggard." With one hand he pulled the Bowie knife from its scabbard, moonlight glinting on the still bloody blade, and with the other he grabbed the neckerchief in the man's mouth. "I'm going to take this from your mouth, and you're going to tell me all about your operation. You get one chance."

Haggard tried to look away.

He turned the neckerchief loose and grabbed a handful of hair. Yanking Haggard's head around and toward him, he moved his face within inches of the outlaw.

"My name is Jack Sage. You may or may not have heard of me, but I spent several years in the Foreign Legion in Algeria. Those folks could teach a Comanche a few things about torture. You answer my questions, or I share with you what I learned. You understand me?"

He turned Haggard's hair loose, and the outlaw gave a vigorous nod.

"Good. Spill it." Jack yanked the neckerchief from the outlaw's mouth.

"Water, please, water."

Jack uncorked the canteen and held it up to the outlaw's mouth, allowing him to drink. The man swallowed several times, water escaping down his chin. Jack yanked the canteen back.

"More."

"No. Talk. Start with who you are."

Haggard looked away again and cleared his throat. "If you release me, there'll be a lot of money in it for you."

Jack did three things. He dropped the canteen, clapped a big hand over Haggard's mouth, grabbed the man's right shoulder, and squeezed. The deep guttural scream came from low in the outlaw's belly. Jack released his grip on the injured shoulder. He kept his hand over the outlaw's mouth until the screams were replaced with heavy breathing.

"I guess you didn't believe me. Try me again, and I'll put a bullet in your knee to match the one in your shoulder. Would you like that?"

The outlaw shook his head.

"This is the last chance you're going to get. I want the whole story, beginning with who you are."

The man gave a long sigh. "I am Major Jayden Phillip Haggard of the United States Army."

Jack couldn't believe it. "Your father is Senator Haggard of New York?"

"Yes."

"He wouldn't be involved in this."

"No, he has no idea." Haggard looked down at the flowing water. "He would be mortified to know what I'm doing."

Jack shook his head. He knew of the New York Haggards. He had met the senator when Jack was a captain, and the senator was a surprisingly good general who had been kind and considerate of his men. He remembered the man had only one son and four daughters. At the time, the son had been a captain and had a bright future. Jack looked at the man in disbelief. "How in the world did you end up in this? How could you kill two little girls? You weren't brought up like that."

Haggard shook his head. "No, I wasn't. War changes people, you know that."

"Don't blame the war. We didn't learn to kill children."

The moonlight struck Haggard's anguished face. "You may not have, but I did. We killed everyone, destroyed everything in our path. It was orders, Sherman."

Jack stepped close to Haggard. The man winced, trying to move away. Jack grabbed his left shoulder to stop him. "Listen to me, Sherman didn't order innocents killed. His march destroyed property, but was not supposed to destroy the people. That's what it was all about. Take away the food, weaken the forces."

Haggard looked away, unable to meet Jack's eyes. "We did. Anything in front of us was killed. Man, woman, or child. As my commander said, 'Nits make lice.' That's what we did."

Jack, still gripping the man, squeezed his shoulder until he winced. "Then you should've been executed yourselves." He released the outlaw and looked up at the treetops. He could hear the tinkling of the stream hurrying to the Gulf of Mexico. Something climbed in one of the trees, scratching the bark. His mind searched for peace, away from the war and killing. He felt dirty just being near this man. To know this had been going on during the war on the side he'd fought for . . . He took a deep breath and stepped close to his captive.

"Forget the war, Haggard. How did *you* get started in this awful business?"

Haggard gave a low, humorless laugh. "It was a friend, a

friend in my regiment. He contacted me. He knew I had gambling debts. He told me there was a way he could make all of my debts disappear, and we could make a great deal of money. I was desperate. They were about to go to my father. It would have killed him. He's never known of my gambling."

"It looks to me, there's a lot about you he doesn't know."

Haggard's head hung. "Yeah."

"Keep going. I want to hear about the operation."

"I don't know much."

"Who's this friend who recruited you? Who's Sanford?"

"One and the same. He said there's a man in San Francisco who runs the business."

"Are you telling me this is some kind of business? You deal in children?"

"Yes, or whatever he's interested in at the time."

"How does this work?"

Haggard hesitated. "If they find out I've told anyone about this, they'll kill me."

"You're not out of the woods with me yet. I may kill you or just leave you here and let you die from your wound. The only chance you have is to tell me all you know."

Haggard looked up toward the cloudless, star-filled sky and back into Jack's eyes. "Alright, I'll tell you, but you've got to promise—"

Jack cut him off with a harsh whisper. "I don't have to promise anything. I can leave you here for the buzzards. Your only chance is to spill your guts, and I'm tired of waiting." His hand started for Haggard's right shoulder.

The outlaw winced away, saying hurriedly, "Alright. My connection and boss is Robert or Bob Sanford. He was a major in the war, a really brutal man. You wouldn't believe what I've seen him do."

Jack leaned into Haggard's face. "Is it worse than what you've done?"

Haggard looked down and continued, "He told me about this man in San Francisco."

"What's his name?"

"He didn't tell me his name."

Jack gave him a disgusted look. "Go on."

"This man wanted girls between the ages of eight and twelve. He paid a substantial amount for each, but if the child was slim, with blonde hair and blue eyes, he paid more."

"How much?"

"For a girl like Marlene, I'd get paid ten thousand dollars."

Jack was aghast. "You had to pay your men out of that?"

"No, they were Bob's men. He paid them. My share was ten thousand free and clear, and he had already settled my gambling debts, which were substantial."

Jack felt sick. "If the guy is in San Francisco, why does he have people grab children in Texas? That's a long way to transport them."

"His buyers like the Texas girls, especially the blonde, blue-eyed German girls. He's willing to pay for the delivery."

Jack was torn. He was sick of listening to Haggard's explanation, but he needed to know how the girls were transported, and who this guy was in San Francisco. "How do you transport them?"

"Never more than four. The story is their parents paid for a school in San Francisco. The man transporting them is a very scholarly-looking gentleman."

"He's no gentleman."

"Well, he looks very educated, and few people ask questions. He has an assistant, a woman who travels with him. The man in San Francisco pays us to provide transportation until they reach a point they can take a stage or train."

"How do you keep the girls quiet?"

Daylight was approaching. Quail could be heard calling in the brush, and squirrels were racing along the tree limbs, only to jump, crashing into other branches. The forest along the creek was coming alive.

"My shoulder is really hurting."

"Tell me how you keep the girls from crying out, or your shoulder is going to be hurting a lot more."

6

Jack's patience was growing thin. He wanted this story to be told and finished. He lifted the point of his knife's blade toward Haggard's gunshot wound.

The outlaw's words came out in a rush. "We tell them we'll go back and kill their entire family."

Jack's hard gray eyes burned into Haggard. "You are worthless, aren't you. Just finish this. I want the names of the people transporting the kids, where Sanford hangs out, and anything you can tell me about the man in San Francisco."

A small voice called softly from the bank above, "Ranger Sage, are you here?"

Jack called back in a low voice, "I'm in the creek bottom, honey. You wait up there. I'll be up in just a moment."

"Alright. I'm kinda hungry."

"It'll be just a moment."

"Alright."

Jack turned back to the outlaw. "I'm going to leave you down here while I go check on her. You can run if you like, I don't much care. Just remember, I've got the food and supplies. You have nothing." Jack nodded at the flowing water. "If you want to do something constructive while I'm gone, you can clean your wound."

He turned, sheathed his knife, and hurried up the hill. Marlene had cleaned a portion of the ground and was placing rocks in a small circle on the cleared area. A pile of sticks lay to one side. "I thought I'd get a fire ready so you could start it when you came back. I'm sorry, I don't have any matches."

Jack kneeled next to her. "You don't have to be sorry about anything, honey. You've done a great job getting everything ready. Thanks."

He watched her face brighten as her mouth broke into a wide smile. "My papa says I can make a really good fire."

Jack nodded. "This looks perfect. It's nice and small so we don't make a lot of smoke, and building it under the trees, like you did, will break up what little smoke there is."

With enthusiasm, her head bobbed up and down. "That's just what I was thinking."

Jack grinned at the little girl. "Your mama told me you were industrious and really smart. She was right." While he was talking, Jack picked up a few of the leaves, placed some thin twigs on top of them, and struck a match. Moments later they had a fire going. The warmth felt good in the early morning chill.

Jack went to Stonewall's pack and opened a large bag. From it, he took several of the biscuits he gave to the horses. He bit into one and gave a couple to Marlene. "We're going to have to be moving pretty soon, but this is something you might like."

He watched her break a small piece off and put it cautiously in her mouth. She rolled the piece around, crunched it, and smiled.

"That's really good. I taste apples."

"You're right. Apples, oatmeal, and a few other things." He took the coffeepot. "I'm going down to the creek. I'll be gone for a while. You'll be alright?"

She nodded, her smile disappearing. "Mr. Haggard is down there?"

"Yes, Marlene, he is. I'm talking to him. I'll bring him back up here in a few minutes. Do you mind?"

Her face turned serious, and the corners of her mouth turned down. "I don't like him. He's a bad man."

"He is a bad man, and I don't like him either. However, I want to try to take him back so he can pay for his crimes. Do you understand that?"

"Yes."

"Will you be alright by yourself for a while? I'll just be in the creek."

"I'll be fine."

Jack took the pot and headed down the bank.

Haggard had managed to remove his coat and shirt. He was grimacing as he tried to wash his wound in the cold creek water. Jack looked the outlaw over. He saw a man weakened from pain and loss of blood. Jack yawned. It had been at least twenty-four hours since he last slept. He shook his head. Coffee would help.

He kneeled alongside Haggard to dip the coffeepot into the creek. "You need to finish your story. What are the names of the man and woman who transport the kids, and where do they pick them up?" Jack glanced at the coffeepot and heard a rasp of scraping rocks. It didn't sound like a man standing, it sounded like—he threw himself to the side and palmed his Remington.

The thought flashed through his mind, *Not as weak as I thought.* His roll to the left brought his revolver to bear as the jagged rock in Haggard's hand swung toward Jack's head. Jack pulled the trigger and continued his roll, his head still in the path of the jagged rock aimed perfectly to splatter his brains all over the creek.

The 80-grain round ball of the .36-caliber Remington New Police exploded from the muzzle in an upward trajectory. The ball struck Haggard's belt buckle. It deformed into a whirling, misshapen projectile, and its direction changed. Had it missed his buckle, it would have driven straight through Haggard's belly. However, it instantly changed its direction. The mass of lead traveled vertically, paralleling Haggard's body. At that point, it could have missed completely, leaving him with only a large and painful bruise on his belly.

Unfortunately for Haggard, not only was his arm extended, but so were his head and neck. They were stretched and turned, his eyes concentrating on the center of Jack's forehead, where the rock would strike and crush the life from the big man.

Jack saw Haggard's face go from a grimace of evil elation to panic at the sight and blast of his revolver. Then Haggard's neck exploded as the jagged piece of lead tore its way through his left carotid artery, spraying blood over the two of them.

But the hunk of lead wasn't through doing damage. Before exiting, it slammed into the top of his spine where it joined the skull, blowing the topmost vertebrae out and away from his body.

The piece of lead, now much reduced in volume and velocity, continued upward until it thunked into a large pecan tree limb. The limb happened to have a red fox squirrel stretched out, legs hanging on each side, soaking its body in the warmth of the early morning sun. The squirrel leaped to its feet, its tiny nose wiggling as it investigated the smell of hot lead, blood, and bone. It stayed only a moment, scurried farther out on the limb, yawned, and dropped into the same position, closing the lids on its little black eyes, and was quickly asleep.

The rock continued, grazing Jack's right temple and dropping harmlessly onto the creek bed. Haggard's body fell lifeless across Jack's chest. He pushed the body farther down and gently felt his head. His hand came away wet. *Not a bad price to pay for being stupid,* Jack thought. With one foot he shoved Haggard the rest of the way off his leg and clear of his body. He rolled over, got to his knees, and splashed cold water on his temple.

Between splashes, he heard the small voice again. "Ranger Sage?"

"I'm alright, Marlene. I'll be up in just a minute. You stay up there."

"Alright."

He picked up Haggard's shirt, soaked an end in the cold water, and held it against the cut on his temple. With the pressure and cold, the bleeding soon stopped.

Jack stood. He felt fine. He was relieved there was no dizziness. With the sound of the shot, they would have to move quickly. If Sanford or his crew was pursuing them, they might be close enough to have heard it, and if that was the case, they could be here soon. He took a quick moment to search Haggard's body. All he found was a letter and two dollars in the man's vest pocket.

He dropped the dollars into his vest and glanced at the envelope. It was postmarked from New York. He'd look at it later. He started to walk away and stopped. He knew many men kept valuables in their boots. He bent and yanked Haggard's boots off, first his left and then the right. The left was empty, but out of the right boot fell a wad of money. A lot of money, folded in half. He picked it up and shoved it into his inside vest pocket. There wasn't time to count it now. That would come later.

Finding nothing else, he left Haggard lying on the rocks of the creek. The man deserved nothing better than burial by buzzard, coyote, and skunk. The senator need never know what his son had become or how he died.

Jack hurried up the creek bank to find Marlene sitting by the fire, eating another biscuit. She turned to watch him as he neared. "Did you shoot Mr. Haggard?"

"Yes, Marlene, I did. He tried to kill me, and I had to shoot him."

"He was a bad man."

"He was." Jack started packing up the supplies. He poured the water he had collected from the creek over the fire. It popped and sizzled and smoked more than he liked.

"We're leaving?"

"Yes." He talked as he worked. Jack didn't want to frighten the girl, but he wanted to be honest with her. "It's possible the friends of Haggard may be looking for us. After that shot, I think it would be safer if we moved along, put some space between us."

"Ranger Sage?" Something in her voice caused him to stop and turn. He saw a quiet little girl, strong, but afraid. "They're coming for *me*, aren't they."

Jack mustered a grin for her. "If they are, Marlene, they're biting off way more than they can chew. You remember what happened last night?"

She nodded her head slowly, and Jack went back to saddling the animals. He was in the process of saddling Smokey when she spoke again.

"Mr. Haggard said there would be a lot more people with Mr. Sanford."

Jack didn't answer, but finished loading the two mules and saddling the other horses. He had brought all the guns owned by the killers. He hung two holsters across his saddle horn, each supporting a .44-caliber Walker Colt. With their heavy loads and long barrels, they were almost like rifles.

"Come on, honey, let's ride."

"I'm thirsty."

Of course you are, Jack thought. *You haven't had anything to drink since you woke up.* "Let me help you onto your horse, then you can have a drink from the canteen. Is that alright?"

She nodded and hurried to his waiting hands.

She was light as a feather when he lifted her into the saddle. He swung up onto Smokey and asked her, "Have you been eating well?"

She shook her head. "I haven't really been hungry."

"No, I'm sure you haven't. Could you eat some jerky while we ride?"

"Oh, yes, and I could eat another one of those horse biscuits, too, if you have one."

Jack turned, reached into his saddlebags, and pulled out two more. He gave her one and took one. "Can you ride fast and eat at the same time?"

She grinned at Jack. "That would be fun."

He bumped Smokey, and the two of them, with their string of animals, took off at a lope, leaving a cloud of dust.

Jack saw it and shook his head. There was nothing he could do about the dust. They had to move and move fast.

They rode east, through shallow valleys, up rocky hillsides, and across plateaus. Deer and turkey raced from their path. Buffalo stood and watched, their shaggy heads following the intruders. On they pushed.

Jack watched Marlene. When they would slow, he'd give her a piece of jerky, a horse biscuit, or a drink from the canteen. She seemed to be doing fine. *Better than me,* he thought. *I've almost fallen asleep a couple of times.*

They halted to change horses, and Jack, with his binoculars, checked their back trail. Nothing, no dust or riders. Maybe they were safe. He started thinking about the possibility of other children, little girls, being with Sanford's bunch.

During one of the periods they were walking the horses, Jack spoke to Marlene. "Do you remember the men saying anything else about the ones who were going to be joining them?"

The little girl's forehead wrinkled, and her lips pursed. After almost a minute, she nodded. "Yes, Ranger Sage, I do." It was like a dam opened. "They said Mr. Sanford would be arriving soon. It sounded like they expected him last night. They were all excited. They talked about him paying them when he arrived. They were like Papa after selling corn or wheat at the market, all planning on how they were going to spend their money."

Yeah, Jack thought, *I bet they weren't talking about spending their money on the same things as your papa.* But Jack didn't interrupt her. He wanted her to keep talking, which she did.

"They also said something about the other men bringing in more girls. I felt sorry for them. Mr. Haggard told me what was going to happen to me, and I suspected the same thing would happen to them."

"What did Haggard tell you they were going to do with you?"

"He said I was really lucky. He said I was going to be rich for the rest of my life." She turned her head to look at Jack, tears threatening to escape her blue eyes. "I don't want to be rich. I just want my mama and papa and my family."

Jack leaned toward the little girl. "Listen to me, Marlene. They aren't going to get you again. You'll be able to be with your folks as long as you want."

She had turned forward to watch their progress. She turned her face so she could look at him. "You promise?"

Jack locked his eyes on hers. "I promise I will do everything in my power to get you home safely."

She searched his face, then broke into a grin. "Good."

"Do you feel like riding fast again?"

To answer him, she kicked her horse high in the flanks with her little heels. The animal broke into a lope, and Marlene turned her head back toward Jack. She gave him a wide, impish grin.

He bumped Smokey, and his entourage was off again.

They didn't stop. Marlene seemed to be born in the saddle. Her little legs stuck out from the horse's sides, but it didn't matter. A smile across her face and blonde hair streaming behind her, she rode like the wind. Time disappeared almost as quickly as they rode. Nearing the Little Devils River, Jack slowed again.

He had made up his mind. He was determined to get Marlene home. He knew the outlaws were taking the other girls to San Francisco, but they had a long way to go just to get out of Texas.

He would put out the word, and after dropping Marlene off at home, he would head back for the other three. He would do everything in his power to rescue the other girls.

They reached the Little Devils River late in the day. He thought about going on, but this country was too rough to voluntarily ride through it at night. They'd camp here and allow the horses to rest.

Jack kept watch through the night. His concern about the outlaws overpowered his body's desire for sleep. Before daylight, he dug a slab of bacon from Stonewall's pack, sliced it, and started it cooking over the fire.

The smell of the cooking bacon awakened Marlene. She had pulled her blanket over her head and was only a small bump on the ground against her saddle. Abruptly the bump moved. The blanket lifted, and her eyes peeped out. She lay watching Jack for a few seconds. "That smells good."

Jack looked up at the little tousle-haired blonde. "Well, good morning, sunshine. How are you?"

She gave him her impish grin. "Your bump is turning purple."

Jack felt where Haggard's rock had struck. It was a large lump and tender. "I guess that makes me colorful."

Marlene giggled. "Is the bacon ready?"

"It is, are you?" Jack started to grin at the girl and then felt a crawling sensation at the back of his neck. That feeling had saved him more than once. He listened, hearing nothing.

That was the problem. There was no sound. The sun was rising. The day was beginning. Birds should be singing. Squirrels should be barking and scratching against the trees, armadillos digging, and he heard nothing. He motioned for Marlene to come over to him quietly, and he drew one of the .44 Walker Colts he had placed next to him.

Marlene slipped over and pressed her little body close to him. He wrapped an arm around her just as a head peeked out from behind a big pecan tree no more than thirty feet away. *The man is so stupid*, Jack thought. *He left his hat on.* The brim preceded his head coming into view. By the time the man's eye cleared the thick trunk of the pecan tree, a .44-caliber round ball was there to meet it. His head exploded.

Jack pressed the girl to the ground as three men charged the camp from different directions.

Instantly, he knew what had happened. Sanford was smarter than Jack had figured. He thought the man would follow him, but Sanford had decided Jack would head back to the Schmidt farm. He did exactly what Jack had done with Haggard, and sent his men to head Jack off at the river.

One man was charging from his left. Gunfire ripped through the glade. Jack felt the whip of a bullet passing too close to his cheek, but the near brush with death was forgotten as quickly as the bullet had passed. He fired. The big .44 ball slammed the charging man back and to the ground, but he still held his gun. Jack shot him again before he could lift the weapon. He didn't have time to see if the man was dead. Two more men were charging, but had slowed after seeing blood fly from their two friends, which was the exact opposite of what they should have done. If they had kept coming, one of them might have gotten him.

But both men slid to a stop and jumped behind trees. Jack took the momentary respite to clear the area behind and to each side of him. No movement. It looked like these four were the only ones Sanford had sent. Which made sense. The outlaw chief needed his other four men as escorts to get whatever girls he might have to the pickup point.

From behind one of the trees, a man called, "Hey, gringo. You done shot two of my friends. We just want to talk to you. We can make you a very good deal. Mucho dinero for you. What you say?"

7

Jack could just see the wide brim of the sombrero of the man talking. It was sticking out on both sides of the tree the man was hiding behind. He took careful aim at the brim with the long-barreled Walker and squeezed the trigger. The round ball sliced through a half inch of the curled outer edge of the sombrero almost as smoothly as if it had been done with a knife. The sombrero jerked, and the foot-long and half-inch-wide piece dangled by threads.

The sombrero disappeared completely behind the tree. Jack could picture the man examining his hat. It brought a grin to his face. He felt the adrenaline of the battle, and had it not been for Marlene, he would almost be enjoying himself.

Jack, still watching the tree where the sombrero had been, laid down the empty Walker and picked up the other, earing the hammer back. While he waited, he pulled the little .36-caliber Remington from his left holster.

"Marlene?"

The little girl looked up from below the brush.

"Do you know how to shoot one of these?"

She nodded her head. "My papa lets us shoot all the time. I like it."

Jack pulled the hammer back and carefully handed it to the girl.

She took it in both hands. Jack could see she knew something about weapons. She was careful to keep the muzzle away from him.

"I think there's two bad men left, but if one tries to slip up on us, I want you to shoot him. Right here." Jack pointed to the middle of his body. "Do you think you can do that?"

She nodded her head again. "I can do it. Papa said I'm a good shot."

"Good. If he keeps coming, you keep shooting until he stops. You understand?"

"Yes."

"Don't you be afraid. We're going to get out of this and get you home."

"I trust you, Ranger Sage."

"Señor," came the cry from the man behind the tree, jerking Jack back to his immediate problems. Before he could continue, Jack heard the sound of hoofbeats racing away from the ambush. If there were only four of them and if this wasn't a trick, things were looking up. The Mexican behind the tree was the only one of the four remaining.

The Mexican continued, "You have ruined my beautiful sombrero. Why would you do such a terrible thing?"

Jack said nothing. He moved his head near Marlene's. "Don't worry. There are no more than two left, and maybe only one."

He could see the fear in her eyes, but the little chin jutted out in determination. "I'm a little scared, Ranger Sage."

"I know. Hold on a bit longer."

"Señor, I think my friend has left me to bring the others. It is just you and me for now."

Jack said nothing. He laid down the Walker and slid his Remington out of the holster. It felt good, like an old friend.

"Señor, we can still make a deal, you and me. My *jefe* will pay you much dinero for the girl."

Jack said nothing.

He glanced toward the horses. They were standing with heads up, watching, but they hadn't broken free from their lead ropes.

"You must do something, Señor. *Mi compadre*, he went after the rest of our soldados. They will be back, and they will kill you. Better if you make a deal now."

Jack knew there were three possibilities. The outlaw could have sent a horse running and was now silent, waiting, or he could have run out on his friend, or he could, like the man said, have gone after the others. Jack had to do something. "Why don't you step out from behind that tree."

"Oh, no, Señor. I think you will keel me if I make such a move. I can stay right here and wait for my friends to come. Then we will all keel you ver', ver' slowly."

Jack said nothing. He bent down and put his head close to Marlene's ear. "I'm going after this last man. Stay right here. Keep your gun ready, and wait for me."

She turned her head toward him. Her face was inches away from his. Her clear, bright blue eyes looked directly into Jack's. "You'll be back. I know you will."

"You're right, Marlene. I'll take care of him, and we'll be on our way to take you to your folks." He turned away and started crawling.

Time ticked slowly by. The sun moved higher in the heavens. The horses went back to grazing, and the wild four-legged animals back to foraging. Jack kept slowly moving forward, hoping, after his sombrero getting shot, the Mexican would not look around the tree. If he did, he would find Jack exposed, an easy target.

He reached the halfway point. His right leg ached from the

old bullet wound. *Hopefully it won't cramp now or when I try to stand up,* he thought, and continued moving slowly toward the Mexican's hideout pecan tree.

His mind ventured back to Algeria, the marshes, and the mosquitoes. How bad those mosquitoes had been. It took all of a man's endurance to resist swatting those vicious little creatures, but the movement or the noise of a smack could bring a bullet. This was hard, but nothing like the marshes had been.

He took another breath and moved forward. Sweat ran from under his gray Stetson and into the cut on his temple, the salt doing what salt did naturally, cleansing and burning, but it wasn't bad. He could take it. It wasn't those Algerian mosquitoes.

"Señor, are you still here? Have you left me all alone?"

Jack was almost there, only feet away. He shoved himself forward with his right foot, his eyes glued on the tree in front of him. He knew the Mexican was worried. He might come out from behind the tree at any time. He brought his left foot up and placed his left hand on the tree and pushed. His right leg cramped. He couldn't straighten it.

The Mexican stepped out from behind the tree to his left.

Not the left, his mind shouted. He had his left hand on the tree to brace himself. His Remington was in his right hand, and his right leg was cramping. The instant he came from behind the tree, the big Mexican saw Jack and his awkward stance. In his hand he held another .44-caliber Walker.

It looked huge to Jack. He saw the man's pencil mustache turn up with a grin.

"Señor." The man paused, his grin growing wider, his head nodding. "I think you are dead." The muzzle of the Walker, only inches away, started to swing toward him.

Good, the fella's a talker, Jack thought. He returned the grin and pushed hard against the tree with his left hand, driving his body back, allowing himself to fall backward. Instantly he swung the

Remington and fired at the bulk of the man. There was no aim, just pull the trigger, throw the Mexican's shot off. His bullet struck the barrel of the big Walker, knocking it from the man's hand.

Jack's right leg still wasn't cooperating. He hit the ground on his back and fired again, but the Mexican had leaped behind the tree. Did the man have another gun? If he did, Jack was probably dead. He fired another shot at the opposite side of the tree just to keep the outlaw from coming out, and flexed his right leg. It moved. The cramp was relaxing. He moved it back and forth. The cramp was gone.

He leaped to his feet and waited.

"Don't shoot, Señor. You ruined my beautiful Walker just like you ruined my beautiful sombrero. I don't think I like you, but you don't have to worry about another gun. I don't have one. I'm coming out."

Jack was ready. Both legs were working. He was feeling good. He had escaped death once again. *I'll take luck over skill anytime,* he thought and laughed to himself. "I'd better see both hands first, and they'd best be empty."

"I have a better deal for you, Señor." The Mexican stuck one hand out. It was empty, but when the next came out from behind the tree, it held a long, thin-bladed stiletto. The big outlaw followed his hands and stepped into the open beside the tree. He looked Jack over and shook his head, the little bells on his sombrero giving a soft jingle. After letting out a low, slow whistle, he said, "You are one big gringo, gringo. You must have had plenty of tortillas and frijoles." He threw back his head and laughed at his own humor.

When he looked at Jack again, the grin was gone and the almost black eyes were hard and serious. "I am going to kill you, gringo."

Jack looked the man over. He wasn't as big as Jack, but he was still big, maybe a couple of inches over six feet. He was heavier, with a small paunch, which meant nothing. He had seen men built like him be as quick as a striking rattler.

"I can see you want to fight me, gringo. You have already killed many of my friends." He laughed a humorless chuckle. "Maybe not friends, maybe just *compañeros*. How you say, companions? I think you are one bad hombre, and you know, I too am a bad hombre." He grinned while he turned the knife slowly in his right hand. "Let's see who is the baddest hombre. Huh? What you say?"

Jack grinned back at the outlaw. "Mister, if I didn't have this little girl to look after, I'd take you up on it, but this is not your lucky day. Drop the knife."

The grin left the man's face, and he took a quick step forward. "You make a big mistake, gringo." The outlaw's hand flashed. It jerked back in a short, underhanded blur.

Jack was ready. The knife the outlaw held looked to be perfect for throwing, and the distance between them was short, making Jack an easy target. The problem for the Mexican was that Jack already had his revolver out, the hammer back and pointed at him. All Jack had to do was squeeze the trigger. Which he did.

The knife thudded into the ground halfway between the two men. The Mexican stood. His left hand moved up to his chest, touched the small bullet hole, and, now bloody, moved so the outlaw could see it. He stood swaying, staring at Jack. Then, as if a supporting string were cut, he collapsed to the ground. His eyes stayed on Jack. His breathing was jerky. "Who are you, gringo?"

"Jack Sage."

"Of Laredo?"

"Yes."

The outlaw's eyes grew wide as he labored to get out his last words. "You killed my cousin."

Jack said nothing.

The outlaw released his last breath, and blank eyes stared up into the fluttering green leaves of the pecan tree.

Jack turned to Marlene. He could barely see the top of her head above the brush. "It's over, Marlene. We'll be leaving shortly."

"Good," he heard. "I want to go home."

∽

LATE AFTERNOON of the same day, they rode into the yard of Wilhelm and Deborah Schmidt. Jack was tired, but not too tired to see the completed barn. It looked almost new with the exception of a few smoke-darkened rocks and timbers.

Marlene had fallen asleep and was unconsciously maintaining her balance on her horse. Jack said nothing.

Dirk, his younger sister Elke following him, stepped from inside the barn. When he saw Jack, he stopped, and then his eyes settled on Marlene. He let out a yell, "Mama! Papa!" and ran straight for Jack and Marlene with Elke's fat little legs pumping to stay up with him.

His yell caused Marlene to wake at the same time Deborah and Wilhelm rushed from the house. Jack pulled the horses to a stop. Marlene yanked her right leg out of the stirrup and threw it over the saddle horn. She slid down the horse's side and hit the ground running.

She ran straight to her mama's open arms and, while at least six feet away, leaped into those arms, which clamped tight around her. Sobs racked both daughter and mama. Arms clutched each other desperately as if they feared someone would try to rip them apart. Dirk and Elke both clung to Deborah's dress, while Wilhelm enclosed them all in his strong reassuring arms.

Jack watched from atop Smokey. He stared at the barn, trying to convince himself it was the remaining smell of the caustic smoke that was causing his eyes to burn. *This is the good part,* he thought. *There is so much bad, so much fighting and killing, but this makes it worthwhile. One of these days, folks like this won't have to worry about their youngsters being stolen, but that day's not here yet.*

Wilhelm finally broke away and walked to Jack's side, extending his hand.

Jack took it.

"Mr. Sage, I don't know how I can ever thank you enough. I hoped, but inside was darkness, knowing what happened to those other two little girls down Austin way. You've given us new life. I'll never be able to repay you."

"Mr. Schmidt, seeing Marlene with her family is all the payment I need. It's more than enough. Seldom does a lawman get to see a family happy because of their visit. This makes the job worthwhile."

Marlene finally released her mama's neck and dropped to the ground. Deborah looked up at Jack, tears of happiness flowing down her cheeks. "Mr. Sage, you have brought our Marlene home. How can we ever repay you?"

Jack smiled at the woman and at Marlene. "Ma'am, like I told your husband, what I've just seen is more payment than any man deserves."

She pulled a handkerchief from her apron pocket, wiped her face, blew her nose, and pushed her blonde hair back. "Well, you'll certainly get more than that. Get off that horse and come in the house. I'm sure you and Marlene could use a good meal and a couple of baths." She rubbed her oldest daughter's blonde head, sniffed, and wrinkled her nose in an impish grin. "Especially you, young lady."

Marlene frowned and turned her blue eyes on Deborah. "Mama, I don't stink."

Deborah smiled down at her daughter. "I don't care how you smell, my little sweetheart. It's a smell I love." She looked back up at Jack. "Well, come on, Mr. Sage." She stopped what she had been about to say and asked, "How long has it been since you've slept?"

Jack swung down from Smokey, flinched slightly when his right boot hit the ground, and said, "Ma'am, I'm so tired, I can't rightly remember."

Deborah turned to Wilhelm, who had taken the horses and mules from Jack. "After you take care of those animals, get a tub of water heating. We'll get two baths going. You can set Mr. Sage's in the barn." She stopped and looked at Jack. "Is that alright?"

"That's mighty fine with me, ma'am. You folks don't have to go to so much trouble. I'm going to have to be on my way pretty soon. There's some more children out there."

His last statement stopped her for a moment. She thought, gave a long sigh, and said, "You'll do those babies no good as tired as you are. Your horses look beat, too. You need to get cleaned up and eat. Then a good long rest. It'll sharpen you up for what you have coming."

I can't argue with that, Jack thought, but he said, "Thank you, ma'am, but I do need to be on my way as early as possible."

Deborah swept her children up like a mother hen. "Come along, kids. Mr. Sage needs to wash up." She looked at her husband. "Why don't you get the water started first. Then the two of you take care of the animals. My goodness, Mr. Sage, it looks like you brought back way more horses than you left with, mules, too."

Jack said nothing. He rubbed Smokey's neck. It was true, they were all tired. A couple of days' rest and a good feed would do everyone good.

Wilhelm led five of the animals into the barn. Jack followed with the rest. There were three additional saddles besides the three Jack had taken when he took Marlene from the outlaws' camp. All of them were loaded with rifles and looped holsters hanging from saddle horns, filled with revolvers. Wilhelm shook his head. "It must have been a war out there."

"The cards fell my way." Jack unsaddled Smokey and removed his saddlebags and bedroll. Next he stepped over to his mule and stripped the pack and saddle from his back. He found a brush and started brushing Stonewall.

Wilhelm was back quickly and went to work on the other animals. "As soon as the water's ready, you can jump in the tub. I'll take care of the rest of this stock."

Jack's hand was brushing along Stonewall's back when Wilhelm spoke. His eyes jerked open. "Oh. Yeah. Thanks." He shook his head, laid down the brush, and walked out to the watering trough. Once there, he removed his hat, took a deep breath, and plunged his head into the water. He blew out underwater, creating loud, popping bubbles, and pulled his head out.

Dirk and Elke were standing close, watching him. He shook his head, his thick hair throwing water everywhere like a dog. The two kids, laughing and screaming, jumped back out of range. He looked at the two grinning faces and smiled. "Sorry, living alone, I sometimes forget."

Dirk stepped near to Jack and stared up at him. "You ain't got any kids, Mr. Ranger?"

Jack's mind, dulled from fatigue, flashed back to a little black-haired baby boy in his arms under a warm star-filled Algerian sky. He could feel his amazement of what they had made together, ten fingers, ten toes...

"Mr. Ranger? Are you alright?"

Jack jerked himself from his past, his mind hazy, and stared at the little boy and girl. Finally, feeling embarrassed, he grinned at them. "Sure I am. Just tired. No, Dirk. I don't have any children."

He figured his face must have appeared sad to the children, for Elke stepped forward and grabbed one of his big fingers in her tiny hand. "I'm sowwy, Mr. Ranger. Don't be sad. We love you."

Jack cleared his throat. *The smoke must be bothering me again,* he thought and rubbed his eyes. "Thank you, Elke. Now I've got to get back to the horses."

He returned to the barn to see Wilhelm look at him with a questioning glance, eyebrows raised and eyes wide.

"Those kids bothering you? I'll shoo them away if you like."

Jack shook his head and laughed. "No, not at all. I just got them a little wet when I dunked my head."

Deborah stepped into the barn. "Will, would you get that water ready, please? Supper is almost on the table, and Mr. Sage needs to get cleaned up." She carried a washcloth and towel in her arms, with a bar of lye soap balanced on top. She placed them on a shelf, turned to leave, and stopped. "Mr. Sage, do you have any clothes besides those you're wearing?"

"Yes, ma'am, I sure do. In my saddlebags."

"Good. Leave the dirty ones on the bench by the door of our house, and I'll wash them with Marlene's."

"Thanks." Jack had decided it was no use arguing with this woman.

Wilhelm nodded his head toward the door. "Give me a hand with the tub, Jack, and we'll have you clean in no time."

8

Light filled the room, and Jack stretched his rested body. From the side table he picked up his pocket watch, unconsciously rubbing the emerald shaped in the form of an exploding grenade set in the top of the case. He flipped it open and gazed at the face. Seven. He hadn't slept that long in ages. After bathing, he had dressed in clean clothes and had a meal that had to have been really good, but he kept falling asleep.

Finally, Wilhelm had shown him to this room and closed the door. It had still been light then, so it couldn't have been later than five. He had slept for fourteen hours. There was a chair pulled up to the side of the bed with his gun belt and Remingtons draped over it. On the seat of the chair were his striped trousers and gray and white striped shirt, neatly folded. Socks lay washed and darned next to his shirt, and his vest, brushed spotless, hung over one corner of the chair. His gray Stetson, also clean and brushed, hung over the opposite corner. His light gray bandanna was ironed and lay folded across his shirt. To finish off his ensemble, his boots, cleaned and polished, sat at the foot of the chair.

Jack lay in bed, eyeing the clean clothes. He shook his head and crawled out of bed. The Schmidts were certainly going overboard to be kind to him. Aching muscles complained, but he knew with a little movement, they'd warm and settle down. He slipped his shirt over his head and pulled it down, put his hat on and pulled on his trousers. Next he swung his gun belt around his waist and fastened the buckle in the same worn spot, moved the belt up and down, left and right, until he had it perfectly situated. After looking at the neatly darned socks, he pulled them on, followed with his boots. It felt good to be clean and in clean clothes.

There was a small mirror on a dresser across the room. He walked over and looked at his reflection. *That face just keeps getting older*, he thought. *Fortunately, the hair isn't thinning. Starting to show a little gray at the temples but not much. Speaking of temple, looks like I'll have me another reminder, thanks to Haggard.* His finger gently felt around the lump on the side of his head. It was healing, not as sore.

He rubbed his hand across the stubble. He looked pretty scraggly. He needed to get on into Fredericksburg. He'd take a few minutes to get a good, hot shave there. Before opening the door, he removed his hat. Then he pulled the door wide, ducked, and stepped through. The smell of fresh ham, eggs, gravy, and biscuits hit him. His stomach growled instantly and loudly.

Marlene and Mrs. Schmidt were working in the kitchen. They turned when he opened the door, and both laughed when his stomach growled.

Marlene was the first to speak. "My mama's cooking makes people's stomachs do that." She looked at his forehead. "Your head isn't quite as purple."

"Thanks, I noticed." He turned to Deborah Schmidt. "Mrs. Schmidt, first, thank you for letting me use the bedroom last night. I slept like a rock. Second is all the cleaning you folks did. I don't think I've been decked out like this with shined boots and clean clothes and hat, all at the same time, in ages."

"Call me Debbie, everyone else does, and it was a small thing for what you did for us. We will always be in your debt."

Jack nodded and said only, "Thank you, ma'am."

Wilhelm came in from outside. "Good morning. I hope you slept well."

Jack grinned at the man. "I reckon I slept well, and long. Thanks for your hospitality. I've got to be getting on into town and report to the rangers' office. Those little girls are getting on down the line."

Everyone's faces grew more serious. Wilhelm said, "Yep, we've got us a bona fide Texas Ranger office right in town. Which horse you want saddled, and I'll take care of it."

Debbie put a hand on her hip. "Just you wait a minute. You need food. Your stomach's already let us know that. A few minutes aren't going to help those poor babies. Sit down and eat before you go."

Jack looked at the pile of biscuits and gravy and relented. "The mind says go, but the belly says eat. The belly wins, but I do need to be quick about it. Sorry, ma'am."

Marlene clapped her hands and ran around to a chair on Jack's side of the table, one chair from the end. She pulled it out. "Sit here, Ranger Sage, next to me."

"Thank you, Marlene. Aren't you pretty this morning."

Her mother had brushed the girl's thick blonde hair and tied it with a blue ribbon that closely matched her dress and eyes. She blushed and looked down at the floor, then looked up at Jack. "Thank you." She walked to the big ranger and took his hand. Her dainty little fingers disappeared in his big paw as she guided him to his chair. "I can take your hat."

"Thanks." Jack gave her his hat and sat in the chair. Wilhelm sat in the end chair. Marlene would be sitting between them. Dirk grabbed the chair next to Jack, and Elke sat next to her brother. Deborah's place was across the table, adjacent to her husband.

As good as the food was, and it was delicious, Jack hurried with the meal. He felt a sudden urgency to be on his way. His mind had switched to the chase. These were nice people, and Marlene was a sweetheart, but there were three more sweethearts on their way to San Francisco. He needed to finish up here and find them. But first he had one thing to do.

He reached into his inside vest pockets, one on each side. Jack pulled out two wads of money and Marlene's picture. He examined the picture one last time and handed it back to Deborah.

She took it, smiled, held it to her heart, and laid it on the table.

Jack watched her, then pushed aside his plate, straightened the bills, and laid them on the table.

Dirk's eyes grew large. The little boy had never seen that much money. "Mr. Ranger, is that real money?"

"It sure is, Dirk. I took it from the bad men." He had almost explained he'd taken it off the bodies of the men he'd shot, but changed it for the kids. The stack also included what he had taken from the other outlaws. With Haggard's, it totaled a significant amount.

He counted it out, dividing it into three piles. When he was done, there was three thousand dollars in each stack. He picked up one stack and handed it to Will. "This won't compensate you for the pain you folks went through, but maybe it'll be a help in the future. Those outlaws won't be needing it."

Will pushed Jack's hand away. "That's blood money. We'll not be benefiting from the profits gained by selling children."

Jack shook his head. He leaned past Marlene, whose eyes were also glued on the money, and held it back out to the man. "Will, money is money. It moves around, doing good and doing bad. Let this money do good. It can help your family. It can help your farm. I saw your orchard. It'll be several years before those pecan trees are producing. I know you for a man who looks to the future. Use this to hang on and build that future while you're waiting for your first crop. Let this money do good." With his last words, Jack extended his hand closer to Will.

Will looked at Deborah. She nodded her agreement with Jack, and he took the money. "When you put it like that, Jack, it makes sense."

"Good." He looked down at the two remaining stacks. "These two will go to the families of those two little girls. It won't replace the girls, but maybe it will help those families and their other children. That's one of the reasons I need to get into the rangers' office." He picked up the two piles of money and put one in each of his inside vest pockets and stood.

Will stood at the same time. "Which horse?"

"The grulla. I'll be along in just a second."

"Take your time," Will said, hurrying out the door.

Marlene jumped out of her chair and ran to get Jack's hat. He watched her run across the room, and thought, *She's springing back. She's a tough little girl.*

He turned back to Deborah. "Ma'am, I'm sorry to have to leave like this. Breakfast was mighty good. I appreciate all you folks have done for me. It wasn't necessary."

She had also risen. "But it was, Ranger Sage. You brought our sweet Marlene back to us."

Marlene ran to Jack with his hat, handed it to him, and held her arms out. He took his hat and reached down for the little girl. When he had lifted her, she threw her arms around his neck and squeezed hard, speaking into his ear. "I love you, Ranger Sage. I know you must be an angel God sent to protect me."

Jack felt the smoke in his eyes again. Through the blue dress, he patted Marlene's back. "Reckon I'm no angel, Marlene, but I know you're a strong girl, and one of these days you'll grow up to be a fine woman, just like your mama. I'm glad you're back home."

He gave her a final squeeze and returned her to the floor.

Deborah, tears at the corners of her blue eyes, moved around the table, tiptoed, and gave Jack a kiss on the cheek. "Like we said, we will always be in your debt."

Jack nodded his head. "I'll see you folks in a while." He stooped, stepped through the door, and took a deep breath. One more stop and he'd be on his way.

∼

Jack guided Smokey to the hitching rail in front of a narrow office squeezed between a bank and a general store. The title, Texas Rangers, was etched on the glass in the upper half of the door. He stepped from the saddle, looped the reins around the rail, strode to and opened the door. He bent and stepped in, looking around.

The office was small. There was barely room for a desk, a couple of chairs, and a potbellied stove, with a steaming pot of coffee on it. A closed door in the back wall allowed access to another office.

The older man at the desk looked up. "What can I do for you?" His question wasn't unfriendly, but it didn't invite wasted conversation either.

Jack pulled the captain's badge from his pocket and tossed it on the desk. He could see the recognition in the man's eyes at the sight of the badge. The man stood and thrust out a hand. "Don't think I know you. I'm Gabe Patton. Most folks know me as Gabby 'cause I don't talk much."

Jack shook the man's hand. "Jack Sage. You in charge here?"

Gabby's eyes widened at the mention of Jack's name. He stared and shook his head, tossing a thumb toward the door in the back wall. "Not a chance. I just take care of the office. Major Wilson, Gordon Wilson, is the man in charge. Let me get him for you."

Before Gabby could move, the door opened, and a man about Jack's age stepped through. He was solidly built. Like most, not as tall or as big as Jack, but solid. He sported a handlebar mustache that was neatly curled and trimmed. He extended his hand. "Gordon Wilson, Sage, glad to meet you. Why don't you grab a cup of coffee and step back to my office." A glint of humor passed through the major's eyes, corners wrinkling. "If you can fit in, that is." He glanced at the older man. "You got an extra cup around here, Gabby?"

"I shore do, Major Wilson." Gabby turned, yanked a dusty cup from the shelf behind his desk, blew the dust out, and handed it to Jack.

"Much obliged." Jack took the cup, grabbed the pot, and poured himself a full cup of coffee, then followed Wilson into his office and closed the door.

The major had moved behind his desk to sit. When he heard the door close, he turned to look at Jack, eyebrows raised.

Jack reached inside his vest pocket and pulled out the two stacks of money, laying them on Wilson's desk.

Before he could explain, Wilson asked, "What's this?"

Jack pulled up a chair. Wilson gave a hand motion indicating for Jack to sit. He eased himself into the chair, never trusting chairs because of his weight. Recognizing it was carrying his weight, he relaxed and eased forward.

"Major, the Schmidt girl is home. We arrived back yesterday."

The man punched the air. "That's one of the best things I've heard. How is she?"

"I'd say pretty good. She's a tough little girl. She had to go through a lot, but the men didn't touch her other than to slap her around."

Wilson's face darkened. "I'd like to get my hands on them."

Jack shook his head. "It won't be necessary. They've recognized the error of their ways."

Wilson's brows lifted. "How many?"

"All told, there were two bunches, a total of seven. That's where this money comes from. Before they passed, they asked me to donate this money to the Schmidts and to the families of the little girls they murdered."

Wilson leaned forward, his forearms on his desk, and stared at Jack. "They asked you?"

"In a manner of speaking. I wanted to get it to you. I've already given the Schmidts their third. I figure you can make sure those families get theirs." Jack eyed the major, waiting for his reaction.

Major Wilson gave a slow, pensive nod. "Yes, I believe I can ensure those families get this money. You say the Schmidts have already received an equal portion?"

"Yep." Jack held the major's stare, his expression blank.

"Do I need to ask what happened to the outlaws?"

Jack shook his head. "Not really. You're a major in the rangers. I think you can figure it out. I do have more information about the leaders of this bunch, unless you feel you need to ask additional questions about the outlaws."

Wilson shook his head slowly. "No. I think I have all the information I need." The major scooped up the money and slipped it into his desk drawer.

"Good, let me tell you what I know, what I think I know, and what I need to pursue the remaining three girls." Jack began explaining, and the captain leaned closer as he spoke.

When he was finished, Jack leaned back in his chair and waited. Major Wilson, his head turned slightly, watched a spider build her web where the walls and ceiling joined. Finally he looked at Jack. "That's a pretty ambitious plan and a massive amount of travel. You think your horses will make it? They'll be carrying quite a load."

Jack nodded. "You haven't seen my horses. Take a look at the grulla tied out front. I have a chestnut and a gray built just like him. I also have a strong and dependable mule, but as strong as he is, he's my weak link. I can't expect him to carry the load he'll be carrying."

Wilson nodded. "You're right, not all the way to California, even El Paso. You're looking at a rough haul."

"That's why I need an additional mule. Stonewall, that's his name, gets along with me and all the horses. I need another one like him."

"I can take care of that. The liveryman we use knows his animals, and he's the owner of several mules. He'll get you a good one." The major opened the desk drawer and took out a stack of the money Jack had just given him. He counted out a thousand dollars and pushed it across the table. "Take this. It'll get you on your way quicker. I'll replace it from the bank later. I'll also have Gabby and another ranger ride out and pick up those horses, saddles, and weapons. When we sell them, they'll bring more money than what I've given you."

"Thanks." He pulled out a list and handed it to Wilson. "I need to get a shave before heading out of here. Is there someone you can get to drop this list off at the mercantile? When I'm done, I'll swing by the livery, pick up the mule, and load him up at the mercantile. Then I'll be on my way."

Wilson stood. "I'll get it taken care of. Don't let me hold you up. I know you're anxious to be after those girls. I wish we had men to send with you, but everyone's out on assignment."

Jack stood. "Thanks, Major. I think it's better with just me, although I could sure use Cart. He's a fine tracker."

"Let's check with Gabby. They're on their way back. Maybe I could send him with you. He probably wouldn't mind seeing California again. He was out there a few years ago."

They stepped into the main office, and Wilson said, "Gabby, what's the last we heard of Cart's location?"

Gabby opened the side drawer of the desk, fumbled through some papers, pulled a wrinkled, sweat-stained note from the drawer, and handed it to Major Wilson.

Wilson read it and looked up. "They've chased the Comanches back into the Oklahoma territory. From this, it looks like they're headed for Santa Angela. They heard of some trouble there between the town and the fort. The military commander would prefer the rangers deal with it."

Jack nodded. "Always better to keep the military out of civil problems if possible, especially in Texas. Is it possible you can get a message out there? Have Cart meet me in Fort Stockton?"

"I can. We'll dispatch a rider today."

"Thanks, Major." Jack extended his hand. "I'm getting that shave."

As they shook hands, the major said, "Good luck to you. I hope you can save those girls."

Jack nodded to Gabby and turned for the door. "And I plan on finding out who's behind this whole thing."

9

Jack pulled his animals to a halt. They'd been traveling for six days over rough country. Off to the north was Seven Mile Mesa, and directly in front of him was Fort Stockton and Comanche Springs. Even from this distance, the gushing water of the springs glistened in the afternoon sunlight, and the light breeze shimmered through the tall grass like waves on an ocean. There weren't many trees out here except along the creeks and rivers, but the grass was plentiful.

He patted Pepper on the neck. They'd made good time. Since leaving the Schmidt farm, they had traveled over two hundred miles and completed it in six days. There were overnight stops, but the nights were short. He had hoped from the start he'd reach Fort Stockton before the outlaws did. Soon, he would have the answer.

Besides the outlaw leader's name, Robert or Bob Sanford, he knew little else. He didn't even know if the outlaws who had grabbed the girls had traveled this far. They were supposed to hand the girls over to a man and woman near the camp where he found Marlene, but that summed up all he knew about their travel, other than the destination, San Francisco.

"Come on, boys, just a little bit farther and you can have you some of that sweet-tasting water to go along with your oats and maybe a little corn." He clucked, and Pepper stepped out, followed by the others. He'd soon know what or who waited for him in Fort Stockton.

Jack rode into the little town. Storefronts were being thrown up along the main street, and several houses were in the building process on lanes running perpendicular from main. People stopped to watch him ride in. He was used to it. A man his size on a horse the size of Pepper, and the other two, would usually bring a bit of gawking. From the first building on the left side of the street, a sign hung, proclaiming Binford's Stable, and adjacent to it, Butterfield Stage. The livery had a covered area extending toward the prairie. It housed a forge, anvil, tub, and a long desk-like structure with tools hanging from the end of it. The owner had an assortment of hammers, and a pair of tongs lay across the corner of the desk.

Jack was glad to see a blacksmith shop. It was about time his whole crew got new shoes, especially knowing how much farther they still had to go. He rode up to the water trough and swung down. The animals crowded around, helping themselves.

"They look to be a mite thirsty," a heavyset man commented as he stepped out of the office.

"That they are. I'll be needing to put them up for the night."

"Twenty cents a day, twenty-five if you're a-wantin' oats or corn. That'd work out to a buck or a buck and a quarter a day dependin' on what suits your needs."

Jack took out a dollar and a quarter, reached across Pepper's back, and dropped them into the man's hand. "I'm guessing you must be Mr. Binford."

"That I be. Most folks call me Binford or Ford, makes no never mind to me. Reckon you must be Ranger Sage."

Surprised, Jack said, "How'd you know?"

Binford nodded. "I figgered. Couldn't be two people in these parts your size. An older fella rode into town earlier today. He described you, said you and him are rangers, and to be on the lookout for you. Said your name was Jack Sage."

"Good, so Cart made it."

"He did, Ranger Sage, and you can find him at the Silver Dollar Hotel. You want I should give your animals a good rubdown? Looks like they could use a good one."

Jack scratched Pepper behind the ear. "Do that. They've come a long way fast. They're tired and hungry, especially the mules. They've been swapping their load all the way from Fredericksburg."

Ford stepped over to Stonewall and started unloading the packs. "I like mules. I'll take good care of 'em. I'll put your gear in the tack room. It'll be out of sight from curious eyes and sticky fingers."

"Thanks. I've got another question for you."

Ford gathered the lead ropes in one hand and the reins in the other. Then he turned to Jack. "Fire away. I know most of what goes on in this town."

"Have you seen a wagon come into town? It would be driven by a scholarly-looking man and woman, with three little girls."

Ford smiled. "Why, sure I have. That's Mr. Clements, he's Bertrand Clements, a college professor from California, and Miss Tidwell, Nadine Tidwell. She's a teacher, and she looks after the girls. Most of the girls are sad because they're leavin' their folks and going to a finishing school, but she works real hard trying to keep them happy."

"Are they still in town?"

Ford shook his head. "Oh, no, they always take the first stage out to California. Mr. Clements tells me he wants to get the girls there as soon as possible so they can get used to their new surroundings and begin learning."

"When did the stage leave?"

"They got on the stage yesterday morning, Mr. Clements,

Miss Tidwell, and the three girls. Saw 'em myself. It's surprising how much these girls look alike. I asked Mr. Clements about that, and he told me it's because most of them are German. It's only them Germans who can afford to send their kids so far away to finishing school."

"Where's the hotel, Ford?"

"Cain't miss it. On this side halfway up the street, Silver Dollar Hotel. When you leaving?"

"Probably in the morning. See you then." Jack turned to leave in search of Cart, when Ford's voice stopped him.

"Mr. Clements and Miss Tidwell have left, but if you wanted to talk to Bob Sanford, he and his boys are still in town."

Jack stopped and spun back around. "Any idea where they're staying?"

Ford chuckled, then said, "You must not know Mr. Sanford. He only stays in the best of places. He'll be in the Silver Dollar, too."

"Ford, I haven't met Mr. Sanford yet. Could you tell me what he looks like?"

The liveryman had removed the mule's pack and was unfastening the cinch on Pepper. He stopped and looked over Pepper's back at Jack. "I'd have to say he's a fine specimen of a man. He carries himself like he's used to having money. Thick black hair, kinda falls out from under his hat, over his forehead. I notice he's always takin' his hat off, fancy black Stetson, and pushing his hair back up under the brim. Like most of us, the sun has his skin mighty dark.

"He'll stand about five ten, and I'd guess he weighs around one-eighty. Thick in the shoulders. Keeps his hair long over his ears. I reckon it's to cover up the saber scar, whacked off the top of his left ear." He put the saddle up and turned back to Jack. "He does wear some fancy boots. They have silver tabs over the toes. He's mostly pleasant unless he gets riled. Looks to be a bad feller to mix it with if that happens. That's about it, all I remember."

Jack looked up the street, anxious to be on his way. "You've got a good memory for people, Ford. Much obliged. Oh, don't mention rangers are in town. Alright?"

Ford picked up a brush and headed for Stonewall. "Sure thing, stranger. Have a good evening."

Jack lifted his hand in salute, turned, and headed up the street. He wanted to find Cart and corral this bunch. Hopefully they could find out more about the route Clements was taking with the girls and get more information on the San Francisco man.

Jack strode down the boardwalk, stepping aside and tipping his hat to the ladies. It surprised him there were so many in this remote part of Texas, but riding into Fort Stockton, he had seen large numbers of cattle and sheep. The more ranches around, the more women, plus the businesses in town. He did hear pianos filling the night, so there were sure to be several saloons.

He made it to the Silver Dollar Hotel without passing a saloon. They must all be on the opposite end of town. He'd thought about stopping at the stage office, but the lights were already out. Turning into the lobby, he was relieved to see Cart sitting on a large sofa with a cup of coffee and a newspaper. Jack walked up to the ranger, whom he could see watching him over the top of the paper.

Cart laid his paper aside and looked up at Jack. "Howdy, I got Major Wilson's note. You been busy. Glad you got the girl back."

"Me too. It was touch and go there for a bit, but it all worked out."

"How is she?"

"Surprisingly well. They slapped her around a little, but physically, that was all."

"Bet her folks were happy to see her."

"Yep." Jack looked around the lobby. No sign of the man he was looking for. "Cart, you seen anything of a black-haired fella?

He's about five ten and weighs around one-eighty. Has silver caps on the toes of his boots."

"I have. He's with four slimy-lookin' characters. They all act tough. You know the type, walk right at other men to make 'em step aside, leer at the ladies, and always loud. The feller you described is the exception in the group. He acts like sugar wouldn't melt in his mouth, all bowing and doffing his hat to the ladies and engaging men like they were long-lost friends. And would you believe, it appears he and the local marshal are on mighty friendly terms."

Jack continued to look around the lobby, though the smells from the restaurant were getting his attention. "How long you been in town?"

"Since morning, why?"

"You sure picked up a lot."

The older man grinned. "Been 'round the patch more'n once. Had a meal back there." He tossed a thumb toward the hotel restaurant. "But most of the day, I've either been sitting here reading my newspaper and drinkin' coffee or in front of the hotel. Those rockers out there are mighty comfortable. Are we after that bunch?"

"Yes and no. You eaten supper?"

"Nope, been hoping you'd show."

Jack nodded toward the restaurant. "Let's grab something to eat and talk. I need to fill you in."

On their way to the restaurant, Jack stopped at the front desk, signed in, and got a room across the hall from Cart. He finished quickly, leaving his rifle with the hotel clerk.

Jack scanned the restaurant as he entered. He noticed Cart was doing the same thing. They were quickly led to a table near the front window, which Jack declined, pointing to a smaller table by the back wall.

Once seated, Jack leaned across to Cart and began speaking in a low tone. "The man I was asking about is Robert Sanford. He leads one of the gangs that are stealing the girls."

Cart leaned forward. "I knew there had to be more than one bunch taking those girls. I suspected there were at least three, but we never found any solid proof."

"All I know of is two. So far, each of them is made up of eight men. Sanford's the leader of this bunch."

Cart slid his chair back. "What are we waiting for? Let's go put an end to some outlaws."

Jack shook his head. "No. I want you to know the whole story, plus I'm hungry." As he spoke, the waiter approached with coffee, filled their cups, took their orders, and left. Jack took a sip of the bitter, steaming brew, and continued.

"This seems to be a well-organized effort, and you're not going to believe how much is being paid to kidnap these girls." He took another sip of coffee, swallowed, and resumed his tale. "But I'll get to that. There are other crooks involved. The outlaws who grab the girls turn them over to a scholarly-looking couple who takes them to San Francisco, where another man is waiting for them. I don't know his name or location."

The waiter returned with their dinner. Jack was hungry, but his concern for the girls overpowered the enjoyment of the food. He ate quickly, filling in Cart between bites. "Sanford grabbed three girls. He was supposed to meet up with the outlaws who took Marlene, but they won't be meeting with anyone except their maker. He got them to the scholarly man and woman and accompanied them here. The girls left with those two on yesterday's stage."

Cart cursed loud enough for the other patrons to turn from their meals and stare at him disapprovingly. He made eye contact with an elderly lady. "Sorry, ma'am."

She gave him a curt nod and turned back to her meal. He returned several hard stares from men around the room and turned back to Jack. "Those girls won't be able to ride that stage all the way through. They'll never make it. They're going to stop several times. That's a long, hard haul. Maybe we can catch up with them when they stop."

Jack finished his dinner. The concern he had been feeling for the girls was growing. With it, the stress. He needed to stop Sanford and his men to ensure there would be no more young girls taken, but he also had to rescue the captives before something terrible happened to them. He took a deep breath. "Any idea where they might stop?"

Cart nodded. "Yep, a couple. El Paso's the first. The girls have already traveled from Central Texas and are tired. After this stretch to El Paso on a stagecoach, they'll be exhausted. I think they'll have to stop." Cart sat up straight, as if an idea hit him. "I'll tell you something else. We need to talk to the stage manager, Ezra Becker. He may know exactly where they'll be stopping."

Jack shook his head. "His office is closed."

"Yeah, but I know where he lives. Let's go." Cart stood, reaching into his vest pocket.

Jack rose at the same time. "Forget it. Major Wilson gave me expense money."

The two men walked from the restaurant and out the hotel door.

"Follow me." Cart turned left and headed toward the first side street and turned left again. At the second house, he stepped through a space in the fence.

Jack could see the fence was new. The gate had yet to be hung. The house had a fresh coat of lemon yellow paint and a high porch. Five steps led up to the porch. The occupants of the house must have heard the clump and jingle of their boots, for as they reached the door, it opened. The man was younger, well dressed, slim, and sporting a full mustache. His gaze fixed on Jack, who towered over him.

"What can I do for you gentlemen?"

"You can let us in, for one thing, Ezra."

The man's head swung to Cart, and his face broke into a grin. "Why, Ranger Cart, it's good to see you. Yes, please, gentlemen, come in." He opened the door wider and followed it, allowing room for both men to enter the hallway.

Cart spoke up. "Ezra, this is Ranger Sage. We're on the trail of some mighty bad folks and thought you might be able to help."

Ezra motioned to the first room off the hallway. "Please have a seat."

A large, blond, pecan desk dominated the office space. In addition, in front of the desk were two green wingback chairs. Behind the desk and on the two adjacent walls were bookcases running from the floor to the ceiling and stuffed with books. Ezra moved to the chair and sat. Jack and Cart followed suit, dropping into the two wingbacks. "Tell me, how can I help?"

Jack spoke. "Mr. Becker, I'm sure this is going to surprise you, but Bertrand Clements and Nadine Tidwell are thieves."

The man's eyes widened. "I cannot believe it. I value education, and both Bertrand and Nadine seem so well educated. It's very hard to picture them as criminals."

"That's why they make such good thieves. They had three children with them?"

"Why, yes, they did."

"Three little girls."

"Yes."

Jack leaned forward, his forearms rested on the desk. "Those little girls have been abducted, stolen from their parents."

"What? I can't believe it. This is the second time Bertrand and Nadine have come through our fair town with young girls. The very first time, Bertrand took great pains to explain they were taking the children to finishing school."

Jack shook his head. "I'm sure he did, but the finishing school doesn't exist. They're taking them to a fella in San Francisco who's paying a pretty penny for them. In fact, part of their gang killed two other girls when the rangers got too close."

"Oh my goodness," the station manager exclaimed. "How can I help?"

Jack leaned back, resting his thick forearms on the arms of the chair. "By telling us how many stops they plan on making."

"Why, sure. Dr. Clements always stops in El Paso, and most of the time in Tucson. He makes several stops along the way, allowing the girls to rest. I can give you a list of his other layovers if you like?"

"That could be a big help," Jack said.

Becker opened his top desk drawer, took out a sheet of paper, a blotter, a steel-nibbed pen, and a bottle of ink. He laid the paper on a leather backing on his desk, opened the bottle of ink, dipped the pen, and began to make a list. After several entries, he picked up the blotter, rocked it across what he had written, examined the result, and continued.

With his last entry, he made one final blot, blew on the paper, shook it, and handed it to Jack. "Please don't fold it for a few minutes, or it still might smear. Will that help you?"

Jack looked it over and thought, *San Francisco is a long haul. I sure hope we can catch them in El Paso, as much for the girls as us and the horses.* He raised his eyes from the paper to Becker. "This'll help."

"Good. It is still hard for me to believe anything bad about Mr. Clements. Why, he has been in our home. He is a very wise and interesting man."

Jack's eyes hardened. "When we get our hands on him, his interests are going back to Fredericksburg. He'll have to use all of his wisdom to keep his neck out of a hangman's noose."

Becker's face turned pale. "You do know he's traveling with two other gentlemen."

Jack looked at Cart and turned back to Becker. "That's the first we've heard of them."

"I must say, they are impressive. Bertrand usually has two such men with him to protect the girls. They're not thugs. They're well-spoken and polite, but large." He looked at Jack. "Almost as big as you. Bertrand says they are necessary because of the dangers of outlaws along the stage route." Realizing what he had said, Becker shook his head. "Unbelievable, they're the outlaws."

Jack said nothing.

Cart leaned forward. "Ezra, what can you tell us about Bob Sanford?"

Becker had been looking at Jack. When Cart mentioned Sanford's name, his head snapped around to the ranger. "Is Bob involved?"

Jack leaned forward again, his concern for the girls growing with every moment he and Cart weren't on the trail. "Mr. Becker, we need to know all you know about Sanford, and we don't have a lot of time if we're going to try to catch those thieves."

In amazement, Becker turned back to Jack. "Ranger Sage, it will be almost impossible for you to catch the Butterfield stage. We have stations no more than forty and sometimes twenty miles apart. At every station, the mules are changed out."

Jack looked at Cart and back to Becker. "How long does Clements stay in El Paso and Tucson?"

Becker thought for a minute. "If I remember correctly, he said he wanted to rest at least two days and no more than four, depending on how tired the girls were."

Jack nodded. "Perhaps we can catch them there."

Becker shook his head. "If they stay four, then yes, you might, but you'll have to push your horses extremely hard. If you miss them in El Paso, I don't think your horses will have the strength to race to Tucson."

Jack looked out the dark windows. *How are we going to save those innocent girls?* he thought. *How do we do it? Did I make a mistake not going back to Sanford's camp when I could?*

"Jack," Cart said, "we can catch them in El Paso. Come on." He stood and watched Becker. "Ezra, tell us what you know about

Sanford, and make it quick." He slammed his calloused hand on the desk. "We need that information now!"

Becker jumped and stared at Cart, then began talking. "Bob Sanford is the cousin of Carter Beake, our town marshal. They've always been close. They fought in the war together. Carter was with Bob when he lost part of his ear. Carter even killed the Yankee who sliced Bob's ear off." His voice changed from passing information to almost pleading. "You can't really be after Bob Sanford. He's the nicest guy in town. Granted, the crew he runs with is pretty rough, but he isn't. He'd never kidnap little girls."

Cart pointed a big finger at Becker. "You tell us where they hang out, right now."

"Bob always stays at the Silver Dollar Hotel. I don't know about his companions. There's a girl he likes at the Last Chance Saloon, Dory Abney. If he isn't at the hotel, he'll be at the saloon. You'd best be careful. The men he hangs out with are tough."

"No, Mr. Becker," Jack said, "those men aren't tough. They're mean little cowards who steal and hurt children. We aim to take 'em back to Fredericksburg or Austin and see them hang. I thank you for your information and recommend you remain in your home this evening. You wouldn't want to be thought aiding outlaws."

Jack turned and headed for the door. Cart gave Ezra a warning look and followed.

Outside, Cart asked, "Where we goin'?"

Jack checked each of his Remingtons, making sure they were loose in their holsters. "We're going to enforce the law."

Cart's face, visible in the moonlight, broke into a grin. "Heh-heh-heh. Now you're talking." He followed Jack's example with his two .44s.

10

Reaching main street, Jack and Cart turned left. Most of the city's citizens had disappeared from the street. Buffalo hunters, scalp hunters, drinkers, drunks, and cowhands were the only ones out at this time of night.

The sounds of laughter and drunken singing accompanied by a tinny piano Jack couldn't stand filled the moonlit darkness. He had never been able to appreciate music. He remembered his mother telling him how, when he was a baby, she had played the piano to soothe him, but instead, it sent him into fits of screaming. She had tried several times to help him appreciate the awful discordant sounds, but, finally, she stopped. She reserved her playing for only when her son wasn't around. He felt bad, because she loved music, as did many people, but he could not stand it.

He reached into his vest pocket, pulled out the ranger badge, and hung it on his vest. "There's at least five in this bunch. We don't have a lot of time. We need to take care of 'em and be on our way, but we can't be careless."

Cart patted his badge already hanging on his jacket. "I've taken care of coyotes before. You just do your thing, and I'll follow your lead." He motioned in front, several buildings ahead where light streamed into the street from the door and windows. "That's the place."

Jack gave a sharp nod. Upon reaching the doors, he pushed them wide and stepped through. Like every saloon, the interior filled his senses. A loud piano banged incessantly from the back wall, competing with the raised, demanding voices of patrons. They wanted a drink, to place bets, or just to be heard over the din.

But he was used to all of this except maybe the piano. This was where much of his work as a lawman had always been done. Smells vied for dominance, unwashed bodies, the rotting stench of buffalo hides, perfumes of the girls, cattle odors from the cowhands, and the smell of sweaty horses from just about everyone. And the sight, men and women laughing, bartering, gambling, and jostling each other.

But he wasn't here to enjoy the sights and sounds, he was here to find Sanford. It took him only a moment to spot the man sitting at one of the tables, a busty blonde hanging around his neck. From behind him, she reached over his right shoulder and lifted a glass of amber liquid to his lips. He carefully took a sip, took it from her hand, and set it back on the table. She laughed and gave him a tight hug, kissing his cheek.

Jack noticed Cart was angling away from him and also watching Sanford. He examined the men at the table. There were two others beside the gang's leader. He was guessing these were the men who rode with Sanford. But where were the other two? There was no way to tell. The saloon was filled with hard men. It would be impossible to pick them out until there was a confrontation. He wanted to keep the bar and Sanford's table in his and Cart's line of sight.

He began to move toward Sanford. As he did, the noise of the saloon started subsiding. Heads turned toward Jack and Cart. The arrival of a Texas Ranger in town didn't go unnoticed, and when two showed up, everyone knew excitement could be just around the corner.

Jack saw the bartender move away from the bar and stretch his arms, placing his hands flat on the counter behind him. *Good, Jack thought, one less we have to worry about.*

The blonde spotted Jack first. He saw her lift the black hat and press her lips to Sanford's right ear. He could see her whispering. Sanford, who was focused on the man he was talking to on his left, turned his head. Jack could see his eyes go straight to the ranger's badge. His face grew solemn, but Jack saw no fear.

By now the shouting and talking had almost ceased, and there was near silence in the saloon. Thankfully, even the piano player had stopped hammering the keys.

Jack saw two men step away from the bar and head toward the door. His voice rang out in the now quiet saloon. "Hold your places. We're Texas Rangers, Sage and Cartwright. No one leaves the building." Jack nodded at the two men. "You two back up against the bar rail and face the mirror. Place your hands on the bar."

The smaller man glared at Jack and started to speak. His partner grabbed his arm and jerked him back to the bar. Both turned and placed their hands flat on the bar top.

Jack glanced back to face Sanford. "You're Robert Sanford?"

Sanford, cool as a cougar about to pounce, leaned back in the chair and motioned to the table. "I am, Ranger. Why don't the two of you take seats, and I'll buy you a drink."

"Robert Sanford, I am placing you and your outlaw friends under arrest for the kidnapping of young girls to be sold as chattel. Stand up slowly, and lay your gun belts and guns on the table."

Sanford spread his arms and held out his hands. "Ranger, you've made a big mistake. I've kidnapped no one. I was hired by a finishing school in San Francisco to escort three young ladies here. I turned them over to a professor and his assistant."

Jack looked at Dory. "Ma'am, you'd best step away. There may be gunfire, and I wouldn't want you injured."

The table directly behind Sanford was filled with gamblers. At Jack's suggestion to the girl, the gamblers jerked erect, chairs flew back, they grabbed at the money on the table and scurried to get out of the line of fire. Sanford patted Dory on her forearm, pulled her around, and gently slapped her on the bottom as he guided her away from the table.

"There's no need for gunfire, Ranger Sage. We'll go in peacefully."

"Stand up. I'll not tell you again." Jack had moved to the side of the table. He was now depending on Cart to watch the room and the two outlaws at the bar.

"Come on, Ranger, my cousin's the marshal in this town. We're not the worthless bunch you're looking for. We're honest, hard-work—"

Jack stepped within range, hooked the toe of his boot under the back leg of the outlaw's chair, and jerked. Sanford flipped over backwards, his hat flying from his head. He started up from a crouch, and Jack hit him. He limited the force of the blow. He didn't want to kill the man. His fist struck Sanford in the chest. *Let's see how smooth-talking you can be with the breath knocked out of you,* Jack thought.

This time Sanford hit the floor and slid on his butt until he came up short against the wall. The two tables behind his were positioned perfectly to allow him to slide between them without hitting either. He sat gasping for air, leaning forward from the wall, and both hands gripping his chest. He looked like a catfish out of water.

The ratcheting sound of a Colt hammer going to full cock and its cylinder rotating filled the silence of the room. When Jack hit Sanford, Cart had pulled one of his .44s. "All right, boys, just like the man said, unfasten those belts and put 'em on the table."

The two outlaws at the table did as they were told. Jack

stepped across the room to Sanford, glancing at the floor where he had slid. Just as he suspected. This was a rough-hewn floor, with plenty of splinters. He could see the bright spots of fresh, clean, exposed wood where splinters had separated from the floor.

Sanford was still gasping when Jack reached him. He bent, grabbed the man by the front of his shirt, and yanked him to his feet. The outlaw immediately bent over, laboring to draw a breath. Jack knew breath came sooner if a man stood erect, but this man didn't deserve help. He grabbed him by the back of his vest and shoved him forward toward the table. "Take your gun belt off and add it to the collection."

Sanford, who was beginning to breathe, unfastened the belt and dropped it on the table. Jack gave him a hard shove. "You know where the jail is, Sanford. Let's go." The man almost fell, but caught himself and straightened. He winced, reached back, and pulled a splinter from his rear.

Cart's attention had switched from the men at the bar to the two men still at the table. "Up, you two. You're going with him." The two rose, started moving, and Cart bent to pick up the three gun belts.

Jack caught a flash of movement from the corner of his eye. The younger outlaw at the bar had spun around and was drawing. Jack's right hand was full of the back of Sanford's vest and shirt. His left streaked for his Remington. He knew he wasn't as fast with his left hand, but it might be fast enough. The .36-caliber revolver slipped free and clear. The moment the muzzle passed the edge of the holster, it started rotating, the barrel smoothly coming up while Jack's huge thumb pulled the hammer back.

He could see the other man's hand was faster than his. The big muzzle of the .44 Colt was staring at him. The thought coursed through his mind: *He's going to beat me!* He braced his body for the impact, and the outlaw's .44 fired. Smoke shot from the muzzle, accompanied by a round ball of lead rocketing toward him. Jack pulled the trigger. He saw a bloom of red on the man's chest and heard a crash to his right.

He kept his eyes on the outlaw, ready to fire as many times as needed. The man's revolver drifted down until it was pointing at the floor. Then it slowly started moving back to the horizontal. Jack waited, and the outlaw's strength faded with his loss of blood. His hand relaxed. The weapon dropped to the floor, followed by the outlaw. His partner dropped to a knee, then looked at Jack.

"You killed my brother."

Jack watched the kneeling man. He was older. There was graying in his hair and in his mustache. "I didn't want to. It's time for you to stand up and put your weapon on the bar. Don't make me kill you, too."

The man stood, unfastening his gun belt. The outlaw lifted the belt and gripped the body of the holster with his left hand. He cast a furtive glance at Jack, turned the holster toward him, and went for the butt of the handgun with his right hand.

Never attempting to draw the revolver from the holster, the outlaw pulled the hammer back. The roar of a .44 Colt erupted behind Jack, and the outlaw slammed against the bar. With the support of the bar behind him, he managed to stay on his feet and yank the revolver from the holster. This time both Cart's Colt and Jack's Remington roared. The outlaw jerked twice against the bar and toppled over his brother.

Jack glanced back at Cart, saw he was covering the shooter, and swung his revolver back toward Sanford and the other two men. All three stood with their hands high, visibly hoping to ensure neither Jack nor Cart made a mistake and shot them.

"Cart, watch these three."

"Like a hawk."

Jack strode over to the crumpled men, knelt, and examined them. The older man was still breathing. The outlaw, bloody froth around his lips, coughed. "I had to try. He was my brother."

Jack dropped his Remington into his holster, cradled the man's head in one hand, and slid the outlaw's hat under his head before he slowly allowed the man's head to rest on the hat. "If he had been my brother, I would've done the same thing."

Jack stared into the man's piercing blue eyes while the man held his gaze. He had another fit of coughing. "I shoulda been a better brother. He didn't deserve to die like this."

Jack nodded at the man. "You should have, and neither of you should ever have taken those children." The man's eyes widened, as if he were seeing the devil himself, and Jack watched the light fade from the outlaw's eyes. He stood.

Both were dead. He retrieved their gun belts, placing them on the bar, followed by two guns, which he slid into the holsters. He knelt again and inspected the holes in the bar. Rising, he looked at the bartender, who had remained calm and stationary throughout the entire incident. "Sorry about the damage. How much you think it'll cost?"

"Five dollars oughta cover it."

Jack pulled a five-dollar bill from inside his vest pocket and dropped it on the bar. "You have an undertaker in town?"

The bartender nodded. "With all the shootin', I expect he'll be showing up shortly."

"Good." Jack dropped a double eagle next to the five-dollar bill. "Give him this and tell him to take care of the bodies. If he has any questions, he can get in touch with the nearest rangers' office." Jack turned and headed back to the prisoners, his boots thumping on the wooden floor the only sound in the saloon.

Reaching Cart and the prisoners, he said, "Let's go."

The prisoners headed out, then Cart. Jack stepped to the door as a pale-faced man with rumpled black hair and a black coat to match burst through the batwing doors.

He stopped and looked at Jack's badge. "Got some business for me?"

Jack pointed at the bodies on the floor. "Two. The bartender has your money."

Where the undertaker had stopped, he blocked the doorway. Jack gently but firmly pushed him out of his way and stepped outside. Cart and the prisoners were waiting.

Cart pointed back in the direction they had come. "The marshal's office is thataway, just a ways from Binford's."

Jack shoved Sanford forward. "Move it." The two rangers followed the three outlaws across the street.

"Ranger Sage," Sanford said, pointing at his rear, "I've got splinters stuck in me, and it's hard to walk. I'm going to need the doctor to remove them."

"My heart's bleeding for you. Keep walking."

Jack watched the man walk. He reminded him of a crab skittering along the beach, except slower. "Sanford, you said the marshal is your cousin?"

Sanford stopped and turned to look at the ranger.

Jack gave him another shove. "Keep moving. You can walk and talk."

When he was moving again, Sanford said, "Yeah, he's my cousin, and he's not going to be too happy with this."

"Is he in on your kidnapping scheme?"

Sanford tried to stop again, but Jack shoved him forward hard enough to make him stumble.

"We're not kidnappers. You shot two innocent men."

Jack gave a short laugh. "Yeah, two innocent men who were set on killing us."

With his Colt, Cart pointed toward a small office front with a light in the window. "That's the marshal's office. I'd suggest you fill your hand just in case the marshal's upset enough to pull iron on us."

Jack drew a Remington.

Reaching the office, Jack said, "You first, Sanford, I'll follow, and Cart, why don't you bring in the other two."

Sanford stepped up on the boardwalk, opened the door, and walked in, Jack right behind him. A man with a deputy badge sat behind the desk with a dime novel in one hand and a cup of coffee in the other. He looked up at the intruders. His eyes hit Sanford, jumped to the huge man behind him with the little gun, and back to the outlaw.

"What the blue blazes is this, Bob?" Then he looked back at Jack. "And who are you? You know you can't come into the marshal's office . . ." His eyes fell on Jack's badge. The other two came in behind Jack, followed by Cart.

Jack dropped his weapon back into its holster. "Deputy, we are Texas Rangers, and these men are our prisoners. I want you to lock them up."

The deputy put his cup on the desk, dropped his dime novel, and stood. "Now, see here. I can't lock these men up. This here is Bob Sanford. He's the cousin of Marshal Beake."

Jack looked around the office. It looked much like any other marshal's office. It had a desk, a couple of wooden, straight-backed chairs, and a potbellied stove with a coffee pot sitting on it. In the back wall was an open door exposing the jail cells. Next to the door, on a wooden peg, hung a large metal ring with keys. "Are those the keys to the cells?"

The deputy looked at Jack, then at the key ring, then back to Jack. "Well, yeah, I guess so, but—"

Jack shoved Sanford through the door, grabbing the keys from the peg. Cart was behind him with the other two outlaws. Jack opened the first cell and tossed the keys to his friend. Cart caught them and moved to the second cell door. He unlocked it and waved the two men in with his revolver. Once they were inside, he locked the door.

The deputy looked back and forth at the now occupied cells. "This ain't right. I'm gettin' the mayor."

Jack stepped into the cell with Sanford. "Take your time, Deputy. We'll be having a little conversation."

Sanford, his voice cracking, called to the deputy as he headed for the door, "Get my cousin, too, Huck. Hurry."

"Cain't, he left town. Gonna be gone for several days." With that, the deputy disappeared into the night.

Jack turned to Cart. "Would you mind finding a soldier boy at one of those saloons, make sure he's fairly sober, and tell him to get a message to the provost. Tell him there are three prisoners here who need to be in their stockade."

Cart started to ask a question, changed his mind, and headed out the door.

Sanford tried to sit down on one of the bunks and grimaced. "I need a doctor for these splinters."

Jack said nothing.

"Why are you sending us to the fort? Fort Stockton won't hold civilian prisoners."

Jack towered over the seated man. "Listen to me, Sanford. I don't have a lot of time. I have questions, and I want answers. The sooner you answer, the happier you'll be. You understand me?"

Alarmed, Robert Sanford looked up into the cold gray eyes of a determined man. "I'm a prisoner. You can't do anything to me."

11

Jack slapped him. The slap was open handed, from a hand that looked as wide as a bear's paw. The crack of flesh against flesh echoed through the jail. The force rolled Sanford off the bunk and onto the floor, leaving the left side of his cheek nearly as red as fresh blood.

Sanford gasped. "You can't do that. It's prisoner abuse. I know my rights. I don't have to answer any of your questions."

Jack bent, grabbed the man by his front, his big left hand closing on vest, shirt, and skin, and yanked him from the floor. He jerked so hard, Sanford, though he wasn't a small man, came completely off the floor.

Jack slapped him again, this time harder, and hung on to him. The man's head jerked to one side, and his nose began to bleed. Jack extended his arm to keep the blood from his clothing.

Sanford had passed out, but only for a few seconds. When he came to, blood was dripping down his chin onto his vest and shirt.

Jack moved his face within inches of the outlaw. "You ready to answer my questions? I can keep this up all night."

Sanford's eyes looked dull. He stared over Jack's shoulder,

blinking like an owl. In a pleading voice, he said, "I don't have any idea what you might want to know."

Jack nodded. "That's a start. First, I want to know how long you've been taking girl children."

"I don't know what you're talking about."

Jack raised his hand to strike again.

"Wait, please wait. My neck hurts. My head hurts. If you hit me like that again, you're liable to kill me."

"You mean like your pardner killed those little girls?" Jack flexed his arm as if to begin his swing.

"Wait, dang it. I'll tell you. Just don't hit me again."

The smaller man in the other cell grabbed the cell bars. "Bob, don't you say nothin'. You'll get us all in trouble."

Jack turned cold gray eyes on the speaker. "If he doesn't, when I kill him, you'll be next."

The man's eyes grew wide. "You're a Texas Ranger. You cain't kill us. We're prisoners."

"Just you watch." Jack drew his arm back again.

Sanford tried to shrink away, but the fist held him close. "No, please. I said I'll talk."

"Then talk, and don't stop, or there's more waiting for you."

Sanford began. "We've taken a total of nine girls, that's Haggard's bunch and us."

"From where?"

"The German settlements."

"How much are you paid?"

Sanford slanted his eyes toward the men in the other cell. "I'd rather not say."

Jack was losing his patience. "Listen, mister, I'm just about fed up with your delays. I've got to be on my way, and I want answers. I want to know how much you were paid for the girls. Tell me now." He extended his right arm again.

"All right," Sanford almost screamed. "We were paid anywhere from four to ten thousand a girl."

The two men in the other cell looked at each other in shock.

"Who paid you?"

"Dr. Clements. He gave us our orders, and he paid us."

"Who does he work for?"

Sanford didn't hesitate. "I don't know. I know he's in San Francisco, but I don't know who he is. Dr. Clements is our connection. He gives us our orders, and he pays us. I don't know anything else. I just pick up whichever girl Dr. Clements orders."

"So he gives you specific orders? He tells you exactly which girl to grab?"

"Yes. We get their names, where they live, and their description. We know a lot about them and their parents before we ever try to take them."

Jack was intrigued by this piece of information. It meant that Dr. Clements or the man he worked for had connections in the areas from where the girls were taken. "How does he get this information?" Jack pulled the man's face close. "I warn you, Sanford, you lie to me, I'll know. I've been in this business a long time."

"I swear, Ranger, I don't know. He never tells us anything except who to grab and where they live. Please, I'm telling you the truth. Don't hit me again."

Jack nodded toward the men in the other cell. "They worked with you?"

"Heck yeah they did. We were all in this together."

The smaller man jerked at the cell bars. "Sanford, you're a dead man. I get my hands on you, I'll wring your lyin' neck."

Jack looked over at the men in the other cell. He could see the hate in their eyes. *He's not kidding. They'll kill him if they get into a cell together,* Jack thought. Still gripping Sanford's front collar, Jack looked coldly at the other two men. "If I hear another word from either of you two, I'm coming into your cell and break some bones. It'll be two against one. Who do you think is going to win?"

He looked back at Sanford. His head hung, and his shoulders drooped. This wasn't the cocky fella he had first seen in the saloon. "What about this Nadine Tidwell?"

Sanford didn't raise his head. "She's a nurse. She gives the girls laudanum to keep them quiet on their trip. It's a long way to San Francisco. We have orders to get rid of any girl who kicks up a ruckus, complains too much, tries to expose us, or ask others for help. Clements told me, the man in San Francisco would be really mad if that happened, but we can't take a chance."

"Do you know where they stop and how long they stay at each stop?"

Sanford shook his head, and Jack dropped the man on the bunk. He moaned as his rear hit the hard mattress. "Can you get me a doctor for these splinters?"

"Yeah." Jack turned to leave the cell, grasped the door, and stopped. He turned back. "Look at me, Sanford."

The outlaw raised his head slowly. His eyes, when they met Jack's, had lost their glint, their pride.

"Tell me the truth. Is your cousin involved in this?"

"Carter? Not a chance. He's about the straightest straight arrow I know. When he learns about what I've been doing, he'll never have anything to do with me again." His head dropped, and he stared at the floor.

Jack pushed the door open, left the cell, and locked the door. He shot a threatening stare at the other two. They moved to the back of the cell. He turned, entered the marshal's office, and closed the door. Almost as soon as the jail door closed, the front door opened. The deputy stepped in with a prosperous-looking man behind him. The man was tall, going to a paunch slightly, and beginning to bald. He looked to be in his mid-forties.

He stepped forward and offered his hand to Jack. "I'm Mayor Grover, Ranger. Could you tell me what's the problem here? I understand you have Bob Sanford and his men in our jail."

Jack took the man's hand. "How do you do, Mayor Grover. My

name is Jack Sage. I'll be glad to explain. Are you aware that Robert Sanford is a child abductor?"

The shocked look on the mayor's face was sufficient to answer Jack's question. "I cannot believe that. I would say it is almost impossible if it weren't a Texas Ranger telling me. Can you explain? Is Marshal Beake involved?"

"No, he's not involved, at least from my interview with Sanford, and I believe he is telling the truth. It seems Sanford has a gang and was joined by another gang. Both groups were employed by Dr. Clements."

"What? I know Dr. Clements. He helps to operate a finishing school for girls . . ." The mayor's face reflected the thoughts coursing through his mind. "Those girls are not being taken to a finishing school, are they?"

"No, they are not. Sanford is paid to catch these girl children and transport them to Dr. Clements and this woman Nadine Tidwell. Together they take these poor little things to San Francisco to be delivered into the hands of another very evil man. I gather the man in San Francisco is the head of this whole operation."

The mayor stood aghast at the tale he had just heard. "I am so sorry we didn't figure this out. Everyone seemed so polite, so educated, and Bob was Marshal Beake's cousin. It all appeared aboveboard. Although, as I think back, all the girls who were brought through our town seemed very subdued. There was no laughing, running, or playing. Dr. Clements explained it as the children being sad because they had to leave their parents, and they would recover once at the school."

Jack flexed his fists at the thought of what the abductors had done and were doing to the children. "They were being given laudanum to keep them quiet. It is also my understanding that if any of them made trouble, that child would not make it to San Francisco."

The mayor was shaking his head when Cart and an army

corporal came through the door. "Jack, this is Corporal Brady. He's in charge. Their provost is on patrol. Corporal, this is Ranger Jack Sage."

Upon stepping through the door, Corporal Brady's face lit in a wide grin. "I know Captain Sage. How are you, sir?"

Jack grabbed the corporal's extended hand, and the two of them pumped with vigor, Jack returning the grin. "Corporal Brady? Mike, the last time I saw you, it was with first sergeant stripes. Those sleeves seem to be missing a few stripes."

"Aye, there's been a downturn in my fortune. Seems a few other first sergeants decided to insult my lineage. As you know, I'm not averse to extracting justice should I feel the need. It cost me my stripes, but I'm working for a good man now. I'll have them returned in no time. Ranger Sage?"

"It's a long story. You know Mayor Grover?"

"Aye," the corporal said. The two men nodded to each other.

Jack laid a hand on the corporal's shoulder. "I'd love to talk, Mike, but time is getting away from me. I've a favor to ask."

"Ask away, sir. Needless to say, if I can, I will."

"Good, I have three prisoners here. I'd like for them to be held by the army until rangers call to pick them up. They're awaiting trial for kidnapping children and more. I don't have the time to go into it, but do you think your commanding officer will allow them to be held in the stockade?"

Mike nodded. "I feel sure he will, sir. He'll have little use for men like these. Do you know how long we'll be holding them?"

Jack thought for a minute. "Do you have any patrols going east?"

"Aye, we do. One is leaving in the morning to patrol between here and Fort Griffin. They'll be stopping in there."

"Good. You can also have the eastbound stage driver take a letter to the first ranger office they come to. They'll send someone out to pick up these men."

"I think the colonel will be fine with your proposal. In fact, I'll take them with me and toss them in the stockade right now."

"Excellent, thanks." He turned to the mayor. "Mr. Mayor, does this suit you?"

Grover nodded. "By all means. I'll be glad to have these men in a federal jail. Now, since this seems to be settled, I'll bid you good day." The mayor turned and left the office.

"That's what I like, a politician who doesn't try to manage every little thing," Jack said. He looked at Cart. "Do we need to leave now, or can we get some rest? I don't want those animals to get out of El Paso ahead of us."

Cart slid his hat to the back of his head. "Jack, the shortcut I'm going to take will put us there long before they pull out even if they stay for only two days. I guarantee it. However, if our horses don't rest up tonight, they'll not be up to what's ahead of them. I heartily recommend we take this opportunity to rest, along with them, and take off in the morning."

Jack turned to Corporal Brady. "It's good to see you, Mike. I wish we had more time. Maybe I'll get back through here."

"It's enough to know you're alive and kicking, sir. You take care of yourself, and I'll take care of the prisoners." He opened the door, stuck his head out, and called, "Private Jankes, get in here."

A young man of little more than twenty years ducked and stepped through the door. The private was as tall and wide as Jack. He paused, staring at Jack.

"I know," Jack said. "You're a surprise to me too, Private Jankes. How tall are you?"

"Four inches over six feet, sir."

Jack laughed. "You're a half inch taller than me. I'll have to say I wouldn't want to crawl in the ring with you."

The private grinned. "No, sir, me neither."

"Private," Corporal Brady said, "there are three men locked in the jail. Take them out and hold them outside. I'll be there shortly."

While Private Jankes was removing the prisoners, Jack asked for two sheets of paper and a pencil from the deputy. He quickly wrote two notes, one for the stage and one for Mike. He signed them both and handed one to the deputy. "Deputy, I'd be obliged if you'll give this note to the stage driver of the first stage headed east. Have him drop it off at the first town either with rangers or at a ranger office. Can you do that?"

"Why, shore."

"Thanks." Jack handed the other note to Mike. "Give this to the appropriate person, and see it is taken east. The sooner the rangers get the note, the sooner the prisoners will be taken off your hands. By the way, one of them has a load of splinters in his rear. You might have the fort's surgeon take a look at him. Also, he's the one who spilled the beans on the whole outfit. I'd keep him separate from the other two, or they'll kill him."

The two men shook hands, and Mike took the note. "It's been good to see you, sir. I'll take good care of your prisoners. Maybe our paths will cross again."

"I'd like that. I look forward to seeing those first sergeant stripes back where they belong."

Mike nodded and stepped into the darkness.

Jack took a deep breath. "Let's head to the hotel. On the way, I'll fill you in. I'm looking for a good night's sleep."

Cart stepped outside and waved Jack out.

Jack pulled the door closed behind him and laughed. Both Mike and Private Jankes were mounted and riding behind the three outlaws, who were walking to the fort. Sanford was struggling along in his crab-style walk. Jack grinned, shook his head, and motioned for Cart to join him. Walking across the dusty street, Jack began his tale of what Sanford had told him.

It was the fourth day of their travel. The early morning West Texas sun was already hot. Jack was on Thunder, and he could tell the big horse had lost weight in the past four days. All three of his horses and the mules were lighter than when they started. He gazed across the continuous prairie grass as far as the eye could see. The wind, which seemed to never stop, whipped the grasses and beat against them, sucking the moisture from their bodies.

Jack reached back, opened his saddlebags, and pulled out his binoculars. "Hold up, Cart. I thought I saw something. Is that the road in the distance?"

Cart pulled over next to Jack, his eyes constantly moving. This was Apache country, and the man who didn't stay alert would end up hairless and dead. "Yeah, that should be it."

Jack lifted his field glasses and scanned the distance. He handed them to Cart.

The older man brought them up, made adjustments for his eyes, and swore. "I never thought I'd see that. The Butterfield Stage has a reputation for always making it through." He kept looking. Then handed them back to Cart. "That's our stage."

Jack took the glasses and looked again. From behind a few low rocks on the opposite side of the stage, he saw a blonde head pop up, look around, and jerk down. "That's our stage?"

"Sure enough, and I'm bettin' it's got a passel of Apaches around it. No tellin' how many, but enough to kill one of their mules. Probably the only reason they haven't killed the others is they want them for a food supply on the hoof. One dead mule in the traces is enough to accomplish what they're after, stopping the stage. I cain't believe it. That stage hasn't been hit in ages. That must be a bunch of renegades."

"How close can we get without them knowing we're here?"

"Shoot, they could be looking at us right now. If they are, we're dead men. We just don't know it yet. Let me have a look again."

Jack gave him the field glasses. Cart studied the area. "Can you believe it? I've got these binoculars, and I still can't see 'em. They're the slyest Injuns there is. You never see 'em 'less they want you to or until it's too late." He brought the glasses down. "Them mules look tired. We've made good time. They've been here for a while."

"What do you think are the chances of the folks on the stage surviving the attack?"

Cart put the glasses back up to his eyes. "Somewhere between zero and none if the next station doesn't get help to 'em pretty quick. No tellin' how long they been down there. Help may be already on the way, but if it ain't, they ain't got a prayer. Look at 'em. The only protection is that pile of low rocks they're in. Them Apaches killed that mule in that spot on purpose. They knew the folks on the stage would head for them low rocks, and they'll just wait 'em out."

Jack took back the glasses. "I think I saw one of the girls. I saw a blonde head stick up and look around. It was a small female. At this distance, I just couldn't make out whether it was a girl or a woman." He took the glasses down, offered them to Cart, who shook his head. Jack dropped them back into his saddlebags. He loosed his revolvers and checked each one, then pulled the Winchester from its scabbard and tried to shove in another round. It was full. He opened the breach far enough to ensure a round was in the chamber, closed the lever, and turned to Cart, who was doing the same thing.

Cart laid his Winchester across his legs and took a deep breath. "Well," Jack said, "you're the Indian fighter. What's the plan?"

12

Cart nodded toward a draw to the west of the ridge. "See the draw, kinda deep and outa the way?"

"I see it."

"We're gonna ride beneath this ridgeline to the bottom of the hill, then circle around the end and enter the draw down there. It's pretty twisty, which is good. It means an Injun can't look down the draw and see any distance at all. Once we're in it, we'll ride until I find the right spot. That's where we'll drop the horses. You need to figure out which horse you can spare. That's the one you want to be riding, 'cause odds are those Apaches are gonna kill our horses first thing. They're not always the best shot, but some of 'em are mighty good. Just depends on how lucky we are. You ready?"

"Let's go."

Cart led off. Upon reaching the end of the ridge, they eased out and around. The two rangers paused several times to check for Apaches, at least any they could see. Then they proceeded until they made it to the draw Cart had pointed out. The lip of the draw was at least eight feet above the dry bed. A few minutes of riding found a game trail that led into the bottom. At the same time they dropped into the draw, a faint sound of shots echoed across the grassy plains and rugged hillsides.

The two men took it slow. They were concerned about the people and kids stuck back in those rocks, but they wouldn't be able to help anyone if they blundered into Apaches. The soft thud of horses' hooves was faint in the sand, but Jack knew what he had heard of the Apache. They had grown up in this desert of grass and rocks. They could hear any out-of-place sound like it was being played on a cymbal.

Jack was anxious to turn and attack the Indians, but he wasn't anxious to lose one of his horses or mules. He was a tough, hard man, but kids and animals were his soft spots. He felt close to all three of his horses. He didn't want to lose any of them, but he for sure didn't want to lose Smokey. That grulla had been with him since Mexico, and if a man could love a horse, he loved Smokey. He felt silly admitting it, but he and that horse had an attachment that went far beyond horse and rider. Smokey knew what Jack wanted before he did. Sometimes it was eerie how the grulla responded to him.

Cart pulled up in a narrow section of the draw. He swung from the rental horse he was riding and tied the leads of Sandy, his linebacked dun, and the other horse he had rented from Ford's place. Jack swung down from Thunder and scratched the big gray behind the ears. He tied Smokey and Pepper and the two mules to roots in the wall of the draw. They were all tied with knots they could pull out if they had to. He swung back onto Thunder's saddle and patted the big gray on its neck. The animal responded by turning its head into his hand.

"It's time," Cart whispered.

"How do we do this?"

"Only one way. Ride straight in, hard and fast. They'll be shootin', but you been in the war, that won't be anything new to you. When you get there, take the time to tie your horse where you can see him. Otherwise, the Apaches will steal him. You got all the ammunition you can carry?"

"Yep." Jack had slipped two bandoliers across his body. They crossed, forming an X over his heart. *Excellent aiming point*, he thought, with a sardonic grin. He also had two extra cylinders in his vest pocket and two of the big .44 Colt Walkers hanging from his saddle horn. He grinned at Cart. "With all this weight, if I fall, I won't be able to get up."

One side of Cart's mouth lifted. "If you fall, I'll just drop behind you. You'll work as good as any horse."

The moment passed. Cart turned the rented horse back the way they had come and started him off walking. Jack rode beside him. Cart leaned close. "When we get to the big boulder I showed you, pretend you're charging a bunch of Rebs. I'll picture me a passel of Yankees."

Jack chuckled and grew serious. "Thank goodness that war's over."

Cart nodded his shaggy head. "I ain't what you'd call a religious man, but I'll say amen to that."

The two rode in silence. They guided their horses to a narrow trail out of the bottom of the draw and followed the rim through the tall grass. At times, the grass touched Jack's boot tops. His head swiveled continuously, and sweat flowed down the middle of his back, but he had yet to recognize the feeling he was being watched.

Maybe it's failing me, he thought. *Or just maybe we might surprise them. The rescue will come from the west, along the road, not out of the northern hills. They may not be watching.* Jack laughed to himself in derision. *Funny, Jack Sage, Apaches not watching.*

They kept riding. Ahead, he could see the massive boulder Cart had pointed out. He reached down to one of the big .44-caliber Walkers and pulled it from its holster, hefting it. He'd had a pair of these horse pistols slung on his cavalry mount during the war. They were powerful weapons, but they were extremely heavy. He was glad to have them now, thanks to the outlaws. He held his hand over the hammer mechanism and cylinder to deaden the sound as he pulled the hammer back.

Cart had the butt of his Winchester resting on his right knee. Jack couldn't think of a better man he'd want to ride into battle with.

They reached the boulder. It was less than a hundred yards from the disabled stage.

Both men, as if on cue, kicked their horses and let out blood-curdling yells at the same time. Thunder charged ahead of Cart's livery horse. Jack eased him up a bit. They needed to be riding on line, side by side. It was more confusing to a shooter even though there were only two of them. The Indian still had to make up his mind which ranger to shoot. That split second of indecision might make the difference, and they needed every edge they could get.

Cart's rebel yell brought back chilling memories of charging men in gray uniforms. He put it out of his mind, himself yelling at the top of his lungs while racing through the grass and rocks. When they were less than thirty yards from the stage, an Apache leaped from the grass, his rifle barrel turning toward Jack. Too slow. The ranger leveled the .44 Colt and fired. The bullet hit the Apache in the forehead, blowing him back and to the ground. Jack had only an instant to think, *I was aiming at his chest,* as he brought the Walker to bear on another Apache who had leaped out of the path of the big gray horse.

Now there were Apaches everywhere. There must be fifteen or twenty, and there was firing from the rocks where the stage passengers were located. Jack saw Cart wheel his horse to the left and run over an Apache who had tried to get out of his way. He heard Cart fire as the two of them were pulling up at the stage. An Apache jumped from beneath the stage, a tomahawk in his hand. Jack shot him in the chest. He leaped from his horse, whipping Thunder's reins around the stage door post and tying them fast. He heard a whish, as if something were sliding through grass, and a weight slammed into his back, a powerful arm circling his forehead. A knife flashed for his throat. He grabbed the hilt and squeezed the brown hand holding it. He heard the Indian grunt in pain, but the opposite hand went for his eyes. He leaped forward, turned, and then rammed his back against the coach with all the force his two hundred and five pounds could muster.

The man's hands relaxed. The ranger leaped away, and the Indian crumpled to the ground. Jack spun and shot him in the forehead. Bullets were slamming into the coach all around him. He felt a sting across his left bicep. He grabbed the other Walker holster, slung it over his head, yanked his rifle from the scabbard, and with the same hand shoved two fingers under his canteen strap. Spinning, he found another Apache charging him with a spear pointed at his belly. He shot him with the Walker and knocked the head of the spear to the side with his Winchester's barrel. It buried itself into the stage door. He spotted Cart just in time to see him diving for the rocks, and dashed for cover. Jack leaped over the rocks and, too late, saw Cart straight ahead, lifting himself from the ground. He slammed into his friend and heard the air whoosh from his body.

Jack's massive frame hit Cart solidly in the chest. He rolled from his friend, dropped his rifle and canteen, and whirled around. There was no time to check on him. Men were fighting hand to hand in the rocks. Jack shot another Apache reaching for one of the little girls huddled in a pocket formed by three of the boulders. His bullet struck the Indian in the right shoulder. He dropped the girl and spun to charge at Jack, but this time Jack shot him in the chest.

And it was over.

The Apaches melted into the grass and rocks. The boulders they were gathered in were quiet except for Cart, now sitting and gasping for breath, blood coming from a knife slash across his chin. Jack looked for the girls. Relieved, he spotted all three. They were huddled together, clinging to each other, looking surprisingly calm. *The laudanum,* Jack thought. Seeing Cart was going to live, he quickly examined the remaining occupants of the boulders.

He picked out the stage driver and the shotgun rider. They were fine. There was one man wounded and one dead. The dead man looked like a cowhand, and the wounded one was probably a traveling salesman who was on his monthly route. Jack had no difficulty identifying the two men hired to protect Clements and his entourage. They were big men, but dressed well, and then there were Bertrand Clements and Nadine Tidwell. Neither difficult to identify, and neither showing any concern for anyone other than themselves. Both were huddled near the girls. Tidwell had a cut on her forehead. It looked like a rock splinter had slashed across the pale skin from a glancing shot.

He removed his hat and eased his head to the side of the boulder he had just leaped over, until just an eye was exposed. The prairie was quiet. Except for the smell of gunpowder and death, there was no sign or movement from beyond the boulders. They had made it, for now. His next thought was Thunder. The big gray stood at the stage door, blood running from a graze across his left hip, but from this view, he looked to be fine.

"Whew-we, you fellers showed up at the right time. Name's Buck Finton. I'm the mule skinner, and that there is Ralph Lonner. He's ridin' shotgun. Don't usually have one, but I'm danged glad Ralph was here today. Him and that greener took out two of those Injuns who would've had us for sure if he hadn't been here."

"Howdy," Lonner said.

Buck pointed to the dead man. "Reckon that poor young feller picked the wrong stage to ride. Them Apaches plugged him about the same time we reached the rocks." Looking at the young man, Buck gave his head a shake. "Danged shame, I'll tell ya." His outlook brightened when he looked up at Jack again. "But I don't mind sayin' it, I was tickled as a pig in slop when I seen you two fellers a-yellin' and a-shootin', roaring in here on them cayuses. I'd say you messed up those Apaches' party, at least for now."

Jack pulled his vest back, showing his badge, and nodded at Cart, who gave him a less than friendly look. Cart was busy getting the bleeding from his chin stopped. "We're rangers. Heard the shooting and thought we'd investigate." Jack looked around at the people inside the ring of boulders. "I guess it's a good thing we did."

"Danged right it is. We're mighty beholdin'. If'n you ain't showed yoreself, our hair might've been hangin' on some brave's lance by now."

One of the guards hired by Clements spoke up. "Not a chance. We would never have let those savages in here."

Buck looked at Jack and rolled his eyes. "Mister, you might not've had any say at all. Them Apaches are tougher than boot leather."

Cart had stopped the bleeding from his chin, and his eyes were sweeping the stage and the prairie outside of the boulders. "They're tough and persistent. I'd suggest we keep a close watch. There's a good chance they ain't done yet. Our group has only been increased by two. They've lost some men, and I'm thinkin' they're not too happy about it."

Buck picked up his Colt and joined Cart and Lonner watching the stillness of the prairie. "Ranger, you may be right. Those fellers out there may be a lot of things, but quitter's not one of them. Especially when they think they've got the upper hand."

Jack, while he also kept watch, nodded toward the girls. "What are three little girls doing out here without their mamas and papas?"

Buck tossed a thumb over his shoulder toward Clements. "He's the headmaster of some highfalutin school in San Francisco. These kids' parents are sending these girlies to get a bunch of school learnin'. Seems like a waste of time to me."

"I beg your pardon. Correct education is never a waste of time. It is important for a young lady to speak her language correctly and to be conversant in languages of other countries."

Jack kept his eyes traveling over the rocks, grass, and brush. "Who are you?"

"I am Dr. Bertrand Clements. I am in charge of the travel of these young ladies. With me is Miss Nadine Tidwell. She is the guardian of the girls."

"Cart," Jack said, "if you'd help keep an eye out, I'm going to speak to these folks."

Cart turned his head slowly. "That's what I'm doin'. You need to watch where you jump."

Jack held back the grin he felt building and thought of the girls. The thought brought a stern look back to his face. "You're right. Sorry."

Cart nodded and resumed his watch. He said, to no one in particular, "Felt like someone dropped a cotton bale on my chest."

Buck couldn't resist. "Heh-heh, boy, I thought you was a goner when I seen that massive hunk of man fly over that boulder right at you. I swear if I'd been you, I'd be dead right now."

Jack turned to the girls and leveled a smile at them. They were no more than twenty feet from him, and he could see the dull gaze in their eyes. They were all blonde and blue-eyed. "Hello, girls."

They said nothing.

Miss Tidwell spoke. "We teach them not to speak to strangers."

"I think that's smart. Miss Tidwell, my name is Jack Sage, Texas Ranger. Would you be so kind as to introduce us?"

Jack noticed the bodyguards grow uneasy as well as Clements and Tidwell.

She looked down at the girls and, in a cold, prim voice, said, "Girls, this is Ranger Jack Sage. He would like to speak to you."

Jack could hear the warning in the tone of her voice. He gave the girls a wide smile. "Hello, girls. You know my name, but you have me at a disadvantage. I don't know yours or your parents'. I'd like to get to know you."

Now Jack could see Clements squirm and glance at his hired guns. They both shifted their handguns where it'd be easy to swing them toward Jack and Cart.

One of the girls finally spoke up. "I'm Catarina."

Jack nodded to her. "Nice to meet you, Catarina. You're a mighty pretty girl. Can you tell me where you're from?"

She looked up at Clements. He glared down at her and nodded.

She gave Jack a lethargic smile. "I'm from San Marcos. Do you know where that is?"

"I do, Catarina. I like to fish in the river. What's your folks' name?"

She looked back up at Clements.

Jack gave her a big smile. "You don't have to look at him, honey. It's alright. Tell me your parents' name."

She returned his smile. "My mama's and papa's names are Olga and Joseph Klein."

"Thank you." He started to ask her another question when the sound of horses could be heard coming from the west.

Buck spoke up. "I'm bettin' that's what we've been hopin' for."

All eyes except Jack's, Lonner's, and Cart's turned to the road. Sure enough, there was a dust cloud large enough to indicate several riders. Hopefully, enough to keep from getting ambushed by the Apaches.

Suddenly, the Indians charged.

13

Jack had been expecting it. This gave them one last chance to get scalps. They were close. Much closer than even Cart expected. Two wide-shouldered men leaped into the circle. Jack fired into the body of one about to impale Buck with a long-bladed butcher knife, he keeled over, and Buck shot him again. The other Apache grabbed at one of the girls, but a bodyguard shot him in the ear. They were so close, the man just shoved his weapon against the Indian's ear and fired.

Others were close, but too far to make it inside the circle of boulders. The men, except for Clements, opened up with a withering volley of fire. The charge lasted only seconds. The Apaches dropped from sight. Occasionally the tops of the grass could be seen moving, but was it the wind or an Apache scurrying away?

The riders came into sight. They looked to be a party of twelve.

Buck let out a sigh of relief. "Looks like they're leading a pair of mules. That'll get us to the station. We can change there and be on our way. Hallelujah!"

The riders pulled up to the rocks. Everyone stood in relief, each glad to see their rescuers.

"Buck," one of the men said, "when I saw you was runnin' late, I started worrying. Finally you was so late I knew something was wrong. I'm sure glad we were able to round up enough men."

"Norm, I'm danged glad to see you. Until these here rangers showed up, I figured our goose was cooked and our hair was gone. We tested lady luck today, and she paid off. Come on, let's get one of them mules hooked up so I can get this stage rolling. Got a lot of time to make up."

Buck and Lonner stepped from behind the rocks. Buck turned and extended his hand to Cart and Jack. "Much obliged, Rangers. You saved us for sure." They shook, and he turned to the other people. "Folks, if you'd hand up that cowhand's body, we'll put him on top. Then go ahead and hop on in. We're goin' to be on our way mighty quick." With that, he turned and strode after Lonner, who was already headed for the stage.

For the first time, Jack spoke to the salesman. The man was examining his arm. "Let me take a look at that arm, mister. Looks like you took a bullet."

The salesman shook his head. "No, thanks, Ranger. It's just a graze. I'll take care of it myself at the station." He nodded to Jack's arm. "Looks like you might need some looking at yourself."

Jack looked down. He had completely forgotten about the wound. He unbuttoned his shirtsleeve and rolled it above the wound. More damage had been done to his shirt than his arm. The bullet had traveled across the side of his bicep and broke the skin only enough for it to bleed.

Cart looked. "I've cut myself worse shaving."

The other passengers were climbing aboard the stage, handing up the girls.

Cart nodded at them. "You think one of us should ride along?"

Jack shook his head. "Where are they going to go? I think we can get our horses and head to the stage station. We may or may not catch up with them, but we'll catch them soon. How's that sound to you?"

"Yep, makes sense, as long as we don't get ambushed or our horses stolen by a bunch of mad Apaches. We messed up their little party, and they'd love to have us hanging over a fire." Cart looked Jack up and down. "Especially you. Shoot, I might like that myself after that lick you gave me."

Jack grinned. "I'm sure sorry about that. It just shows you're mighty tough. An average man would have a caved-in chest."

The team was hooked up and the passengers aboard. Buck waved one last time and popped the whip over the mules, and the stage was off with all of the men except one. He had ridden over. "You rangers headin' to the station? If you do, I'll gin you up a fine meal. This stage line owes you big. We ain't never lost a passenger to Indians. This could've been the day."

Jack shook his head. "The stage line owes us nothing, but we'll see you in a while."

The rider waved and raced after the stage.

Jack had untied Thunder from the stage and took a few minutes examining him. The only thing he found was the wound on the big gray's hip. He poured a little water over it, carefully cleaning away the blood and examining the scratch. Thunder's bullet wound was like Jack's, enough to bleed a little, but hardly qualifying for wound status.

Jack looked across Thunder's back at Cart. "How's your horse?"

"Great, not a scratch anywhere. He's one lucky animal. If he were a little faster, I'd think about buying him from Ford. You ready?"

Jack nodded and swung aboard. The two of them headed back the way they had come, eyes constantly searching.

Cart glanced at his partner. "You didn't want to take the girls now, huh?"

Jack shook his head. "I thought about it, but we were so close,

I didn't want to take a chance on one of them or someone else getting shot. I noticed how jumpy all four of that bunch got when I started asking questions. Those bodyguards were ready to start blasting at the first hint of suspicion. It was just too dangerous for everyone else."

Cart continued to search the countryside. "I agree. I noticed Clements. He kept looking at one of his gunmen. He was real edgy. It was a smart move to wait. Like you said, there's nowhere for them to go."

They continued north. Jack's mind labored over his decision. *Was it the right thing to do? Maybe I could've killed both the gunmen before they made a move, and maybe not. I feel sure we'll get another chance, but what if, after those questions, Clements decides to stay on the stage instead of stopping in El Paso?* Jack rode on, knowing he'd free the girls if it was the last thing he ever did.

∼

THE TWO RANGERS pulled up in front of the stage station. Jack had hoped the stage might be there, but the empty yard was witness to his hope being baseless. They would have moved out as soon as the mules were changed.

He and Cart headed the horses to the watering trough. Reaching it, they swung down. It had already been a long day, but they had to catch the stage. If they didn't, Clements would leave them in the dust.

Jack was riding Pepper, and the red horse drank like he hadn't had water for a week, as did all the animals. "You have any more shortcuts to get to El Paso?"

Cart looked up and shook his head. "Nope, from here it's a straight shot. The road's the shortest route. Just in case Clements doesn't stop, we've got to run the horses. It's going to be hard on 'em and the mules. Fortunately, we're only looking at about twenty miles, and the last five, the stage will have to slow to a walk. That'll help."

The station manager stepped out the door. "Leave your horses, Rangers. I'll have a man take good care of them. Come on in, and I'll fix you up with a meal for a king. You fellers have earned it."

Jack had switched the packs on the mules, with Stonewall getting the load for this last run. The mule looked at him like he was being betrayed, but stood quiet, accepting his lot. After finishing Stonewall, he pulled the saddle and blanket from Pepper and moved them to Smokey. He pulled the cinch tight, fastened the end, and stepped into the saddle. With Cart having followed suit, Jack pulled Smokey to a stop by the manager. "We're much obliged, but we've got a stage to catch."

The manager raised his hand in salute. "You fellers stop by anytime. I promise you a free meal and drinks. Your money will be no good here, and after we get word around the stage line, it won't be any good anywhere." His last words were said to Jack's and Cart's backs. They both gave him a wave as they disappeared around the bend.

The two rangers rode hard. Every mile and a half or so, they'd slow to a walk, watching the breathing of the horses. When their breathing was almost normal, they would be off again. The horses and mules had started the run tired, but they were giving it all they had.

Jack could feel Smokey's breathing accelerating. It was time. He slowed to a walk and looked at the mules. Stonewall was breathing hard. Each period of walking was taking longer until the animals' breathing dropped back near normal.

Cart pulled up next to him. "We need to be moving."

"We'll kill these horses."

Cart's face was grim. "Think about the girls, Jack. We've got to catch 'em in El Paso. If they don't get off that stage, we'll never catch 'em. Once they hit town, we'll gain some time because the coach will have to slow down, but we've got to get moving."

Jack could feel Smokey's chest. It wasn't heaving like it had been, but it hadn't reached the point he would like. He looked back at Stonewall. The mule's head was still up, but it had drifted lower than normal.

Cart looked at him. "Jack?"

"Let's go." He kicked Smokey in the ribs. They were off. This run seemed to last forever. He could feel his horse straining and the pull of Stonewall on the lead getting heavier. He leaned forward, near the grulla's ear. "Come on, boy, you can do it. Just a little farther."

At last he could see the edge of El Paso. Smokey was covered in lather, his sides heaving. Jack looked back at Stonewall. He was still coming, but under the load, he was having a hard time.

Cart yelled. Jack looked up again. Ahead was the stagecoach. It had entered town and had slowed to a walk.

Jack immediately slowed Smokey to a walk. His lathered horses' sides were heaving. "How far to the station?"

"Not far, and I know a shortcut. Follow me."

Cart turned up a side street that looked like they were traveling perpendicular to the stage's travel, but Jack didn't question his friend's lead. He had learned Cart knew this country, and if he said he knew a shortcut, he knew a shortcut.

They walked the animals for about a quarter of a mile and turned right. This was a straight shot, with no traffic. Jack knew the stage would have to occasionally stop, passing all of the people, horses, and wagons on main street. He felt elation. They were going to catch Clements and rescue the girls.

Rescuing the children was his first goal, but his next was getting information on the leader of this worthless bunch and putting him out of business. A smile drifted across his face at the thought of shutting them down, when ahead, from the left side of the street, wandered a sheep. He thought nothing of it. One sheep? No problem. Then another and another joined it until the street was packed.

Jack watched them clog the middle of the street. His heart dropped. There was no way they'd be able to get through that mess.

Cart started cursing. He rode to the edge of the snow-white animals, even trying to push through, but Sandy balked. The sheep pushed under the horse and around its legs. Cart managed to back him out before he was trapped and his horse went crazy with the little white monsters.

The only thing they could do was pull up and wait. But waiting seemed futile. They just came pouring out from left to right. Their constant bleating threatened to be the last straw. He needed to get through. There were too many to start shooting, and realistically, he wouldn't shoot them anyway, though he felt sure Cart would.

Smokey's breathing was slowing. Jack looked back at Stonewall. It looked like his mule was recovering. *Just a little longer, boy,* he thought. Stonewall looked better, but really tired. There was no way the mules could make another run like they had just done, not in their condition. Jack didn't know how much weight his animals had lost, but he was looking at ribs on all of them. They needed a solid week or more to rest up and eat. Even then, it would be a while before any of them would be able to make another run like they had these last four days.

Jack turned to watch the sheep. Was he wrong, or were they thinning? A gap between two of them appeared, then another. Then there was only a single line crossing, and at last, two shepherds with crooks walked into the street, singing to the sheep. When they saw the two men waiting on them, one of them a giant, they stopped singing and hurried the last of the sheep across.

Their way was clear.

Jack and Cart took off. They couldn't run the horses, but they could walk them really fast, which they did. Chickens and pigs searching for food in the El Paso side street were shocked when the horses loomed up charging at them. Squawking, the chickens flew in all directions, and the pigs, young and old, little and big, grunted their displeasure as they raced from under the horses' hoofs.

They kept moving, and off to the right, down the narrow cross streets, Jack could see the main street. The road they were on angled toward it, and they were getting closer.

Cart swung next to him. "The station's close. We've got 'em."

"Good. Be ready. This may be quick and bloody. Make sure your badge is visible. The main thing is not to hurt the girls or Clements. He's got some questions to answer."

Cart nodded, flipping the leather loop from his revolver's hammer. Jack did the same.

The stage station came into view. They would enter the main road next to the station. He looked for the stage. His heart skipped. It wasn't there. Thoughts raced through his mind. *Are they already gone? How far is the stage ahead of us? I'll have to have a fresh horse. I'll leave Cart to take care of the animals, and I'll rent a horse to catch them. It'll be easy because I'm so close.*

Jack breathed a sigh of relief. The stage was pulling up to the station. Cart's shortcut, even with the sheep, had managed to get them here before the stage. Cart looked back at him and grinned. Jack knew the man was looking forward to the fight with these outlaws. Not outlaws, vermin, scum. Jack knew Cart believed in the law, but his friend believed in justice more, and he was ready to mete it out. *So am I,* Jack thought.

He saw one of the bodyguards step from the stage, followed by Clements. After reaching the ground, Clements took two steps, turned, and stopped. The bodyguard helped Nadine Tidwell and then the girls. They looked even more tired and disheartened than they had in the boulders. *Probably the sight of us leaving was almost too much for those little girls to take,* Jack thought.

They rode to the barn, which was located behind the station. The view of the stage disappeared behind the corner of the building. Stage hands had already disconnected the mules and were about to lead out a string of fresh ones. Jack swung down and tied the animals. He walked over to the wranglers. "Hold up with the string. This stage isn't going anywhere until we're done."

The wranglers looked up at Jack and at Cart. Seeing the badges, they led the animals back into the barn. Jack waved one of the hands over. He pulled out a five-dollar gold piece and held it out to the man, who immediately extended his hand. Jack dropped it into it. "I'd appreciate it if you'd see to our animals. They need water, but they've been ridden hard, and they'll try to drink too much. Just make sure they take it slow."

"Yes, sir, Ranger. We'll be glad to take care of your animals."

"Thanks. It also might be smart if you stayed back here until things quiet down."

The man nodded again and moved toward the horses.

Cart joined Jack, and the two of them strode toward the stage yard in front.

Cart was smiling. "I don't think I've had this much fun in a long time, though you might have to remind me again about Clements. I'm thinkin' I might have to shoot him just a little bit."

Jack couldn't help but grin. "Don't shoot Clements. He has valuable information. I want to catch the headman and stop this forever."

Cart shook his head as they stepped into the stage yard. "You're a hard taskmaster, Jack Sage."

Clements had Catarina by a tiny arm and was shaking her. Jack could see tears streaming down the child's pale cheeks. He looked around for the bodyguards and the woman. The yard was empty. Evidently they were all inside.

Cart walked straight to Clements and hit him hard in the

right kidney. The man snapped to the right, almost doubling over, and Cart hit him in the same spot again.

After the second punch, he looked at Jack and held his hands out, palms up. "You said not to shoot him. You didn't say anything about not hitting him."

Clements crumpled to the ground. He lay moaning, holding his side.

Cart bent over to the surprised little girl. "Hi, honey, do you remember me?"

"Yes, you're the rangers. Are you here to rescue us again?"

"We sure are." He picked her up and sat her inside the coach. "You duck down and don't look up until one of us says it's all clear. Do you understand?" He pushed the door closed.

She looked out the window to Cart, her face solemn. "I sure do," and dropped down to the seat, out of sight.

One of the bodyguards stepped out the stage station door.

14

The bodyguard took in Clements on the ground moaning and Cart turning toward him from the stage, and went for his gun. Jack, who was standing by the office door, threw a short punch to the man's head. Short though it might have been, it had the power of his thick, muscled shoulders, and his anger behind it. The blow struck the bodyguard on his right temple. With satisfaction, Jack watched him collapse in the doorway.

Less than a second later, Cart's revolver blasted into the doorway past where the fallen bodyguard had been standing. It was followed by a second and third shot. Jack, weapon now drawn, watched as the second bodyguard fell through the open doorway across his partner. Jack stepped over the fallen men and into the stage office.

All the people had scattered away from the doorway. There were several under the tables to the right of the door. Jack saw Nadine Tidwell and the other two girls. He pointed his revolver at Tidwell. "Get out from under the table, and get over here." She was slow in moving. Jack's voice rose. "I said get over here, and do it now."

The woman duck-walked, as rapidly as she could, from under the table, rose, and stumbled toward Jack. She was carrying a small bag. When she reached him, he jerked it from her hands and used his weapon to point to a bench by the door. "Sit down there."

Without uttering a word, she walked to the bench, smoothed her dress, and sat, attempting to recover her composure.

Jack turned to the girls, who sat on the floor, their knees drawn up, with arms wrapped around their thin legs. He knelt and spread his big arms. "Come on, girls. You're safe. We're taking you home."

At the mention of home, the girls slowly crawled from under the table and walked sedately to Jack. Neither of them stopped until they had their arms around his neck, squeezing like their lives depended on it.

Jack's big arms closed around the girls like an angel's protective wings. "You don't have to worry about anything. In a few days you'll be home with your family, and this will be nothing more than a bad dream for you to forget."

The girls began sobbing. Jack was keeping his eyes on Tidwell when Catarina walked in, smiling. She never stopped, walking straight to Jack. He opened his arms, and she joined the other two.

After a moment, Catarina said into Jack's neck, "Thank you, Ranger Sage. I knew you'd come for us. When you asked me about my family, I just knew."

"I'm sorry we had to leave, but it would have been too dangerous for us to have tried to take you in the boulders. You might have gotten hurt, and we didn't want that to happen."

The girls finally released his neck, but remained close. He stood as a slightly overweight man approached. The man looked down at the corpse half in and half out the doorway. "Ranger, I'm Leland Hackett. I'm the station manager here in El Paso. Could you tell me what's going on?"

The girls clung to Jack's trouser legs, their eyes fixed on Nadine Tidwell.

"I'd be glad to, Mr. Hackett. These young girls have been stolen from their parents and were being taken to San Francisco to be sold."

Hackett's eyes opened wide with shock. "Mr. Clements and Miss Tidwell, kidnappers? That's impossible. They work for a finishing school for girls in San Francisco. This is the second group of girls they have escorted to the school." The shock gradually disappeared as what Jack had told him sank in. "What are you planning on doing with them?"

"I'm planning on asking them a few questions and then getting on your stage to San Francisco."

Hackett thought for a moment. "That means you are going to be delaying our departure."

"I'm afraid so. Do you have a room I could use to question these two?"

"Why, yes, I do, but I imagine Marshal Ruff will be arriving soon. Gunfire usually draws his attention. You might want to use his office."

A hard-looking fella Jack figured was a rancher spoke up. "Ranger, we know how to take care of folks who steal little girls. You leave 'em to us. We'll invite 'em to a bonfire. I bet they'd like that."

Jack eyed the man. The rancher wasn't joking. Jack knew exactly what he had in mind. He had heard of a Texas town where the townspeople had burned a rapist alive, and he had no doubt that was what this rancher was thinking. "I appreciate the thought, but they're going back to either Fredericksburg or San Marcos to stand trial. I'm sure they'll be getting the justice they deserve."

The man nodded, took a final sip of his coffee, and gave Nadine Tidwell a hard look. "Just offering a little help." He rose, dropped a nickel on the table, and strode from the station, nodding to Hackett as he passed.

Cart had walked in while Jack was talking. He had Clements by his collar, the man's hat was gone, and he was dirty and disheveled. It looked like he had fallen more than once. Cart shoved him toward Jack. "He wants to talk to you."

Nadine Tidwell spoke up, her words sharp. "Bertrand, you keep your mouth shut. Don't you say a word."

Cart was standing next to the woman when she spoke. His Colt magically appeared, and he thrust it against her neck. "Lady, I'm a Texas Ranger. I ain't ever killed a woman, and mostly I uphold the law, but I swear, if you open your mouth again without being asked something, I'll blow your ugly head off."

A gruff voice spoke up from the doorway. "What the blue blazes is goin' on here?" A large man with a mustache and goatee glared down at the blood-soaked floor. His head came up, examining the interior of the room before stepping over the one dead and one unconscious body in the doorway. He nodded to the departing rancher and looked at Cart with Clements in tow, and then Nadine Tidwell. On his chest was a marshal's badge.

The little girls crowded tightly around Jack's legs. He patted them on the head and nodded to the marshal. "You must be Marshal Ruff. That fella with a man in tow and his gun against the woman's neck is Ranger Taylor Cartwright, and I'm Ranger Jack Sage. Those two fellas in the doorway were bodyguards for these kidnappers." Jack pointed at Clements and Tidwell.

Cart motioned a warning in front of Nadine Tidwell's face with his Colt and slid it back into the holster.

Clements spoke up. "We most certainly are not kidnappers. You know me, Marshal Ruff. I am an honest educator who is being malign—"

Cart slapped Clements across the face. "What I said to your woman goes doubly for you. Please, just for me, say one more word."

Clements's mouth shut with a pop.

Jack gave the marshal a brief explanation. Time was precious. He needed to get moving.

Marshal Ruff nodded as Jack talked, his face growing darker. He took several glances at the culprits while Jack explained. When Jack finished, the marshal slid his hat back. "You're welcome to leave 'em here. We haven't yet hanged a woman in El Paso, but I think we can make her the first. You say you need to get on to San Francisco?"

Jack nodded. "I do. Right now, I'm holding the stage until I talk to these two. Hopefully I'll be on my way soon."

Marshal Ruff nodded toward the bodyguards. The one Jack hit was starting to moan and move. "I'll take care of those two." He glanced at Hackett. "Leland, why don't you let them use your office. That'll be faster than draggin' these two"—he motioned toward Clements and Tidwell—"down to my office and back. You want that stage out of here as fast as possible, don't you?"

Leland Hackett nodded to Jack. "Like I said, you're welcome to use it."

"Thanks." Jack looked at the marshal. "You mind watching the woman while we talk to Clements? I'd like for both of us to be involved so we can both hear the confession."

"Be glad to."

Hackett spoke up again. "My office is right back here." He headed to the rear of the building.

Jack followed Hackett. "Bring Clements, Cart, and we'll have a little conversation."

Cart shoved the man after the big ranger and followed him across the stage station. He stopped at a table with a still steaming coffeepot and clean cups. He poured two cups of coffee and hurried after Jack.

Jack and Clements were already in the room, the prisoner seated in a straight-back chair facing the desk. Cart walked in and set one of the cups on the desk next to Jack. "Thought you could use this."

"You're not kidding." Jack picked up the cup and took a long sip of the coffee. Before setting it down, he lifted it slightly to Cart. "Thanks." Then he turned to Clements.

"Mr. Clements, your short reign of terror over Texas families has come to an end. I don't know if you heard what the rancher in the stage office had to say before he left, but it wasn't pleasant. His suggestion was to burn you two to death in a bonfire."

Clements shrank from Jack, fear filling his eyes. "Please, Mr. Sage, I can tell you a great deal. I can tell you who is in charge, where he lives, and how much he pays for the girls. I can tell you all of that. Just let me go free."

Jack barked a humorless laugh. "Mr. Clements, I want you to understand what's awaiting you. You're going to travel with Ranger Cartwright or a ranger much like him back to either Fredericksburg, San Marcos, or Austin. There, you will receive a trial before a jury of your peers. You will be found guilty, and you will hang by a very tight rope until dead."

Clements's face had gone ashen. He stared at Jack with wide, tear-filled eyes and suddenly turned, bent over, and heaved his previous meal all over the floor. When he looked up, his body was shaking. "May I have some water, please?"

"Not a chance." Cart looked like he was ready to tear the man limb from limb.

Jack knew how he felt. The man in front of him had delivered frightened little girls to a life of fear and pain. It was all he could do to keep from exacting his own retribution from this poor excuse for a man. "Now, Clements, that's the best scenario. That's what happens if you tell us everything, and I mean everything. But it happens weeks, probably months from now. Not only do I want the information on the man in charge, but I want the names of the girls, their parents, and where they're from. I also want to know where the girls are going. If you give me all of the information, you'll have the opportunity to hang." Jack looked at Cart, who was calmly drinking his coffee while one leg of Clements's chair, shorter than the others, rattled against the floor. "If you refuse, then we will probably let you escape to a crowd of people ready to light you up, and that can happen today. I know, that's not much of a decision, but that's what you've brought on yourself. Today or a few months, your choice."

Jack saw the paper, pen, blotter, and jar of ink on Hackett's desk. He shoved them over to Clements. "Start talking and start writing. Make it clear and understandable."

Clements looked up at Jack, eyes pleading. "Could I please have a cup of water, *please*?"

Jack glanced at Cart, who frowned, shook his head, finished his coffee, and left the room. Moments later he returned with a glass of water and a fresh cup of coffee. He slammed the water onto the desk. A third of it splashed out.

The frightened man's arm shot out, and he pulled the glass to his lips, emptying it. He set the glass on the table and looked up at Jack, his face pleading. "Another, please?"

"Write."

Clements picked up the pen and started writing. He talked as he wrote. "Ranger Sage, I am employed by Mr. Clinton W. Ainsworth."

Jack was elated. His mind went over the name, *Clinton W. Ainsworth. We finally have the name of the mastermind of this bunch. Your days are numbered, Ainsworth.*

"He is a very well-to-do attorney in San Francisco. I have been in his luxurious suite on the second floor of the Occidental Hotel. He located me shortly after I arrived in the city, and explained his needs. He offered me a salary impossible to turn down."

Jack interrupted him. "How much, and write it down, also your duties, including Nadine Tidwell's."

Clements hesitated, then began haltingly, "I am paid by the person. I—"

The old-time mountain man was having a hard time containing himself. He strode over to Clements, who was talking. "You mean by the head, by the girl child. Ain't that what you mean?"

Keeping his head down and his eyes focused on the paper, as if that action would make Cart disappear, Clements, his lower jaw shaking, muttered, "Yes."

Jack gave Cart a stern look and mouthed, "Let him talk."

Cart glared at his friend, spun around, and stalked to the back of the room.

Jack tapped his big finger near the paper, causing the bottle of ink to jump. "Tell us, and write down, how much each of you were paid."

Clements's nervous nod indicated he understood. He continued to write. "I was paid five thousand, and Nadine was paid twenty-five hundred."

Jack, barely restraining himself from attacking the man, asked again, "Per child?"

He nodded. "Yes, per child. We deliver them to a warehouse on the waterfront. There, they are taken from us. From that point, I no longer know their disposition."

Jack moved menacingly closer to Clements and put a fist on the table. "Don't lie to me, Clements. I swear if you lie to me, you may not make it to a mob."

"No, please. I'm telling you the truth. I'm being honest with you—completely."

"How many gangs of outlaws do you have stealing the girls?"

Clements stopped writing and looked up at Jack. "Just the two groups, that was all."

Jack looked down at the quivering man and thought, *He's telling the truth. There is no way anyone that scared would lie.*

"How did he determine who to steal? Did he have an inside man?"

"I do not know." His voice quivered and rose at the sight of

Jack's face. "I swear. I am telling the truth. He never told me. He told me I didn't need to know. I only needed to be at the meeting place to pick up the girls and get them safely to San Francisco. Once I did that, my job was done."

"You were only working in the German area of Texas? No other areas or states?"

"No other. The operation was new. We had just started. Mr. Ainsworth told me that if we were successful in Texas, we'd branch out. He said he could develop new markets."

Jack looked down at the paper to make sure Clements was writing down every word. He looked over at Cart. "Can you think of anything else?"

"Yeah, who else is in it with you?"

Clements nodded again and started writing. "The only other person I can think of is the lady to whom we release the girls at the warehouse."

Jack poked the man, who almost jumped from his chair. "Put down her name and the warehouse number and directions to it. Does it have any guards around it?"

Clements nodded. "Oh, yes, it does. Two guards are there when we deliver the girls. I assumed they were there for protection for Mrs. Crisp." The man continued to write for a few minutes more.

Finally, he sat up, reached for the blotter, and blotted the page he had written. Jack looked at it. "Sign and date it."

Clements obediently scrawled out the date and his signature and blotted the almost full page.

Jack picked it up and scanned it. "Nadine Tidwell, how did Ainsworth locate her?"

"I knew her. I had worked with her before and felt she would be a good fit. It's a long way to travel for two people. You must be able to coexist pleasantly."

Yeah, Jack thought, *and you have to be willing to harm frightened children.* He glanced at Cart. "Could you get the marshal?" He continued to read the page of neat writing. He laid it back on the desk. "Make two more copies, date, and sign them."

Clements had begun on his second copy when Cart and Marshal Ruff walked in. The marshal closed the door behind him. Jack picked up the dried sheet of paper and handed it to the marshal. After he finished reading it, Jack said, "We need your help. Do you know if there are any rangers in El Paso right now?"

Ruff shook his head. "You two are the only ones. We had a passel of them in a couple of weeks ago, but they left for North Texas, Comanches."

Jack shook his head. "We have a logistics problem. I'm headed to San Francisco to catch this piece of garbage who is dealing in children, but we also need to get these youngsters back home to their folks. On top of this"—he motioned toward Clements and his partner—"they need to get back to the Fredericksburg, Austin area for trial. You see our predicament?"

15

The marshal nodded. "I can help with one of those problems. I can hold this one and the woman until the rangers get back, then turn them over."

Jack nodded to the marshal's response. "The problem is whether or not you can hold them. What about a mob? When word spreads, and I figure it has already hit the streets, hot blood and whiskey are going to whip up a mob pretty quick, maybe by tonight."

Marshal Ruff crossed his arms over his thick chest. "I understand what you're saying, but I can guarantee there will be no mob taking any prisoner from my jail. When I tell you I can hold 'em, I can hold 'em. I've got a good deputy, and several of the citizens will step up when I ask. I can do it."

Jack turned to his partner. "What do you think, Cart?"

Cart nodded his head toward the marshal. "I don't personally know Marshal Ruff, but I do know he has a good reputation. If he says he can do it, then I believe him, but here's the rub. I'm not real excited about taking care of these little girls all the way back to San Marcos. That's a long haul with a bunch of kids. I ain't been around kids since I was one."

"Cart, I don't have any other solution. I've got to leave on the stage right now. The girls are in your hands. The end."

The mountain man turned ranger gave Jack a wry grin. "Well, guess I'd better get busy. You need to introduce me to 'em so's they ain't half scared to death of me."

Jack breathed a sigh of relief. It was all starting to fall into place. He turned back to Clements. "Is there any special knock or code you use to get the woman at the warehouse to open the door?"

Clements nodded. "Yes, I forgot that. It's simple. I give two knocks, pause, three knocks, pause, and end with two more knocks. That's it. It works every time. It's almost like she's standing on the other side of the door waiting. She immediately opens it."

"How many girls have you delivered to her?"

"We have only begun. This is our second group of girls. We took the other three girls a little over a month ago."

"Do you know if they're still holding them, or have they already sent the girls somewhere?"

Clements shook his head. His body had stopped quivering "I don't know. As I said, Mr. Ainsworth tells me very little."

Jack looked up at Cart. "You ready?"

"As much as I'm ever gonna be." He looked at the marshal. "You know what time the next stage leaves for Fort Stockton? If it's gonna be a while, we need a place for the girls to stay."

Before the marshal could speak, Jack jumped in. "Oh yeah, whoever keeps them needs to know the professor here and Tidwell have been keeping them sedated with laudanum."

The marshal looked at Clements like he was ready to personally take the man apart, and then he looked at Jack. "Sure I do. My missus will dearly love to take them. They'll fit right in with our other four, two boys and two girls. Of course, if they've been on laudanum, they'll sleep for a while, but they're gonna be a handful when they start coming off of that stuff." His thick eyebrows rose, and he glanced at Cart.

Cart was staring at Jack. "I ain't thought about that. What am I goin' to do with those little things comin' off that junk?"

Jack had pulled Clements out of his chair and started for the door. "See the doctor. Maybe he has an idea or something you can give them to make it easier."

Marshal Ruff added, "The doc's a good man. He'll be more'n happy to help you."

The three lawmen followed the kidnapper into the large area set apart for the office and passenger waiting and dining. Jack could see the mules were hooked up to the stage, and several of the passengers were upset, talking to Hackett and the driver. *They're just going to have to wait,* he thought. *When I'm finished, we can be on our way.*

Hackett, flushed and agitated, rushed up to Jack as he entered the office. "Ranger Sage, are you about ready? My passengers are anxious to be on their way, and so is the driver. Can you tell me how much longer you'll be before you're ready to leave?"

Brusquely, Jack shook his head. "Nope. I'll be ready when I'm ready. Do you want to take care of these criminals and the little girls?"

Hackett jumped back. "No, no. I mean, isn't that your job?"

"You're right. That's what I'm working on. I wouldn't be too pushy, Mr. Hackett, since the Butterfield Stage Line provided transportation for this bunch of kidnappers and their victims."

Jack walked away to a sputtering station manager. Reaching Nadine Tidwell, he dropped his hand to her arm, yanked her up, and thrust her toward Marshal Ruff.

Her dull brown hair pulled back in a severe bun, she looked up at him, dark eyes cold and calculating. "You don't find it necessary to interview me, Ranger Sage?"

"No. I'm out of time. Any interviewing you'll get will be during your trial." He turned to the marshal. "They're all yours.

Good luck. Let the rangers' office know you've got them, or Cart will. I've got to get out of here."

The three little girls were sitting on the bench next to the door, swinging their legs, eyes glued on Jack. He took a deep breath and made his face relax into a wide smile. He turned toward them and watched each face brighten. He motioned to Cart. Jack walked over to them, grabbed a chair, and pulled it into position facing them. Cart did the same.

Catarina smiled at Jack. "Are you ready to take us home, Ranger Sage? We've been waiting for you. We're ready when you are." At the shake of Jack's head, her smile disappeared.

"Catarina, girls, I'm not going to be able to take you because I've got to go on to San Francisco and catch the bad man up there."

The smallest of the three, her wide blue eyes focused on his face, brushed a strand of blonde hair behind her right ear and made a slight tilt with her head. "Like you did here, Ranger Sage?"

Jack turned his smile on her. Thrilled this one was also talking. "Just exactly like *we* did here. That way no other little girls can be taken from their homes.

"Ranger Cartwright"—Jack threw his arm around his friend's shoulders—"here, is going to take you all back home. He's got to get everything ready, and then you'll ride the stage to Fort Stockton and take a wagon from there. Doesn't that sound exciting?"

No nods came from the girls. Even if they had been traveling with Jack, the prospect of the long trip back to San Marcos had to be daunting to all three of them.

Jack patted his friend on the back. "Cart here, Ranger Cartwright, knows a lot about the country. He'll be able to keep you safe. Have you heard about mountain men?"

The girl who had not spoken raised her hand. Jack said, "Go ahead, honey, you don't have to raise your hand with us to speak."

She swallowed and began. "Mountain men are strong and brave. I know because my grandpa is a mountain man, and nobody messes with him."

Jack grinned as he looked at all three. "You are so right. See how much bigger I am than Ranger Cartwright?"

All three of the girls nodded solemnly.

"I'm telling you the truth when I say *I* wouldn't mess with Ranger Cartwright. He's too tough for me. He'll keep you real safe. No bad men will come around. I promise you."

Cart leaned forward and removed his beat-up, dirty hat. His long salt-and-pepper hair fell in all directions. He brushed it out of his eyes. "Would you girls let me take you back home? I'd be right honored. I know a lot about the west, Texas and the mountains, but I don't know much about girls. Would you help me learn? We'll have plenty of time."

Catarina gave Cart a big smile. "We'll teach you all we can, Ranger Cartwright, but you are pretty old. You know what they say, 'you can't teach an old dog new tricks.' Are you sure you can make it back to San Marcos?"

Jack strained to hold in the laughter. He had to look away, and his sides moved once. When he looked back, Cart was staring at him, but said nothing.

Cart showed the girls a big smile. "I'm pretty sure I can make it, sweetie, but if I get tired, will you help me?"

Catarina nodded. "I like you, Ranger Cartwright."

The other girls nodded along with her and smiled at Cart.

Jack leaned forward. "Girls, I'm going to have to leave. Can you all give me a big hug?"

The three of them jumped forward into his arms. Thin arms laced around his neck. In a loud whisper, Jack said, "I'll miss you all, but maybe I'll see you and your folks when I get back."

The smallest leaned closer. "That would be nice. I know Papa would like to thank you for catching these bad people."

"Thank you. Now, even though Ranger Cartwright is old, he's

still strong, and with your help, I know he'll get you home safely." Jack could feel Cart's stare burning into his back. He started to stand. The girls held on for a few more moments and turned him loose. He straightened, officially turning the responsibility and the girls' affection over to Cart. The three of them watched the older ranger and congregated around him. Jack felt both relieved and sad, but there was a job to do. He turned to Leland Hackett.

"Mr. Hackett, sorry about everything, delaying the stage, snapping at you. It's been a little hectic."

Hackett waved his hands in front of him. "Think nothing of it, Ranger Sage. This has truly been quite a day. What can I do for you?"

Jack glanced over at Cart, who was surrounded by the girls. "Cart." The ranger looked his way. "If you're riding the stage to Fort Stockton, what are you doing about your horses?"

Cart shook his head. "Hadn't thought about that."

Hackett spoke up. "May I make a suggestion? If you leave all the horses with me, I can look after them until Ranger Sage gets back. He can then take them with him back to wherever you might be. How does that sound?"

Cart nodded his head. "Sounds terrific to me. I'll be renting more horses at Ford's place in Fort Stockton." He thought for a few moments. "But I have Binford's rental horses here."

Jack added, "And a mule."

Hackett shook his head. "Not to worry. We move horses back and forth between stations. It might take a while, but we'll get them back to Fort Stockton."

Jack listened to the stage manager's suggestions. "That's really big of you, Mr. Hackett. I've got a fine mule, besides Ford's, and my three horses. When I get back, I'll pay you for their upkeep and Cart's animals too. If someone could exercise and give 'em some oats and corn every once in a while, I'd be much obliged."

Hackett gave him a big grin. "I'll be glad to, and let me assure you, it will cost you nothing."

Hackett must have seen the surprise on Jack's face. His grin grew bigger. "Ranger Sage, you and Ranger Cartwright saved the Butterfield stage and their passengers from being killed and scalped by Apaches. You will never spend a dime on this line, and you and your friend are welcome to ride anytime."

Jack shook his head. "We were just doing our job. That's mighty generous, but not necessary."

"It is done. Anytime you want to ride this stage, just tell them who you are, even if you're no longer with the rangers, free rides, forever."

"Well, thanks."

"You are most welcome. Are you ready to board?"

"Just give me a few minutes to grab my saddlebags, and I'll hold you up no longer."

Jack strode out of the office to the barn. The stage hands had already cooled and brushed the animals, and his gear was placed in a corner of the tack room. He thanked them, grabbed his saddlebags and Winchester, and made a quick stop with his horses and mule. After taking a little time patting and talking to them, he gave each a treat and hurried for the stage.

Cart was waiting by the stage door. He thrust out his hand. "It's been a good ride, *compadre*. Luck to you." He leaned forward and in a low voice continued, "Between you and me, when you find this fella, you should loose him in that big ocean. His kind doesn't need to be around. Take care of yourself."

"I'd prefer the law, but we'll see how the chips fall. Safe trip." Jack grinned at his friend. "Don't push yourself too hard. I wouldn't want your age to be a problem."

Cart pushed his hat back and glared at Jack. "You can sure try a feller." Then he broke into a grin.

The stage driver leaned over and looked down at the two rangers. "You fellers wanta hug and kiss? I got a schedule to keep, and it's already ripped to shreds 'cause of you."

Both of them glared up at the driver. Jack jumped into the

stage. Hackett, Cart, and the girls stood nearby. The driver popped the whip. The coach jerked and jerked again, leaning first to the left and then right. Jack thought, *Feels like being on rough waters.* He looked around the inside of the coach at the other passengers, all men, a couple of them irate because of the stage being held up but not willing to say anything to the giant ranger. He gave a general nod to the interior, put his saddlebags behind his feet, and his rifle next to him. He leaned back, tilted his Stetson forward over his face, and, for what seemed like the first time in days, fell into a deep sleep, with the stage pitching and rolling.

∼

THE DRIVER YELLED, chains rattled, and the stage pulled to its final stop at the station in San Francisco. For the final six hours of his thirteen-day trip from El Paso, the stage had been packed with riders. So much so that Jack's long legs were either pulled up next to him or carefully stretched between the gentlemen on the facing seat. Jack grabbed his saddlebags and rifle and stepped down from the cramped stage.

In his growing years, from about fourteen till when he left the ship in Algiers to join the French Foreign Legion, Jack had served on a clipper ship. As he stood on solid ground, after riding the pitching and rolling stagecoach, his legs felt much like they had felt after a long voyage when he first stepped ashore from the clipper.

He surveyed the busy streets of San Francisco. Jack was not a country boy from West Texas. He had traveled Europe and seen much of North Africa. The bustling scenes of the burgeoning city did not faze him. People here rushed more than they did in Texas, but much less than was the norm in New York City. This was a bustling new city, seams stretched with the influx of money.

Jack stepped up to the stage line window. "Which way to the Occidental?"

The harried man pointed to his right. "Two blocks up the street, take a right. You can't miss it."

"Thanks." But the man had already turned and was directing the moving of baggage.

Jack swung around, and his long legs stepped out to the hotel. He felt a movement against his saddlebags. He was also familiar with the trade of pickpocketing. It had been rampant in Algiers and Paris. He swung the barrel of his Winchester, striking a twelve-year-old boy across his shoulder and knocking him to the ground. In the boy's right hand was one of the rolls of bills that Jack had been given by the Texas Ranger major in Fredericksburg. Before the boy could leap to his feet, Jack planted a big boot on his chest, not without some force.

He could hear the air rush from the boy's lungs. He released a bit of pressure, allowing the boy to breathe, but held the youngster on the ground, flat on his back.

An older woman rushed up. "You are hurting that poor boy. Can't you see he can't breathe?"

Jack, while keeping his foot on the boy's chest, leaned over and jerked the money from his hand, stood erect, and turned to the woman. "Ma'am, this 'poor boy' just tried to steal money from me. Can you tell me the location of the marshal's office?"

16

The woman glared up at Jack, which had to be a strain on her neck, since she was barely five feet tall. Her voice was prim and stern. "Young man, this is a city. We do not have 'marshals,' we have police. Furthermore, you do not need to be taking this boy to the police. They will only throw him in jail with all those miscreants. There is no telling what might happen to him."

Jack nodded in agreement. "Thanks for letting me know about the police, ma'am. Since you care about him so much, would you like him?"

"Hey," the kid yelled, "I can take care of myself. Let me up." The boy had both hands on Jack's boot, trying to move it, and was jerking his body around like a bronc attempting to unseat a rider.

Jack looked down. "Be still." He increased pressure on the kid's chest, and the boy stopped moving. He held on to Jack's boot, but stopped pulling on it.

"That hurts," the kid croaked.

Jack eased a little pressure from his chest, but held enough to keep him down.

The older woman was carrying an umbrella. She turned it

like a sword and began poking Jack. "You're hurting him. Let him up right now."

Jack was trying to carry his rifle, his saddlebags, and hold the money he had yanked from the kid's hand, so both of his hands were occupied. His gaze and his voice turned stern. "Ma'am, stop poking me with that umbrella. It's not a sword. I don't want to have to hold you down too."

The woman gasped. "Are you threatening me, young man? I have never been so rudely spoken to in my whole life." She looked around, spotted what she was looking for, and reached into her purse. Drawing out a whistle, she took a deep breath and, from the earsplitting sound, must have blown with all the air her old lungs could muster. She stopped blowing and started waving and yelling, "Police. Police. Help. Help me."

Jack stood watching the action play out before him like he was a spectator. He thought, *Is this really happening to me? I'm trying to slip into town as quietly as possible, and now I'm the center of a comical farce. You can't make this stuff up.* He watched a uniformed policeman walk purposefully across the busy street, holding his hand up to stop wagons, buggies, riders, and delivery vans. They all stopped, giving him plenty of room. In his right hand, attached to his wrist with a leather thong, was a billy club. He swung the truncheon with rhythm and timing.

He's done that many an hour, Jack thought.

Deeming the police officer in range of her strident voice, the woman began. "Hurry, Officer, oh please, hurry. This huge man is crushing this poor little boy."

Jack could see the "poor little boy" was no happier to see the policeman than he was. The kid watched the officer approach with a cautious and fearful expression.

The officer touched his hat to the woman. "I am Officer O'Rourke, madam. What is going on here?"

She took a deep breath and began. "I'll tell you what is going on. This brute of a man, unshaven, and probably a vagrant, is crushing this poor lad with his monstrous foot."

Jack looked at his foot. It wasn't that big.

The officer looked down at the boy. "Tsk, tsk, tsk, Rodney, me lad. Haven't I told you before not to be placing your hand in others' pockets?"

The woman, puzzled, her forehead wrinkled, stared at the policeman. "You know this poor boy, Officer?"

"'Deed I do, ma'am, 'deed I do. It is many a time I have found him taking those things earned by others. I don't know what it is I'll be doing with him this time. He just doesn't listen to me." He looked up at Jack. "You can let him up, sir. I think he's been down there long enough." The officer leaned over toward the boy, his hands folded behind him. "Will you be still when you stand, Rodney?"

The boy nodded as he sat up and then jumped to his feet.

"There's a good lad." O'Rourke placed a kindly hand on Rodney's shoulder. Jack could see the hand tighten when Rodney acted like he might take off. "Now give your apologies to this gentleman."

The boy's lips poked out slightly, his eyebrows pushed closer together, and a few wrinkles appeared on his forehead. He said nothing.

"Now, now, lad, it's a choice you have for yourself this fine day. You can walk with me down to the station and force me to fill out a mess of paperwork I would prefer not to be seeing, and then you can end up in the jail. But the prevention of all that unpleasantness is in your hands. You only have to apologize to the gentleman, lad. Apologize."

At the last word Jack saw the humor disappear from O'Rourke's face. His grip tightened further on the boy's shoulder.

Words shot from Rodney's mouth like they had been squeezed out by O'Rourke, which in fact, they had. In a bit of pain when he began, his voice moved down to its normal timbre at the end of his declaration. "I apologize. I'm sorry."

Jack watched Rodney and didn't see any regret in his face. All he saw was relief he was being released and annoyance he'd been caught.

"Get along with you, Rodney, and be understanding, if I catch you lifting some poor soul's earnings, the next time it'll be the jail for you."

Rodney had already started to move. "Yeah, yeah, I understand."

Jack's hand shot out, and he grabbed the boy by the right bicep, then glanced at O'Rourke. "I need a horse. You seem to know Rodney, here. Can I trust him?"

O'Rourke thought for a moment. "Aye, he's a good lad except for his sticky fingers. You can trust him."

Jack eyed Rodney. "You see my size. I need a good horse, a stayer. He doesn't have to be fast, but that would be nice. I need to rent him for a few days. I don't know how long yet. Can I trust you to rent him for me and bring him to me at the Occidental Hotel?"

The boy eyed Jack in return. "Yes."

"Good, do you know horseflesh?"

O'Rourke laughed. "There'll not be many of his age who knows the horses as well as he. He sometimes jockeys over at the club. He's actually won a few."

Rodney, defensive, spoke up. "More than a few. I've only lost twice, and those were the horses' fault."

Jack turned Rodney's arm loose. "All right, how much to rent a horse?"

"Have you ridden much?"

Jack thought back on his chase of the gang to El Paso. *Too much here lately.* "I've been known to ride a bit."

"Then it'll be three dollars a day, or eighteen for a week. That's for a good horse."

Jack counted out eighteen dollars and put it in Rodney's hand.

He added a five-dollar gold piece on top. The boy's eyes bugged out at the money.

"You're paying me five dollars just for getting you a horse?"

"I need a horse. I don't know who to see or where to go. It's worth five dollars to me not to have to search around for a good animal. Have him at the hotel by six thirty this evening."

Rodney looked down at the money, then back up to Jack. "Yes, sir." He turned and trotted off.

The old woman had been watching all of the proceedings. "I may have made a mistake in judgment where you're concerned, young man."

Jack turned to face her. "Ma'am, I hope you did. My name is Jack Sage, and just for your peace of mind, I've been on that stage for two weeks. Hopefully, I'll look much less like a vagrant after I get a shave, a bath, and a new set of clothes."

The elderly woman's cheeks colored. "Pardon me for being a little brusque. According to my sister, Doris, I tend to be that way when I am excited. My name is Isabel Wagner. Thank you for helping with that young man. I see him around frequently. My sister and I have tried to help, but he is so independent."

O'Rourke had been patiently watching and listening. "Aye, the boy has fallen on hard times. His sweet mother, God rest her soul, passed last year. Times being what they are for the poorer folks, they were only barely making it. It's the streets he mostly lives on. He is a fine little jockey, but has no manager, so hard it is for him to get work, but it's much too much talking I'm doing. I'll be moving on." He touched his hat. "Mrs. Wagner, Mr. Sage."

Jack raised a finger. "If you have another moment, Officer O'Rourke, I have a question for you."

Mrs. Wagner smiled at the two men. "It was interesting to meet you, Mr. Sage." She removed a small card and handed it to Jack. "I'd like to invite you to a cup of tea with me and my sister. Say tomorrow at three?"

Jack took the card, looked at the delicate writing on it, and back at Mrs. Wagner. "I don't think I have anything planned for then. I'd be delighted. Thank you for asking."

Mrs. Wagner nodded. "We'll see you then. The address is on the card. Have a good day, gentlemen." She turned and, shoulders back, marched away.

"Quite a feisty lady," Jack said. "It's her kind who opened the west."

"Yes, for a truth it is, Mr. Sage. Is there something I can do for you? I must be on my rounds."

Jack had been appraising O'Rourke throughout the altercation. He knew people, and he felt he could read them fairly well. He might be in need of someone's help, so he had made the decision to tell the police officer his identity. He reached into a corner of his saddlebags and removed his badge. After making sure there was no one watching, he showed it to O'Rourke.

"May I?" O'Rourke asked, reaching for the badge.

Jack handed it over. The officer handled it, turned it over, and examined it closely, then returned the badge, and Jack slipped it back into the saddlebag.

"Why, Captain, are you showing me this? Of course, you have no jurisdiction in California."

"I realize that, but I'm in pursuit of a man who is either heading up or close to the top of a ring of evil men. We had several girls, ages between nine and twelve, kidnapped over the past few weeks. They were all taken from German communities. There were two groups grabbing children from different towns. Most of them decided to fight it out rather than surrender, but several will make it to the gallows."

O'Rourke's face had darkened. He had stopped swinging the billy club and was gripping it with both hands, his knuckles white. "I detest the likes of such animals. God preserve the wee ones, but why are you here?"

"The leader has a suite at the Occidental Hotel. Here's the rub. I'd like to grab him and get him back to Texas—"

"Hold up, lad. I have to tell my sergeant about this, and he'll want to be involved in the man's capture."

"That's just it. He might not want to be. This man is a prominent attorney here in San Francisco. I know in most places, prominent attorneys have powerful friends, both in and out of politics. Anyone involved with this is probably going to get burned, and burned badly."

O'Rourke rubbed his chin. "Aye, it's truth you're speaking for sure. Let me think." Moments later he asked, "What is it you have planned?"

Jack looked around again to ensure there was no one listening.

"I'd prefer not to discuss it out here on the street. Your uniform and my getup are pretty obvious. Come to the hotel later this afternoon, and we can meet. I'll explain what I can without your commitment one way or the other. If you decide to join me, I'll give you the whole thing. If you're not interested, don't show up."

O'Rourke regarded Jack while again rubbing his chin. "Intrigue, it is what I'm feeling. I'll be there. Say about four o'clock? Now, I must get moving."

"One more thing. I need a nice suit, a pair of boots, and . . . forget it, I need everything. Is there a place you can recommend nearby? One that can do the work quickly."

O'Rourke stopped and turned back. "There is, and it is close to the hotel. The name is Antonio's. Don't let him fool you. He'll try to tell you it will take days, but he can turn a suit out in hours. It's a large family he has, and they all work with him. You can't miss it, across the street from the hotel. Tell him I sent you." The officer raised his truncheon in salute and strolled down the street. Jack watched him go. He spoke to almost every person he passed. Jack turned and headed for the hotel.

Checking in began as a problem until he took out several double eagles. From that point on, he was no longer considered a broke cowhand trying to pull a fast one on them. While checking in, he ordered a tub of hot bathwater and shaving gear. Also he asked a bellman to run across the street to Antonio's and ask the tailor to come to his room.

His bellman tried to take his saddlebags, but he shook his head and, with his rifle, followed him to his room. The bellman unlocked the door and led him into the suite. *Very nice,* he thought. *Not as nice as in Paris, but this will certainly do in a pinch.* He smiled to himself. A couple of weeks ago he had been sleeping under the stars among Texas cactus and coyotes. The bellman handed Jack his key, and Jack dropped a quarter eagle into the man's hand.

"Thank you, sir. My name is Mitch. Ask for me anytime. I will be at your service."

"Thanks, Mitch. The service I need right now is a tub and hot water. I've got two weeks of stagecoach grime I need to get washed off."

"Yes, sir, it should be arriving any moment." He walked to the door and looked toward the stairs. "Here it is." Two hefty teenagers clutched a large pail of steaming hot water in each hand. A third was carrying a long tub with a high back at one end. Jack looked it over as he came into the room. It actually looked like he might be able to stretch his legs out in it. He hadn't seen one that long before. They took it into the dressing room. Moments later two more young men came in with more room-temperature water. The procession continued until the tub was full enough to allow him to sit in steaming hot water without flooding over the side. He gave each of the boys four bits. They were excited and profuse with their gratitude. The bellman shooed them out.

"Mr. Sage, towels, soap, shampoo, fresh from Paris, are all on the dresser next to the tub. Enjoy your bath, and when you are ready for it to be taken from your room, just pull the bell. We will be right up." The bellman leaned forward to Jack and lowered his voice. "It will be the same young men. You were extremely generous to them when they brought the water up. It will not be necessary to provide an additional tip."

"Thanks." Jack followed him to the door, closed it, and looked at the tub and then the bed. It would be so easy to stretch out on the bed and sleep for a week. He shook his head. There was much to do, and he needed to get busy. The tailor would be arriving soon.

Jack closed the curtains on the windows that provided a view of the street from the dressing room and stripped in front of the mirror, tossing his clothes into a pile he would throw away. He examined the new scar on his right temple. The rock had come close but, fortunately, not close enough.

On his right thigh and left shoulder were pucker wounds from bullets. He rubbed the back of his head and felt the permanent indentation where his *friend* had hit him. He thought, *With a friend like that, I'd prefer enemies.* All three wounds were the result of one trip, his first and, so far, only cattle drive. Financially it had paid off beyond expectations, but he wondered if the blood and cracked skull were worth it. He chuckled to himself, remembering the Legion and the wars he had been through without a scratch. *Life is full of surprises,* he thought as he lowered his sore body into the hot water. He let his muscles relax, allowing the heat and the water to do their work before he helped them out with a little elbow grease.

Twenty minutes later he was out of the tub, clean, feeling better, and dressed in the clean trousers he had brought along with him. His broad chest and muscular arms and back were bare as he went to work on his stubble. He'd managed to keep it mostly in check on the longer stage stops, but it felt good to have hot water and lather. Halfway through his shave, there was a knock on the door. He stepped to the chair where his revolvers hung and withdrew one. Opening the door, he held the weapon behind him.

17

The man before him was in his mid-forties, balding, and at least forty pounds overweight, most of which looked to be around his belly. In one hand he carried a stool, and in the other what looked like a tool chest. Before Jack could speak, the man introduced himself. "Good afternoon, I am Antonio Giuseppe. It is my understanding you need some clothes, no?"

"Come in, Mr. Giuseppe, I am Jack Sage. Yes, I need everything, but first I need to wipe off my face. I'll finish shaving when you're through."

At Jack's mention of his needs, the man's face lit in a wide smile. "Please, finish your shave. I myself must get ready. As far as clothing, you are a lucky man, for Antonio has everything." Which he followed with a big belly laugh.

Jack closed and locked the door. He crossed the room to the dresser and slid the Remington back into its holster. "Please accept my apologies for the weapon. I cannot be too careful." Jack continued drawing the sharp straight razor across the stubble on his remaining cheek.

Antonio held his finger to his lips, pointed at Jack and then himself. "You and me, we cannot be too careful. I work for many people who must be very careful. I say nothing about what we do, and what I see, for I see nothing." He laughed again and regarded Jack solemnly as he wiped the remnants of shaving cream from his face. "You are a big man. You take a lot of cloth. What would you like?"

Jack held his hands out, palms up. "I have nothing." He pointed to the filthy clothes in the corner, what he was wearing, and the shirt on the bed. "This is it. I have nothing else. I'll be here for several days. I don't know how many. Then I go back to the plains, where this is what I wear. No suits, so I only want one suit, maybe three pairs of trousers, shirts to go along, bandannas, ties, socks, underwear. Everything." He held up his saddlebags. "When I leave, what I take must fit in these, and, most importantly, I need it today."

Antonio slapped both hands over his mouth and stared at Jack. "No. It is not possible. You ask the impossible. You are too big. For a smaller man, maybe, but not you. If I had all the seamstresses in San Francisco, it would be impossible." He threw his hands up and shook his head. "No."

"Officer O'Rourke recommended you to me and said you could do it."

Antonio began speaking rapid Italian, and Jack was pretty sure he should be happy he couldn't understand him. Finally, still shaking his head, he bent, pulled a measuring tape, a pad, and a pencil from the toolkit and pointed Jack toward the stool. "Get on it. We have no time to waste."

The fitting went quickly. Throughout, Antonio was muttering and writing in his book. After twenty-five minutes, the fat man stepped back and snapped his book closed. "There, the easy part is done. Now we must pick out the clothing."

Jack shook his head. "I have another meeting. The gentleman should be arriving soon. You pick out the clothing. I trust your tastes. Here are the only restrictions. I'm looking for a very conservative look, dark. One of the shirts should also be very dark."

Antonio beamed. "You are a smart man, Jack Sage. I have very good taste. You will have two of the nicest suits, two." He held up two fingers. "Two. I will not fix only one." His head tilted slightly, and he brought his hands together in front of him. "It will be expensive."

Jack stepped off the stool and slipped his one remaining clean shirt on over his head, pulling it down snug over his thick shoulders. "Don't worry about the money. How much do you need now?"

The man's chubby hands waved in front of him as if he were swatting away a swarm of mosquitoes. "No, no, you are a friend of Officer O'Rourke. I trust you." He packed up his case and stool and turned for the door.

"What time can I expect them?"

"I am thinking eight this evening. It will be a terrible rush, but we can have them then."

"Could you make it before six?" Jack knew he was pushing it, but he needed the clothes soon.

Antonio let out a sharp breath, shaking his head. "You make it very difficult, Mr. Sage. But, yes. I will have one suit and accoutrements *before* six."

"And boots?"

The fat man looked to the ceiling as if he were imploring heaven's aid, but reached for the door. "Yes, Mr. Sage, I will have the boots. But I am leaving now before you make any other demands upon me." He rushed out, yanking the door closed behind him.

Jack locked the door, grabbed a boot cloth from the closet, and wiped his boots down the best he could. These had been good boots, but the heels and sides were worn, and the toes had lost most of the leather. He was looking forward to seeing his new boots. Hopefully they would fit. Considering all the measurements Antonio had taken of each foot, they should fit like a glove. Jack pulled his old boots on, stood, and stomped. They slipped easily past the heel. They were really comfortable, but looking down, he had to admit, really worn out.

He reached for his gun belt and thought better of it, pulled one of his short-barreled Remington New Model Police revolvers from its holster, checked the loads, and slid it behind his waistband. These were excellent revolvers. He had made the right choice. His friends had told him he needed a heavier caliber, but he knew the little .36-caliber ball, put in the right place, would do all of the damage he would need.

Next he slipped on his vest, buttoned it, and pulled the front down. It would have to do. The butt of the Remington caused his vest bottom to pooch out slightly, but many men in the city carried weapons. He lifted his gun belt with his remaining revolver and hung it in the armoire. He also stored his rifle in the corner, just behind the belt. He grabbed his saddlebags, removed some of the money, and hung them over the hangar bar, and looked around the room. Most of his things had been put away.

Jack, moving past the pull cord, gave it a yank. *They'll be up soon,* he thought, *to empty and get rid of the tub. Hopefully O'Rourke isn't on time.* Moments after pulling the cord, there was a discreet knock on the door. He opened it, and Mitch stood smiling, carrying a tray on which sat a pot of steaming coffee, cream, and four cups. Behind him stood eight brawny young men, four carrying two buckets each.

"If we may clean out your room for you, Mr. Sage. It will only be a moment."

"That's a lot of water, Mitch."

"Only a moment, sir." Mitch stepped past Jack and placed the tray on the edge of a small table in the sitting room. With one hand he balanced the tray and with the other placed the pot, cream, and cups in their appropriate positions. The table was surrounded by four green wingback chairs.

Jack watched as four of the young men, one at a time, shoved their buckets into the water, tipped them slightly to get rid of excess so it wouldn't splash on the carpets as they walked, lifted them, each carrying two, and headed for the door. Once they were done, the other four grabbed the handles on the tub, and with the remaining water in the tub, lifted it and walked to the door, straining no more than if they were taking a walk with their girlfriend. They disappeared down the hallway.

Mitch looked around the room. He spotted the clothes Jack had heaped in the corner, strode to them, rolled them in a bundle, and placed them under his arm. He marched back to Jack. "Anything else, sir?"

Jack looked into the neat, cleared, dressing room. "Quite a job, Mitch, but you didn't have to grab those dirty clothes or bring a pot of coffee, although I'm glad you did." He pointed at the dirty clothes under Mitch's arm. "I was planning on throwing the clothes away, but thanks." He fished another quarter eagle from his vest.

The young man held up a hand and shook his head. "Not necessary, sir. You have previously taken care of me quite well."

"Take it. This was well worth the price just to watch. I also enjoyed the bath. Plus you're hauling those filthy clothes out of here."

Mitch took the money and dropped it into his pocket. "Thank you, sir. I'll make sure those who did not initially bring water receive their portion."

Jack nodded. "Good man."

"Good day, sir." Mitch stepped through the door, softly pulling it closed.

Jack walked to the window. He had a good view of the Occidental's entrance. He had been there only a minute when he saw O'Rourke walk up. The officer's clothes were too nice to call them just plain clothes. *Compliments of Antonio, I would imagine,* he thought. *I'm sure O'Rourke sends him plenty of business.*

Jack watched O'Rourke stop and speak with one of the doormen. The other walked up to join in. O'Rourke had both men laughing before they had spoken for five seconds. They talked a bit longer, and the officer shook hands with the doormen and disappeared under the awning to the hotel entrance. Moments later there was a knock at Jack's door.

He opened the door, and O'Rourke stepped inside.

"It's much better you're looking, Captain Sage. I'm thinking if you had looked like this earlier today, Mrs. Wagner wouldn't have been poking you with her umbrella."

Both men laughed. Jack replied, "I think you're right, Officer O'Rourke." He immediately went to the subject of the meeting. He didn't have a lot of time. "Since you're here, I suspect you're interested in what I have to say."

"Aye, most interested. These are my streets, and I strive to protect all people, but especially the wee ones. It's this monster, I'm thinking, no matter how big he is, we need to get off the streets. I would prefer he be in jail, but under it is not a bad thing either."

Jack nodded. "My thoughts exactly, so if we're going to be working together, I think this 'captain' and 'officer' need to be replaced. Call me Jack."

"'Tis a good idea. Patrick is the name me mother gave me. I go by Pat."

"Then Pat it is." Jack motioned to the two wingback chairs by the small table. "Coffee?"

"Aye. What Irish copper doesn't like his coffee?"

Pat poured his cup full of black coffee, and Jack took three heaping spoons of sugar and three dollops of the thick cream Mitch had brought up with the coffee.

"You're liking a bit of coffee with your sugar, Jack?"

He grinned at Pat. "I'll tell you the truth, the stuff we drink on the prairie is always black with a few grounds floating in it. Cream and sugar are never an option. So when I have an opportunity like this, I'm not one to pass it up."

Both men took a sip of their steaming coffee, Jack's sip a little longer that Pat's.

"Tell me, Jack. Do you have a plan?"

"Since you don't know me, Pat, I'll tell you. Most of my plans are simple. I've found that a plan goes up in smoke the minute the battle starts."

Pat nodded his agreement. "Aye, the Irish have a saying, the plan is gone when that first punch lands on your nose."

Jack gave a short laugh, then grew serious. "That's pretty much it. My plan is to find if the girls are still here in San Francisco. I'm praying they are. If so, we need to take them and then take our attorney. The girls are the most important. There should be three of them. I want them safe before the attorney is approached. Otherwise, he might be able to get orders to his people to do away with them before we can save them."

Jack took another long sip of his coffee. "Are you ready for his name?"

"Laddie, I've been waiting."

"Clinton W. Ainsworth."

The Irishman let out a long, low whistle. "When you go after a big fish, you waste no time. He's connected all the way to Washington. He made big donations to the campaign of one of our senators. They are too friendly, if you know what I mean."

Jack nodded. "Unfortunately, it's all about money, power, and appetites, and I've seldom seen a politician who didn't have a wide girth."

"So where might we find the girls?"

Though he had it memorized, Jack pulled out the paper with the address of the waterfront Clements had given him and handed it to Pat. The policeman looked it over. "This is a rough neighborhood. You can find anything here. There are people here who will do any dastardly deed required for only enough money to buy their next opium hit. It would probably be best if we visit this area after dark."

Jack nodded his agreement and finished his coffee, filling his cup once again with the same concoction. He lifted the pot to Pat, who shook his head. Jack explained while he stirred. "My thoughts also. There's a woman who holds the girls, and two toughs who protect her. We'll have to take care of them, but I'm thinking that will be no problem. Once we take the woman and men, if the girls are there, we'll need a place to hide them until we take care of Ainsworth. It needs to be with people who can keep their mouths shut about this, for we will still need to cut the head off the snake."

Pat stared out the window. The room was quiet. Jack could hear a mockingbird singing away. He marveled at the bird. He had heard it at home in Virginia, in Texas, Missouri, Mexico, and now out here. The mockingbird's changing songs were accompanied by the flapping of wings and then the coos of several pigeons.

Finally Pat spoke. "We'll need a wagon. That will present the need for three people at least. There'll be one to drive and wait. You and I will enter the warehouse."

"Do you know anyone you can trust with this?" Jack leaned forward to Pat, his thick forearms on his knees. "Nothing can get out about this, or it could all be blown."

"Me brother is also a copper. He'll be happy to pitch in. As far as the girls, of course they'll be a-staying with me bride. She would chase me with a rolling pin if I was to take them anywhere else. My cousin delivers milk. He'll loan me his milk wagon no questions asked as long as I return it for his morning collection and deliveries. Will that do it?"

Jack shook his head. "How big is your family?"

"It is bigger than most, smaller than some. We all get along. Of course, we throw the fists now and then, but we're over it in no time. Jack, family is all a person has. Without the love of family, life can be pretty bleak."

Jack pushed the thoughts of his small family, long gone in a far land, from his mind, and brought the thought of the girls to the forefront. Pat was right, but for him, the girls were his family, at least for now.

Pat leaned back in the chair and sipped his coffee quietly, watching and waiting. Finally, Jack spoke. "When can you make the arrangements?"

"Right now. I'll send one of the bellmen, he's a cousin, to my house. Shannon, me bride, will send one of our children to my brother and cousin to let them know our needs. When is it we'll be doing the deed?"

"Can it be arranged for tonight?"

"I'm seeing no reason it can't. What time will work for you?"

"Since the stage got in today, they might be expecting the girls from Texas to be on it and a delivery tonight. Let's say around ten o'clock."

"Good. That gives me time to make the arrangements myself. I know you set up a horse with Rodney, but I'm thinking the rest of us will ride in the milk wagon. It's enclosed, and there's a bench in the back where we and the girls can sit."

"I like it."

Pat stood. "I'd best be going. Be sure to be armed. I'll come get you around eight. That should give us plenty of time."

"I'm looking forward to this, Pat. This ring, from what my prisoner said, is just getting started. They grabbed nine girls, and we've accounted for six. These three will do it, and once we get Ainsworth, it will shut them down."

Pat stepped for the door and grasped the handle. "There's one thing. I was speaking to the doormen when I came in, and they were talking about a big shindig happening this evening. Seems your Ainsworth is getting some kind of high muckety-muck award."

Jack frowned, then a thought came to him. "Do you have access to anything that might go in Mr. Ainsworth's drink to induce sleep?"

"I do. I've seen it used, and it even gives a man time to get to his room if he's not too slow."

"Good, bring it."

Pat nodded. "By the by, I spoke to my cousin the bellman."

"How many cousins do you have in this hotel?"

18

O'Rourke let a conspiratorial grin lift the corner of his mouth. "Several, I prevent thieves from stealing the owners blind. They appreciate it and have hired several of my family members. Anyway, my cousin tells me that your Mr. Ainsworth is just around the corner from you. He's in suite number four."

"Excellent, with him close, it should simplify our grabbing him. Who's your bellman cousin?"

"I think you know him, Mitch." With a twinkle in his eye, Pat opened the door and was gone.

Mitch, Jack thought, *I might have known. He's keeping an eye on me, smart. I'd do the same thing with those resources.*

Jack closed the door as his stomach rumbled. He stepped back to the coffeepot for one more cup of his coffee, sugar, cream concoction and pulled out his watch, his thumb drifting across the Legion symbol, and opened it. Five thirty, Rodney would be showing up with the horse soon. He reached for the coffeepot, and there was a knock at the door.

"Who could that be?" he said to himself and strode to the door. Opening it, he found Antonio accompanied by a tall young man loaded with boots, a very large box, and clothing on hangars.

"Come in. It's good to see you."

"You are a man in need, Mr. Sage. It is Antonio's responsibility to serve you. I have three shirts, two pairs of pants, boots, as you asked, braces, and something special. Do you have time to try them on?"

"Yes, but we must do it quickly. I have an appointment at six."

"First the shirts."

Jack began trying on the new clothing. The dark gray, faintly striped frock coat emphasized his wide shoulders, thick chest and slim waist. It fit perfectly. He was amazed at the quality of the seams since it had been done so quickly. Antonio had him button the coat, looked at it for a moment, and nodded with satisfaction. Everything looked and felt fabulous.

Antonio spotted the incredulity on Jack's face. "You are surprised, Mr. Sage? I don't know if I should take that as a compliment or an insult."

Jack shook his head in wonder. "Take it as a huge compliment. I know Officer O'Rourke told me you could produce clothing quickly, but I certainly didn't expect it this fast, nor did I expect this superior quality."

Antonio's chubby face widened with a smile. "Quality is what I do. Now, try on the boots. I did not make these, but I have a good friend who is a superb craftsman."

The boots were a solid rich brown leather, polished to a high luster. The heels were high enough to hold any stirrup in any condition, but low enough to walk comfortably. He sat and, after Antonio's helper removed his old boots, pulled on the new ones. They were tight just at the ankle, where they should be, but with a little work, his socked foot slipped right in. After slipping the other boot on, he stood and walked around the room. They were comfortable. He'd never felt a comfortable new boot.

"Marvelous, Antonio. Tell your friend these boots are the

most comfortable I've ever owned, and I have worn out many pairs of boots. Also, this clothing is superior and done in such a short time. I truly am amazed and in your debt. Now, let me pay you, for I have another appointment in only a few minutes."

"There is one more thing, Mr. Sage. The surprise I spoke of." Antonio moved to the box and removed a large, gray, western hat, made much like a Stetson, but with a slightly wider brim and a bit shorter and flattened crown. Jack had never seen one like this. The sides of the brim had a modest curl.

He took the hat. The felt, certainly of the finest beaver, was soft but firm enough to maintain its shape in a hard Texas downpour. Lifting it to his head with one hand at the front, and the other at the back, he leveled and adjusted it to his normal position. He liked it. He made a small change to the hat's position. It felt good. He liked it a lot. He turned to Antonio and gave him a big smile.

Antonio handed him a slip of paper with a list of the price for each item and a total at the bottom. Jack glanced at it only for a moment to determine how much he owed. He counted out the double eagles. Antonio's eyes glinted at the gold. When he dropped the final one in his hand, he paused, then dropped two more.

The tailor looked up at Jack. "This is much more than necessary."

"You have outdone even what Pat O'Rourke said you could do, and you have done it exquisitely. This is a way for me to express my gratitude."

Antonio turned to the young man, who formed a cup with his hands, and dropped the gold coins into them. Then he spun around and grasped Jack's hand in both of his, giving it a vigorous shaking while he spoke. "Thank you, Mr. Sage. You have been more than generous. Antonio is beyond speech. I hope you will also be pleased with the remainder of your clothing, which I will have to you tomorrow morning." When he stopped talking, he dropped Jack's hand and waved the young man toward the door. "We will not keep you. Again, thank you for your business and your generosity." He followed his helper through the door and pulled it closed.

Jack took a quick check of himself in the mirror, removed his hat, and placed it carefully on the bed. He slipped the frock coat off and hung it in the armoire. After sitting in one of the wingbacks, he slid the new boots from his feet and removed the trousers and shirt, each of which he carefully laid alongside the hat. He quickly dressed in his clean, but old clothes and boots, finally grabbing his old hat as he headed for the door.

Jack thought, *I have a lot to do, and not much time to do it in. Rodney should be waiting with the horse, and Pat will be along soon. Those girls have got to be rescu*—Jack stepped through the door. Immediately his arms and legs were pinned in powerful grips, no chance to move or break free. A dirty rag emitting a tart but sweet odor was thrust over his face. His mind screamed, *Ether! I've got to break free. Who could know? I only told . . .* Jack's vision narrowed. The four huge men, two holding him on each side, faded from view until he could only see the smile of the man he recognized shoving the rag of ether into his face.

He collapsed into darkness.

∼

RODNEY, waiting for Jack, stood at a hitching rail at the opposite end of the street from the entrance to the Occidental Hotel. He held a big, dark brown bay gelding. He couldn't be still, switching from first one foot and then the other. He didn't want one of San Francisco's finest rousting him, claiming he'd stolen the horse. He felt the money in his pocket. It had been a long time since he'd had money in his pocket that didn't belong to someone else.

Rodney felt a bout of sadness coming on. He missed his mother. She'd been a wonderful mother, but then she had to die.

He hung his head, a tear threatening to slip from his eyes. He gritted his teeth. His jaw muscles stood out like cords under the fair, young skin. He reached up and rubbed the bay's nose. He liked horses. One of these days he planned on having a big stable filled with lots of horses. He would come out in the morning and have his groom pick out and saddle a horse for him, and he'd take a long ride in the surf. Rodney always felt better when he thought of the surf. He didn't much care for getting into the water, it was always too cold, but he liked the beach where the trees came down close to the sand. He glanced at the Occidental's side entrance.

The hitching post he had chosen was right on the corner, which gave him a view of one of the side entrances of the hotel. His head jerked up. He looked again. Those first two men coming out of the side entrance were toughs Rodney knew. "I wonder what those fellas are doing at the hotel, Cocoa?" he said to the bay. They had gotten his attention. There was a carriage pulled up not far from the door the two men had exited. They came out and stood by the open carriage door, like they were waiting for something or someone. He absently rubbed the bay's nose. "What do you think those thugs are up to?"

Several seconds passed before four more men came from the side exit. His eyes bugged when he recognized who led the other three. What was he doing with this bunch? Two men held a bigger man under each arm, dragging him toward the carriage. This time Rodney jerked forward, stunned at what he saw. "Cocoa, that's Mr. Sage being dragged into the alley!"

He watched four of the men struggle, trying to load Jack into the carriage. With a final shove, he rolled inside. Two joined the driver up top, and the other three climbed inside. The door was shut, and the carriage started off. Rodney could see all the curtains were pulled closed. He leaped up to the stirrup and climbed into the saddle. Then stopped. What did he owe Sage? He had hit his shoulder with that rifle and knocked him down. He was lucky it hadn't hit his head. Why, he might be dead now. His shoulder still hurt. Then he'd held him on the ground with his big foot planted on his chest. He had even pressed harder when Mrs. Wagner came up. Sage could have broken his ribs.

But he didn't. He had surprised Rodney when he asked him to rent a horse for him and had given him the money to do it. Rodney's thoughts went back and forth as he sat on Cocoa, watching the carriage pull away. "We can at least follow them, Cocoa. There's no trouble in doing that."

He started the horse after the carriage, keeping well back so he wouldn't be noticed. After he had been following for a short time, he could see they were heading for the waterfront area. "There's nothing good down there," he said to the horse as he contemplated turning around and taking Cocoa back to the barn. He could get the money back for the horse, and with what he had been paid, he'd be set for a month at least, maybe two. He thought about that. With what he'd been paid. Sage had trusted him enough to give him all that money and pay him. He continued to follow the carriage.

Rodney was correct and nervous. The waterfront warehouse district was a tough place where a boy and a big horse like Cocoa didn't belong. He kept his eyes moving, watching for anyone who might be strolling toward him, acting strange. Of course, everyone acted strange down here. Furtive glances were tossed his way from the scattered inhabitants brave enough to venture onto the streets. He followed the carriage until it pulled into an alley between two warehouses. It stopped and disgorged its occupants.

The leader jumped down first and marched to a warehouse door. Rodney watched the man knock using a sequence, two knocks, pause, three, pause, and ending with two. Immediately the door sprang open, and the man said something, then turned and waved for the others to bring Jack. Rodney could see the big man was still unconscious. They dragged him across the alley, disappearing through the warehouse door.

"All right, Cocoa. We know where they took him, but what can we do about it? We sure can't go to the police." He sat on the big horse, thinking, until he caught movement from the corner of his eye. Just in time he kicked Cocoa, and the horse leaped forward as three boys, they looked to be three or four years older than him, leaped for him. "Run, Cocoa, run," he yelled into the horse's ears, and Cocoa ran, his hoofs ringing on the cobblestone streets. Cocoa had run for two blocks when Rodney slowed the gelding to a walk. He looked back over his shoulder. He could see the boys still standing in the street, watching him. He raised his hand and waved in derision. He saw the oldest lift his arm. He couldn't make out the sign the boy made, but he had a good idea what it was.

"What are we going to do?" he said again, racking his brain for someone to tell who might know a way to help Jack. As the horse walked away from the waterfront district and up one of the many hills in the city, Rodney noticed he was unconsciously guiding the animal toward Mrs. Wagner's house. She and her sister, Doris, who insisted he call her Aunt Doris, had fed him on several occasions, even offering him a room since they had so many. He couldn't accept it. A man has his pride. But maybe she and her sister might know someone. "I don't think they can do anything, Cocoa, because they're way too old, but you never know who a person knows."

He bumped the horse into a ground-eating trot. The big animal moved up and down the hills with little effort, although Rodney felt like he was getting his guts bounced out of him. Finally they reached the old ladies' home. Relieved and sore, he pulled Cocoa to a stop, threw a leg up and over the pommel, and slid to the ground. Once down, he tied Cocoa to a hitching post, walked up the long rock walkway, climbed the tall stairs, and knocked on the door. The third time he knocked, he balled his hand into a fist and hammered on the door with the side of his hand. From inside, he heard one of the sisters call, "Isabel, would you get that door?"

The call was followed by, "What?"

It was repeated in a shout. "Isabel, I am up to my elbows in flour. Will you *please* answer the door?"

Rodney could hear Isabel respond with, "Humph. It is very impolite to shout in the house, Doris."

He heard a chair squeak, and moments later the door opened.

Mrs. Wagner's motherly but often severe face lit with a smile.

"Why, Rodney Beckham, it is so good to see you. Won't you come in?"

"Yes, ma'am, thank you." Rodney stepped into the entranceway of the large, mostly empty house. It had been like this as long as he could remember. Only Mrs. Wagner and her sister, Doris, had ever lived in the house, as far as he was concerned.

"Doris, Rodney is visiting."

Immediately from the kitchen came the reply, "Take him into the parlor, Isabel, I'll bring some cookies and milk and join you." Moments later Doris Newell appeared with a glass of milk and a large plate of cookies.

"Hi, Aunt Doris," Rodney said dutifully. He was preparing to ask for something really big, and he needed them as much on his side as he could manage. Since being on the street, Rodney had become an excellent manipulator.

"Good evening, Rodney. It is awful late for you to be out, isn't it?"

"Yes, ma'am." His eyes had been drawn immediately to the glass of milk and cookies she had set on the small table between him and Mrs. Wagner.

"Help yourself, Rodney. That's why I brought them in here." Using just her fingertips and touching no other cookie except the one she wanted, she daintily lifted it to her wrinkled lips and took a bite.

The aroma of cooking filled the house and had grown even stronger when Doris had brought the plate of oatmeal cookies into the room. Rodney's mouth had already begun watering before he'd made it through the front door. He'd been fortunate today. He had money, which meant he'd eaten lunch. But lunch had been hours ago, and his stomach and mouth were responding to the delectable aroma. He grabbed a cookie and took a bite. He reminded himself not to put the entire cookie in his mouth, so he bit only half of it. It was loaded with sugar and butter and immediately started melting even as he began chewing.

Instantly, Mrs. Wagner said, "Now, Rodney, you shouldn't take such big bites. It will give you a stomach ulcer. Stomach ulcers can be very painful, and some people even die from them. Small bites are better for your health."

Rodney chewed and nodded his head, and he could not wait. He shoved the remainder of the cookie into his mouth. It was so good. He picked up another cookie and bit off half of it. He saw Mrs. Wagner look toward Aunt Doris, who caught the look and said to Rodney, "Would you like to eat supper with us this evening? It is almost ready."

He loved eating with them. Their food was delicious and endless.

"Yes, Rodney," Mrs. Wagner added. "It is getting dark. You might want to stay with us tonight."

The "getting dark" portion of the old lady's suggestion yanked Rodney out of his cookie oblivion. He jumped to his feet and turned to Mrs. Wagner, who sat on an old couch where she had a lot of knitting stuff scattered. "I forgot. Do you remember Mr. Sage at the stage station?"

"Yes, Rodney, I do remember him." She turned to Doris. "He's the one I was informing you of who accosted Rodney, knocked him down, and held him down with his massive foot. He's a giant of a man, although not bad looking if he had a shave and a bath."

Doris nodded. "Oh yes—"

Rodney's head moved back and forth as each woman spoke. Finally, he shouted, "He's in trouble."

Startled, both women jerked to an erect sitting position and stared at the boy as if some monster had been released in the room.

19

Mrs. Wagner was the first to recover. "Tell us, Rodney, how can the huge Mr. Sage be in trouble?"

Picking up on her skepticism, he leaned forward in his chair so he could get closer to them both, and his observations spewed forth. "I saw him knocked out and dragged from the hotel. They put him in a carriage with all the curtains closed. Mr. Sage was unconscious. Two big men had him under his arms and were dragging him out the side exit of the hotel. They had a hard time getting him into the carriage because he's so big, but they finally shoved him in, and then they drove off. They took him to the waterfront, actually a dark, unfriendly-looking warehouse at the waterfront. The leader had a secret knock he used to get in. Then they dragged him inside and closed the door. That's when three older boys tried to jump me, and I ran away and came here."

Doris, brow wrinkled from deep thought, asked, "You outran older boys?"

"No, ma'am. I mean yes, ma'am. The horse I was on outran the older boys not me." He shook his head. "I couldn't outrun boys that old."

Mrs. Wagner leaned forward. "Did you recognize any of the men, Rodney, other than Mr. Sage?"

"Yes, ma'am. I recognized two of the toughs. They're out of work and hang out around where I stay." His eyes grew bigger, and he stared directly at Mrs. Wagner because he knew she was the decision-maker in the house. "I also recognized the leader."

Mrs. Wagner said, "Is it anyone we know?"

"Yes, ma'am."

Losing her patience, Mrs. Wagner said, "Well, come on, Rodney, tell us. Don't keep us in suspense."

"It was Officer O'Rourke!"

Mrs. Wagner flopped back onto her couch like she had been shot. Doris looked at her sister. "Who's Officer O'Rourke?"

Still in shock, Mrs. Wagner turned disbelieving eyes on her sister. "He is the police officer I told you about meeting at the stage station today."

"Oh, the nice one who helped you."

"Yes, that one." She turned back to Rodney. "Are you sure it was Officer O'Rourke?"

"Yes, Mrs. Wagner, I'm positive. I saw him clearly. He was wearing plain clothes, but it was him. I'd know him anywhere. He's arrested me several times." The last was said with a touch of shame.

"Isabel, if he was a police officer, then he was probably making an arrest."

Rodney shook his head vigorously. "No, Aunt Doris, I've seen arrests. I've even been arrested. This was no official anything. They were taking him down to that warehouse to hurt him. I can promise you that, and we need to do something, or we may never see Mr. Sage again."

Doris Newell shook her head and spoke to her sister. "Oh, that would be a shame. You asked him over for tea tomorrow, didn't you? I was so looking forward to meeting him."

Rodney stared at Aunt Doris in amazement.

Isabel Wagner leaned toward her sister. "Doris, are you mad?"

Doris's cheeks colored. Rodney thought it looked funny for an old woman to be embarrassed.

Doris shook her head. "I'm sorry. I've been in the kitchen all afternoon, preparing pies and a cake for Mr. Sage's arrival tomorrow, and I had the tea on my mind, sorry."

Isabel jumped to her feet. "Well, I know what I'm going to do. Rodney, eat more cookies. Doris, make a pot of coffee. I'll be right back."

Doris rose to go to the kitchen as Isabel disappeared into the hallway, and moments later the front door opened and slammed shut. Rapid footsteps could be heard clicking as she went down the stairs and onto the walkway.

When Doris turned toward the hallway, Rodney stuffed three cookies into his pockets and picked up two more, stuffing a whole one into his mouth. Then he rose and followed Doris into the kitchen, where he found her making a pot of coffee. "Where did Mrs. Wagner go?"

Doris talked while she worked. The wood stove was already hot from the previous pies. She loaded the pot with coffee, took a teakettle full of hot water, and filled the top portion of the coffeepot. "She's going down the street three houses. We have a police captain whom we've known since he was a boy who lives there with his family." She turned and smiled at Rodney. "He also likes my cookies."

Rodney was standing, shaking his head. "But he's police. Officer O'Rourke is police. He could be in on it. What if he is? They already have Mr. Sage, and soon they'll have us. I'm leaving."

Doris Newell turned to face Rodney. "Listen to me, Rodney. You can't go through life not trusting anyone. You have to believe in others. Sometimes you make mistakes, and the person you believe in hurts you, but you have to remember most people are good."

"No," Rodney said, shaking his head. "Most people are bad. You've got to watch out for yourself."

Doris looked at the young lad, her head also shaking. "They aren't, Rodney, but if you believe that, you'll attract the bad ones."

The door slammed open. Rodney spun around, and a large man, almost as big as Mr. Sage, came into the room, following Mrs. Wagner. "Captain Barrett, this is Rodney Beckham. Rodney, this is Captain Lawton Barrett. He's a good friend. We've known him since he was a baby, and we knew his parents. They're all good and honest folks."

The captain glanced at Mrs. Wagner. "Thank you." He turned to Rodney. "Hi, Rodney. Sounds like you've had an exciting day. Is that your horse out front?"

Rodney gave his head a shake. "No. I rented it for Mr. Sage."

Captain Barrett gave the two ladies a questioning look. "Is it all right if we stay in the kitchen to talk? I've always loved the smells in here."

Doris beamed. "Of course it is, Lawton, and we can all have a piece of blackberry pie." She motioned to the chairs around the table.

Rodney liked the idea of staying in the kitchen and the pie. He could save his cookies.

Captain Barrett sat down across the table from Rodney. "Would you tell me the story you told Mrs. Wagner and Miss Newell, Rodney?"

Rodney started from the beginning. The story was broken between sips of milk and bites of blackberry pie. "That's it, Captain Barrett. I know they're going to hurt Mr. Sage. I suspect they might even kill him. We've got to hurry, or it'll be too late."

"You'll come with me to show us the building?"

"I sure will. I even have Mr. Sage's horse." He stopped. "Oh, you already know that."

"And you sure about the coded knock?"

"I am. I watched. That was it."

Captain Barrett stood. "Thank you, ladies. As always, I love coming here. Aunt Doris, that blackberry pie is delicious. It tastes as good as the first one I ever tasted."

She smiled at the police captain, love brimming in her eyes. "Oh, Lawton, you were such a good little boy, and you've grown into a fine man."

He reached out and gave her a hug, holding her for a moment. They parted, and he gave Mrs. Wagner a quick hug, not as long, but as sincere. "We've got to get out of here. I need to pick up my men, and we'll be on our way."

Rodney looked up at the big man. "You're not taking any friends of Officer O'Rourke, are you?"

"Absolutely no friends of O'Rourke. Let's go. We'll walk and talk."

Rodney had to almost jog to keep up with the captain. There would be no talking. They reached Cocoa, and Captain Barrett picked Rodney up and tossed him into the saddle. He handed him the reins and adjusted the stirrups to fit the boy. "Stick with me. I need to stop at my house and get my horse and gear. It'll take me a few minutes. Can I trust you to wait?"

"Yes, sir. I'll be waiting when you come out. I ain't going nowhere. Mr. Sage has been nice to me and trusted me. I'll wait."

"Good." It took only a few minutes to reach his house and no more than five for Captain Barrett to come out of the back, walking his horse. He wore his uniform, and Rodney had to admit, even in the dark, he looked impressive all decked out in his revolver and belt and billy club.

"You all right taking it up to a trot?"

"I sure am." And they were off.

Within minutes they were at the station. Captain Barrett dismounted, tied his horse, and found Rodney standing next to him, Cocoa already tied.

"Come on," the captain said. He led Rodney into the station. This was one Rodney had never been in, so no one gave him a threatening look or ordered him to sit down and shut up like they did at the places he had been. Barrett opened the door to an office. "Go in here and wait for me. I'll only be a few minutes."

Rodney hadn't even relaxed when he heard the sound of multiple running feet.

The door flew open, and the captain stuck his head in. "Let's go."

He dashed alongside Captain Barrett, who again tossed him into the saddle and swung up into his. After a short time, the barn door opened, and six mounted horsemen and an enclosed wagon blasted out. The police officers and one sergeant stopped.

Captain Barrett said, "Men, I've explained what we need to do. We'll try the code first. If that doesn't work, the door goes down. Any questions?"

No one spoke.

"Let's go."

Rodney's heart was beating like a drum, but not from fear. This was exciting. They were going to rescue Mr. Sage.

~

Jack's first indication he was alive was his splitting headache. Moving his head made it worse, so he held it still. Faint light penetrated his eyelids until finally he cracked his right one open. He was in a small room, but he heard a lot of moving and talking beyond the closed door. He squeezed his eyes tight. That helped the headache. Opening them again didn't make it worse. Maybe he'd survive. He raised his head and looked around the room. It appeared to be a storage room. No, scratch that, it was a junk room. He could see nothing of the least value.

He was sitting in a chair. He must have been here for a while, because his rear was hurting. *How long have I been here?* he thought. There were no windows, so he couldn't tell if it was daylight or dark outside. He tried to think of how long a dose of ether could knock out a person. He couldn't remember.

Jack shook his head and thought, *I've done it now. They know I know what they're up to, and I'm dealing with smart people. They know if I know, others know, and it is only a matter of time before someone else comes knocking at their door. They have only two options, kill the girls or get them out of the country, never to be seen again, and they'll have to do it quickly. Boy, did I mess up again. Where's that great ability to judge people I brag about all the time?* Just when he was about to berate himself more, the door opened.

"It's happy I am my Texas Ranger friend is wide awake. I was afraid it was a touch too much of the ether I might have given you. You dying would have been a bit of the luck for you, but not for this old Irishman. I'm looking for answers, my friend, and now that I've got you, I've got all the time in the world."

"Pat, there'll be other rangers. They'll find you and drag your carcass back to Texas for a nice high gallows."

O'Rourke threw back his head and bellowed with laughter. "Hey, Abigail, I need a light in here." The officer's face was no longer rosy and friendly. His cheeks were hard and his lips pursed thin. In the dim light of the warehouse, his eyes looked tiny like those of a hog.

Jack joined him by throwing his head back against the high-backed chair and roaring.

O'Rourke stopped laughing. "What, laddie, is it you have to be laughing at?"

Jack grinned at his turncoat friend. "Pat, I'm laughing at an Irish idiot who doesn't have the sense to know he's a dead man."

O'Rourke's face went from grim to angry. Red spots appeared on his cheeks and under his eyes. His lower jaw shot out. His fists balled, and he strode toward Jack, slowing only when he was in range. He threw a wide roundhouse blow that packed all of his anger and strength. If it had hit Jack, it would have, at the very least, shaken him to his toes.

He watched the man approach and saw the swing coming. He had moved his head forward toward his aggressor as he taunted him. At the last second, he jerked his head back and snapped it to the right. The blow missed Jack's face completely. O'Rourke had twisted his body into the blow like a top, and his feet weren't braced. He was expecting Jack's head to be his additional support. The momentum carried him around, and Jack had enough leverage to jerk the chair into the man's right leg, tripping him. The cop sprawled face-first on the filthy floor.

O'Rourke scrambled to his feet, his face mottled with rage. He reached to his hip and yanked away the billy club he kept hanging there.

A woman rushed into the room. "O'Rourke, save that for later. We've got to get these girls ready to travel. Mr. Ainsworth said he wants them out of here now, while his party is taking place. Move it!"

The Irish cop, still raging, pointed the club at Jack. "You'll not be getting the last laugh, Sage. I'll see to that."

Jack's wide face broke into a threatening grin. "Dead man, O'Rourke, and there's nothing your Mr. Ainsworth can do for you."

O'Rourke stared a moment longer, then spun, and slammed the door behind him. Jack had felt relief flood through his body at the woman's mention of the girls. Hopefully they were all safe and hadn't been hurt. He again looked around the room. He needed something to help him break loose, but O'Rourke or his men had tied him tight to chair. His legs were secured to the legs of the wooden chair, and his arms were tied so tightly, his hands were feeling numb. The thought came to him, *A wooden chair. I've broken chairs before by only sitting in them.* Without another thought, Jack, using only what little flexion he could get in his legs and his large feet, propelled himself up and back.

The chair and his body traveled only a short distance above the floor, but his weight, when he crashed to the floor, splintered the chair. He felt a jab in his back but ignored it and leaped to his feet. The rope was slack. *Thank heaven for small favors,* Jack thought. *They used one rope. If a cowhand had done this, he'd have used piggin' strings on each part, and I'd still be tied to the chair, broken or not.* The pieces of chair were falling away. He went to work on the knots tying his hands and, though he had to do it by feel, quickly had them loose. He untied the knots on one leg, and he was free, the rope lying on the floor.

Jack picked up one of the chair legs and hefted it, too light. He stopped and listened. He faintly heard voices, but they sounded far away. His heart jumped. *Maybe they didn't hear me. There wasn't much of a crash since my body muffled most of the sound, mainly just a thud. If they're busy, maybe I'm having a bit of the Irish luck.* He grinned to himself. He was going to enjoy giving Mr. O'Rourke a little of his luck back. He began looking for something in the junk room that would make a better club than the chair leg. He found it.

Lying in a back corner was a piece of iron pipe. It was perfect. Thick enough for his big hand to get a good grip and long enough, a little over two feet, to do some real damage either used like a jabbing sword or a blunt club. He moved to the door. It was locked. He examined the fit and construction. There were no hinges on the inside. It opened out. It was an old wooden door, a door that had been absorbing moisture here on the waterfront for no telling how many years. He had no doubt he could break it open or break through it, but that would make enough noise to get O'Rourke's attention. Maybe—

Jack checked the space between the door and the facing. There was no way he could get the pipe into the narrow space to use its leverage. He went back to the junk and began digging through it. In one of the boxes he found a broken screwdriver blade. It was long, more than eight inches. He tried it, and it fit into the end of the pipe. There was a little slack between the screwdriver and the inside edge, but maybe it was tight enough to work. He moved to the door.

The first time he tried his fabricated lever, the screwdriver slid down the length of the pipe, sticking in whatever damp debris had collected in the closed end. He turned it upside down and gave it a hard tap against the floor. The screwdriver slid out.

The next time he shoved the flat point of the screwdriver into the facing, penetrating the wood. Then he eased the pipe over the screwdriver until he had about four inches of the screwdriver inside the pipe.

Slowly Jack began applying pressure on his lever. The door moved and stopped. *It must have come against the lock hasp,* Jack thought. He continued to apply pressure to the pipe. Bang, it happened. A large piece of the door facing, where the screwdriver had been pushed into it, flew off, and the pipe banged against the back of the door. Jack stood silent, listening. The faint voices continued. He couldn't believe his luck.

He looked down at the floor. The screwdriver wasn't there. In the dark room, lit only by the dim light entering around the door, Jack dropped to his knees and began to scour the floor for the screwdriver. It had to be here. Desperate to find it, he crawled from corner to corner. Along the back wall, he searched every inch of the floor. The screwdriver was nowhere to be found.

He stood, and disgusted, leaned his hand against the wall, and stopped. About eight inches before his hand reached the wall, something poked it. Jack leaned toward the wall until he was less than a foot away. There, barely visible, was the screwdriver, embedded in the back wall like a spear. He shook his head, pulled it out of the wall, and went back to the door. This time he positioned the screwdriver directly opposite of where he figured the lock was located. He shoved the screwdriver tip deeper into the wood, slipped the pipe over the exposed end, and braced it against the door's frame. This time, instead of easing his weight onto the pipe, he decided to give it one hard shove with all of his force behind it.

Jack took a deep breath and slammed his weight against the pipe. He heard a ping as the hasp broke, and the door crashed open, slamming against the outside wall of the junk room. He saw the lock skittering across the floor, still attached to the hasp. Too much noise. He looked around the warehouse.

Boxes were stacked in rows along the walls and at eight-foot intervals across the building, the tall stacks extending to the opposite end. A hallway was left in the middle, large enough to drive a wagon through, and there was light at the end. Jack stood still, listening. Silence, then the sound of running feet coming in his direction. *No surprise*, he thought. *They heard me*. A group of men charged into the light, rushing toward him.

20

Jack dodged to his left behind a row of boxes that fronted the wide path the running men were using. They had passed his position behind the boxes when a loud crash erupted from the end the junk room was located on. Jack heard the running footsteps of O'Rourke's men slide to a halt just past his location. He was too far down the row of boxes to see the main door, but he knew someone had breached the door.

Confirming his assumption, a strong voice sounded off. "O'Rourke, this is Captain Barrett. Throw down your guns, and no one will be hurt."

Jack heard steps on the other side of the boxes start back the way they had come. He crashed into the stack of boxes adjacent to him. They were stacked vertically almost ten high. They tilted and began dropping. A man screamed as they plummeted to the warehouse floor. Jack followed them. He saw O'Rourke, wild-eyed, searching for a path through the scattered boxes, trying desperately to escape this Captain Barrett. The Irishman looked up as Jack broke through the boxes.

Seeing it was Jack, he went for his revolver. Jack grinned at him, took two quick steps before he could level his revolver, and drove a massive right fist into the side of O'Rourke's head. The Irishman collapsed like a sack of potatoes. Jack grabbed the nearest man to him by the back of his shirt and threw him into another who had just cleared a path, knocking them both to the floor. Two more stood with their hands reaching for the rafters as Barrett's squad surrounded them. Jack spun and dashed to the back. The woman wasn't here. Where were the girls? He heard Rodney scream, "Don't shoot. That's Mr. Sage."

He yelled over his shoulder, "The girls are back here." He went through a door, wide enough to allow a team of horses and a wagon into a room, smaller, but still large. There was a table, chairs, and five beds. He saw the girls and the woman in time to throw himself to the floor and roll. She had a shotgun and fired just as he saw them. He felt a burning sensation in his left shoulder as he rolled across the floor, ending up behind another stack of boxes.

Captain Barrett's voice boomed into the building. "Throw that shotgun down, or you'll have so much lead in you it'll double your weight."

Almost as quickly as Barrett spoke, Jack heard the shotgun strike the floor. He stood quickly and dashed over to the girls, who were being forced to stand, as a shield, in front of the woman. He reached past them, grabbed the woman by an arm and whipped her in an arc, throwing her toward Captain Barrett, where she hit the floor and rolled, stopping at his feet.

Jack knelt in front of the three little girls, whose eyes were wide and dull. "It's all right. I'm Texas Ranger Captain Jack Sage, and you are safe. I'll be taking you back home to your families."

All three girls looked at him like they couldn't understand, then one slowly stepped toward him, then another, and finally the last. They put their arms around him and gently laid their heads on his wide chest. He could feel hot tears on his neck and tiny chests heaving in sobs.

Rodney ran up to him. "You're a Texas Ranger?"

Jack grinned at the boy. "I sure am, and these girls are why I'm here."

Rodney looked at him and frowned. "You came all the way from Texas for a bunch of girls?"

Jack could hear the chuckles of the policemen around him.

"I sure did, Rodney, but it looks like to me, I wouldn't have been successful if it hadn't been for you. Thanks, pardner."

Jack watched the boy turn red and scuff the toe of his worn-out shoe on the warehouse floor. "You're welcome, I guess."

Jack looked up at Barrett. "Did you bring a nurse or a woman with you?"

Barrett shook his head. "No. We had no idea this was a kidnapping ring. We were here to save you." He placed his hand on Rodney's shoulder. "Thanks to Rodney."

Jack looked at the boy. "When things slow down, I want to sit down with you so that you can tell me everything that happened and how you knew. Thanks again." He stood, holding on to the girls, who wouldn't turn loose of him. "These girls have been fed laudanum since they left Texas. They need to go to the hospital and have a doctor look at them."

Captain Barrett waved the sergeant over. "Sergeant Monk, you've got the largest number of kids, so you'll probably be the best with these girls. Why don't you take two men and get them straight to the hospital. Make sure the doc knows how important these girls are, and keep watch on them. Use the wagon."

"Sure, Captain." He raised his eyebrows to Jack.

"Listen, girls, this is Sergeant Monk of the San Francisco Police Department. He's going to take good care of you. We still have some of the bad men to catch, so we need to go before they get away, but you can trust Sergeant Monk."

One of the little girls leaned back and looked up at him. "No bad persons can take us again?"

Jack shook his head. "Never. We've caught these, and we're going to catch the others. After they're caught, neither you nor any other little girl will ever be taken by them again, but we have to get going."

He set them on the floor of the warehouse, and Sergeant Monk picked up the smallest while the other two hung on to his pants legs. "Let's go see the police wagon. It has some pretty horses."

The girls seemed to brighten a little. The four of them disappeared around the corner into the hallway.

Barrett looked at Jack's shoulder. "You're bleeding. Looks like she caught you with that shotgun."

Jack pulled up his collar and looked at the wound. There was only one entry and exit. The double-aught pellet had gone all the way through. The bleeding had stopped for now. "I'll get it taken care of when this is over."

Barrett nodded. "Suit yourself. I'll have a doctor on scene at the hotel. He can take care of it in your room if that works for you."

"Great idea. Now you need to know this is convoluted. It's a long story, but we don't have time for it all. There are several people you need to arrest, and O'Rourke and this woman, I heard O'Rourke call her Abigail, her last name is Crisp, are going to tell you the names of the others."

Two of the police officers had just dragged O'Rourke, still unconscious, into the room with Jack. He pointed to the floor. "Lay him down." They dropped him to the floor, and one of the officers walked over to Jack, carrying his Remington.

"Is this yours?"

Jack took it. It felt good to have it in his hand again. "Thanks." He checked the loads and slipped it behind his waistband. He grabbed one of the chairs, sat, and pulled off his left boot. Reaching deep into the boot, he grabbed a sheet of paper, the confession of Clements, and handed it to the captain.

Captain Barrett took it, saw the signatures, and looked up. "You're a captain in the Texas Rangers?"

Jack nodded. Barrett began reading the sheet of paper. He interrupted his reading several times to stop and look at Jack. At last he finished. "Clinton Ainsworth?"

Jack nodded, took the paper back, and slipped it into his pocket after pulling his boot back on. He looked around, saw what he was looking for, stood, and walked to the drinking water bucket. He picked it up and walked to O'Rourke and started pouring slowly. The aimed stream of water hit O'Rourke between his nose and lip, much of it going into his nose. It didn't take long before O'Rourke started spluttering, and his eyes jerked open.

The dirty cop held his arm up to protect his face and yelled, "Stop it!"

At that point Jack dumped the entire bucket of water on the man's head. He set the bucket, upside down, next to the now sitting O'Rourke and sat down on it.

"Hello, Pat. It seems the tables have turned." Behind the fury, Jack could see the fear in the man's eyes. "I'm giving you one chance. Who, besides Ainsworth, is involved in this scheme to sell children?"

O'Rourke looked away from Jack. "I'm not saying a word, laddie, and you can't make me. You're not in the wilds of Texas now. We have rules in the pol—"

Jack hit him. Not real hard, but harder than a love tap. It knocked him over. Jack reached out, grabbed the man's sleeve, and dragged him back, setting him up again. He turned to the captain. "Captain, I was being held in the junk room just inside the entrance. You might want to take your men and see if you can find any evidence. I'll call you when it's time to stop looking." He looked at Rodney. "You go with Captain Barrett."

Rodney didn't argue. He nodded and stepped to the captain's side.

Barrett answered Jack, but kept his eyes locked on O'Rourke's. "That sounds like a good suggestion, Captain Sage. Give me a shout when you think we've looked long enough." He waved for his men to follow him, and placed his hand on Rodney's shoulder. The boy and the captain, side by side, strode for the junk room. His men, grinning at each other, stepped out behind them. Several turned and waved to O'Rourke before they disappeared down the hall.

"Now what were you saying, Pat?" Jack stiffened a finger and poked the bruise that had formed on the man's face.

"Look, I just work for them. I'm not the ringleader. If I tell you anything, they'll kill me."

Jack folded his finger and punched the scarred edge of the first joint hard against the bruise, and O'Rourke jerked his head, trying to get away from the pain. "I swear I can't say, or I'm dead. My family will be out in the street. They'll starve to death without my connections. I didn't know they were going to be selling little girls."

All the other may be true, Jack thought, *but you just lied to me.* He slapped O'Rourke hard with a calloused hand. He could imagine the pain generated across the dirty cop's bruised head. Mimicking O'Rourke, he said, "Lie to me again, laddie, and it's the fist you'll be getting."

O'Rourke shook his head. "I can't."

Jack stood and grabbed the man by his shirtfront, jerking him to his feet. He made a fist with his right hand and drew back, preparing to hit O'Rourke with all of his force.

Just before he let fly, O'Rourke cried, "All right, all right. I'll talk. I'll tell you everything."

Jack backed the man to the chair and turned him loose. He dropped into it. Jack turned his head toward the doorway. "Captain."

Captain Barrett stepped from around the corner with one of his men, who carried a pad and pencil, and walked to O'Rourke. "Start talking, and don't leave out anything."

O'Rourke gave every detail he knew. He talked about how his

brothers and cousins, some police and some not, were involved. He gave names and places, filling in detail after detail.

Barrett looked at Jack. "The senator and his personal secretary are at Ainsworth's party." He took out his watch and checked it. "We can still make it. I need to stop at a judge's house to get the warrants, but this won't take long."

The officer who had been copying every word of O'Rourke's confession finished and handed it to the captain, who handed it to O'Rourke. "Sign it."

The man started reading.

"I said sign it, not read it."

O'Rourke took the pencil and signed at the bottom of the page.

Captain Barrett signed it and handed it to Jack, who took it and wrote his title, followed by his signature.

Barrett said, "Let's go. We've got a party to crash."

Striding out, Jack said, "Wait, I've got one more question for him."

He grabbed O'Rourke and turned him so he could stare into the man's face. "Who was the contact in Texas?"

O'Rourke's face remained blank. "I don't know. Ainsworth never told me."

Jack searched the man's face for a lie. He couldn't find it. "Pat, if you're lying to me, I'll travel back from Texas and finish this. I mean it. If you know who it is, tell me now."

He shook his head. "Jack, I swear he never told me. Ainsworth is an attorney. They're always closemouthed."

Jack shoved the dirty cop back to his escort, turned, and, with Captain Barrett and Rodney, headed out of the warehouse.

Two of the men stayed to guard the warehouse. The sergeant and the two assigned officers had already left for the hospital with the girls. One of the men, who had ridden back to the station to get another transport for O'Rourke and the woman Crisp, was pulling up in the wagon with three more mounted police officers when Jack and the others walked outside. The captain took only a moment to assign an additional man for the wagon. They loaded their prisoners on board, and the transport clattered away.

Jack looked down at Rodney. "You want to ride with me?"

The boy grinned. "You bet."

Jack readjusted the stirrups, stepped into the saddle, reached down, and swung Rodney up behind him. "Hold on tight."

Rodney wrapped his arms around the big man. "I'm ready."

Jack nodded to Barrett, who was mounted and waiting with his men. Within moments they were racing through the streets of San Francisco to the judge's house.

Traffic was light. There were few wagons, carriages, or other horsemen out. Fog was settling over the damp streets, giving an eerie feeling to the ride. It was as if they were riding through deep canyons with tall cliffs on each side. Leaving the waterfront, the smell of dead fish disappeared, and the welcome aroma of baking bread, from the many bakeries preparing for the next day's business, filled his nose.

Only a short time passed until they were in a much nicer, almost ritzy residential part of town. Lights glowed from the windows of homes, and the buildings had been replaced with trees. They pulled up in front of a massive three-story home with a long circular driveway. Captain Barrett looked over to Rodney. "Switch horses. Only Jack and I will go in to see the judge."

Jack swung Rodney to one of the officers and, along with Barrett, trotted up the driveway.

"I didn't want a squad of men galloping up to the judge's home. No use frightening the family."

They reached the massive front door, stepped down from their mounts, tied them, and hurried to knock. A butler appeared, and they disappeared inside.

A short time later, the door opened, and the judge followed them out.

Jack and Barrett mounted. The judge said, "It's a pleasure meeting you, Captain Sage. I am sorry you are here under these circumstances, but I thank you for bringing us this information so that animals like this can be removed from our society."

Jack was anxious to get moving so they could catch Ainsworth and the senator while they were together. "Glad to do it, Judge, and thanks for the additional John Doe warrants."

The judge nodded and turned to Barrett. "Get those degenerates, Captain. Take them off our city's streets."

The captain saluted, and he and Jack raced down the driveway. Their men were listening and ready. The officer passed Rodney back to Jack, and they were off again for the Occidental.

After a ten-minute gallop through quiet, foggy streets, they neared their destination. The fog gave the hotel a ghostly appearance. Its glow, first faint and then growing brighter, finally broke through the mist into a defined shape. Jack rode straight to the main entrance and swung Rodney to the street, following him immediately. "You stay behind us. I don't think there will be any shooting, but you never know. They may have bodyguards."

Barrett stepped up. "Let me go first. I know you're anxious to put these two away, but this is San Francisco, and I'm in charge here."

Jack checked his revolver. "Just don't take too long. I've traveled a long way to make sure these snakes go to jail."

Barrett turned and waved his men forward. Five police officers, a Texas Ranger, and a boy dashed up the steps of the classiest hotel in San Francisco. The Occidental was the center of posh on the West Coast. It catered to the wealthy from around the world. Jack's lips were pulled back slightly in a half-smile. *They'll be talking about this for a long time,* he thought. *The night the police and a Texas Ranger arrested a senator of the United States and his attorney. Look out, Ainsworth, here I come.*

21

They burst through the doors into the Occidental's main ballroom. It was filled with men in tuxedos and women in colorful gowns. At the head of the gathering, on the dais, were several men, accompanied by their bejeweled ladies. The thought flashed through Jack's mind, *I've never seen this much exposed flesh except in a saloon.*

An elderly man was at the podium, his voice booming when they burst in. It dwindled until it was silent. But for only a moment. Then it rose to an angry, authoritative shout. "What is the meaning of this intrusion?"

Barrett kept moving, with Jack right behind him. Barrett dashed straight to the podium, stopped, and yanked a warrant from his blouse. "Senator Woodrow T. Cowden, I am placing you under arrest for the trafficking of minors with the intent to sell."

Barrett turned to Jack and pointed to a fine-looking man sitting between two women. The man had twisted around, his soft blue eyes wide and his full mouth slightly open. Jack's smile widened. He said, "Mr. Ainsworth, we finally meet."

Ainsworth's forehead wrinkled in consternation. He began to stand. "I don't think I know you."

Jack's fist struck the man in the middle of his forehead, splitting the tight skin and sending a shower of blood across the brilliant white of the nearby tuxedo shirts and the colorful, low-cut gowns and exposed skin. Screams reverberated through the ballroom. Ainsworth sailed over his half-finished dessert, across the low railing, and landed on a circular table occupied by eight members of San Francisco's upper crust.

Head wounds tend to bleed profusely, and Ainsworth's was no exception. Falling, his head jerked and twisted, attempting to aid in balance. Blood was flung in all directions. No one at the target table was unscathed. The screams heightened.

Barrett gave Jack an annoyed glance while gripping the senator's arm. "You didn't need to do that."

"Didn't you see? He was standing up to attack me."

Barrett shook his head just as two bodyguards became aware they should be protecting the senator. They ran along the dais, one from each end, toward Barrett and Jack. Barrett shouted, "Police, back off." Jack smiled again and hit the oncoming bodyguard in the belly. The man doubled over, gagging, and the Texas Ranger brought his not-so-small knee into the man's face. The audible sound of flesh striking flesh and cartilage breaking caused a lady sitting at the table on the dais to faint. Jack shoved the bodyguard away and bent to help the woman. He carefully lifted her face from her half-eaten crème brûlée, moved the dish to the side, and gently laid her superbly coiffed head on the table.

The other bodyguard had halted and, with his hands half up, was backing away. Jack leaped over the table to Ainsworth, who was struggling to lift his body from the surface.

Ainsworth lifted his hand to his forehead and moved it in front of his eyes, which widened further in astonishment and fear. "I'm bleeding. I'm hurt." Jack neared the attorney. "Someone help me. Stop this monster!"

Jack grinned at the bloody man and grabbed him by the front of his no longer elegant and no longer white shirt. Then his grin disappeared. "No one's going to help you, Ainsworth, just like no one helped those poor little girls you stole, and the two you had killed, but you're going to help me."

Senator Cowden, in the grips of Captain Barret, marched down the dais, yelling, "Don't you say a word, Ainsworth. If you don't keep your mouth shut, you'll be dead before morning."

Jack, Ainsworth in tow, looked toward Barrett. "Can't you shut him up?"

To which, before Barrett uttered a word, the senator responded, "You listen to me. I am United States Senator Woodrow T. Cowden, and you have made yourself a big mistake, mister. My attorney will be waiting at the police station. I'll never go to jail, and I'll have your job."

Barrett made it to Jack's side. Jack had Ainsworth gripped in his right hand. His left hand shot out like a striking snake, closing around the senator's wizened old throat. The man, no longer worried about jail, but his life, stared at Jack with fear, eyes bugging out like a lizard watching a hawk swoop and knowing it was too late to move. Jack leaned forward, his face inches from the senator's. "You listen to me, you shriveled-up old degenerate. I'll see you in hell before you ever touch another little girl."

Barrett, shocked, regained his composure. "Jack, turn him loose." He reached for the big arm, but Jack dropped it as soon as he finished speaking.

Ainsworth tried to lag behind, but Jack jerk him closer, glancing at Barrett. "Where are you taking the senator?"

"To the precinct."

They walked their prisoners to the door, unfazed by the commotion in the ballroom behind them. At the door, Barrett pulled the warrant for the senator's aide and the three John Doe warrants from his pocket and handed them to the officer next to him. "Arrest him, Mitch O'Rourke on the hotel staff, and any others who give you trouble. Meet us out front at the wagon."

Once they were clear of any people, Jack leaned close to

Barrett and nodded at the senator. "You know you'll never be able to ask him a question once you get him to your precinct. It'll be all over."

"You have any suggestions?"

"Both Ainsworth and I have a suite here at the hotel. I suggest we search Ainsworth's place and then question him. Then we can question the senator without interruption. We won't have long, but perhaps it will be long enough."

Barret mulled over the suggestion. "Good idea." He turned to the two policemen who were standing at a discreet distance. "When everyone is arrested, put them in the wagon, and wait for us. We'll be along in a few minutes. Take Rodney with you." He pointed at one of the men. "Come with us."

The boy looked at Jack, who gave a short nod. He returned the nod, turned, and followed the officer.

Ainsworth moaned. "I'm hurting bad. I need a doctor."

Jack gripped the attorney tighter. "Here's my suggestion. Take Ainsworth up to his room. The senator can go in mine with your officer watching him. We ask Mr. Ainsworth a few questions, then we bring in the senator and ask him a few. Then you can take them both to your precinct."

"Let's go. You lead the way."

Jack led his entourage to his room first, and let Senator Cowden and the officer inside. Barrett gave his officer orders. "He's old, but he's cagey. Keep your eyes on him at all times. If you have to use force, don't hesitate. I'll be back shortly."

The officer nodded, and Ainsworth led them to his room. He unlocked the door and stepped inside. Jack followed, and Barrett closed the door behind them.

Jack walked inside and looked around. Expensive paintings hung on the walls, with plush couches and chairs around the sitting room. He walked to the study, which was overwhelmed by a huge, ornate desk. Coming back into the sitting room, he thrust Ainsworth toward the couch. He picked up a towel lying on the dresser and tossed it to the attorney. "I'm going to ask you a few questions, Mr. Ainsworth, and I want you to answer them quickly and honestly. There are times when I've been called on, as I've patrolled the Texas wilderness, to be judge, jury, and executioner. I don't like it, but when justice cries to be answered, someone must respond."

Jack moved in front of Ainsworth and seated himself on a footstool. "Though we're in San Francisco, I feel this is one of those moments. My recommendation to you is give me a straight answer the first time."

Without further preamble, Jack began. "Who concocted the scheme to take children, girls, from the Texas German communities?"

Jack waited a moment. He took a deep breath. "Mr. Ainsworth, does your head hurt?"

Ainsworth nodded to Jack. His eyes indicated he was getting some of his confidence back. Asking and answering questions was his bailiwick. "Look, Ranger Sage, I'd love to be able to help you, but you see, I don't know anything about kidnapped children." He shrugged, his hands held out in a gesture of willingness to answer.

Jack hit him. He drove his fist into the man's belly. Ainsworth snapped double, his chin past his knees, gasping in short silent jerks.

Jack waited. He knew they didn't have much time, but he didn't want to smash the man's face up too badly. Two minutes passed, and he gently straightened Ainsworth until his back was against the couch. "Feeling better?"

Ainsworth didn't answer.

"Do you remember my question?"

The man nodded.

"Well?"

Barely audible and in gasps, Ainsworth said, "You heard what the senator said. He'll have me killed."

Jack shook his head. "He won't be able to, because when we finish with you, it'll be his turn."

Ainsworth was finally able to take a deep breath. He sighed and began. "The senator came up with the idea. He likes young blonde girls, especially of Germanic descent, but he didn't want to grab them around here. It was too close to home."

"You paid a lot of money to get them out here."

"The senator is richer than Croesus. He owns gold mines all over the west. He can afford anything. That's why he'll have me killed. He'll buy off every judge he goes in front of, no exception. He'll never go to prison."

"Is there anyone else involved?"

Ainsworth gave a slight nod. "You can start with his aide, but there are more. I set it up. I know everyone."

Jack nodded toward the desk in the study. "Would you get us writing equipment?"

Barrett strode to the desk and was back as Jack was asking his next question. "Who, and write them down."

Ainsworth wrote. He listed eight other names, most in or from San Francisco. They included Bertrand Clements, Nadine Tidwell, O'Rourke, Haggard, and Sanford. He stopped writing. "That's all I know about, but I'm relatively certain that's everyone." He looked at Jack, and his voice took on a pleading tone. "Please, Mr. Sage, I swear. That's all I know. The senator owns an island in the northeast where the girls were to be kept. He has a house manager there." He pointed to a name. "That's him." He pointed again. "This last one is our contact in Texas. He's the one who found the girls. He would send pictures. They're in my desk with all their information. The senator would make his choices, and then either Haggard or Sanford would grab them. It took time, was involved and expensive, but Senator Cowden didn't care. He wanted those girls. They were all for him."

"What drawer?"

Ainsworth looked confused. "What?"

Jack frowned. "What drawer in your desk? The photographs."

"Bottom right."

Jack stood, walked to the desk, opened the drawer, and pulled out the folder. He found Marlene's photograph on top, a pretty little ten-year-old blonde with a big smile. It was a duplicate of the photograph Mrs. Schmidt had given him to use to identify the girl. He looked at the corner. There was writing. He looked up at Barrett. "Do you have a photographer on staff with your police department?"

"Absolutely, the best."

"Good, I need two clear copies of each of these." He walked back to Barrett and handed him the folder. "This will convict and hang the man I'm after." He nodded at the paper Ainsworth had finished. "Why don't you sign this after Ainsworth does, then I'll sign it, and we'll get the senator."

All three men signed the paper. Jack was signing when the sound of two shots cracked through the room, close. Jack yelled, "Cowden."

Barrett burst from the room toward Jack's. Before he reached it, his officer staggered out, holding his side with one hand, his revolver in the other. "Sorry, Captain Barrett. The senator had a derringer hidden. Whoever searched him missed it. He got off one shot. He won't be shooting anyone else."

Jack pulled Ainsworth toward the room. "Get your man on the couch, and then get that doctor up here. I'll watch Ainsworth."

After helping the officer to the couch, Barrett raced from the room. Jack had drawn his Remington and waved it at Ainsworth, then pointed the barrel toward one of the wingback chairs. "Sit down, and don't make a move."

Ainsworth moved rapidly to the chair and sat. Jack stood over the officer. He slid the Remington behind his waistband, yanked the officer's shirttail from under his trousers, and unbuttoned first the shirt and then the long johns' top. He pulled them aside until he could see the wound. It was in the man's muscled left side, not far from the edge of his body. "I'm no doctor, Officer, but from the looks of this, as far as bullet holes go, I think you're a lucky man."

The officer looked up at Jack. He was pale and weak, but managed to work up a smirk. "Captain Sage, no reflection on your doctoring ability, but I ain't feeling too lucky."

Jack returned the grin. "I've been shot a couple of times, and I understand what you're saying."

The doctor rushed through the open door to the officer's side. Behind him were two men with a stretcher. Jack looked up to see people gathering in the hallway, gawking at the wounded officer. Most of them, however, were pointing at the dead senator lying in a pool of blood. Jack motioned to one of the stretcher bearers to close the door. The doctor gave the injured man a quick once-over and signaled the bearers to his side. "Take him to the hospital." He patted the officer on the shoulder. "You'll be fine. You got lucky this time."

The officer looked at Jack and gave him a conspiratorial grin. Jack rolled his eyes and chuckled. The stretcher bearers loaded the injured man, and the doctor let them out of the room. He stood to check on the senator's body and saw the blood on Jack's shoulder. "Sit down here." He pointed to the sofa seat next to him.

The pain from the shoulder wound had slackened. Jack still felt it, but it wasn't as bad as it had been. "Doc, I don't think it's bad. It was one shotgun pellet, and it went all the way through."

"Take off your shirt."

Jack complied and sat down next to the doctor. With practiced skill, the physician examined the entry and exit wounds, noticing the other healed and puckered bullet holes in Jack's shoulder. "You make your shoulder available for target practice?"

Jack said nothing.

The doctor continued to work, checking the wound for debris. Jack held his peace as the probe ventured deep in the churned flesh of the bullet hole. Eventually his probing ceased, and he pulled out a bloody piece of Jack's shirt. He held it up in front of him. "That's why you have a doctor look at these bullet wounds. That little piece of cloth could kill you." He put bandages over the entry and exit and stood. "If the pain increases, or the wound turns red or begins draining more than it is now, come see me. If you're not here, get to a doctor, quick." He stood and headed for the senator. He looked down at the body before kneeling.

The senator was lying facedown, a pool of blood around his chest. There was a hole through the back of his coat. The doctor looked at it and turned the dead man over. "What kind of cannon was the officer shooting?"

Jack said, "Colt .44, looked like to me."

The doctor shook his head and looked to the door as it opened again. Barrett entered with another pair of stretcher bearers and Rodney. Jack frowned when he saw the boy.

Barrett, seeing the frown, said, "Rodney's seen dead bodies before. He's been living on the streets of San Francisco. We have murders all the time. Shootings, knifings, they don't stop. What with the shipping trade and gold miners, there's a lot of toughs in this town."

Jack shrugged and watched the doc give the stretcher bearers the go-ahead to take the body. They unceremoniously rolled the dead U.S. senator on the stretcher, lifted him, and headed for the door. Rodney opened the door for them, and Barrett called to the two policemen standing outside, "One of you come get Ainsworth and take him down to the precinct. I'll be along shortly."

A short husky man in his mid-thirties stepped into the room, grabbed Ainsworth by the arm, and hauled him out of the chair.

The attorney looked at first Jack and then Barrett. "What's going to happen to me?"

Barrett stared at the man in disgust. "We can't hang you, but

I'm guessing the rest of your practice will take place in San Quentin."

Jack, who had stood, shook his head. "Too bad you aren't in Texas. You'd stretch a rope." He glanced at Barrett. "Maybe you could arrange for me to take him back to Texas with me."

Ainsworth gasped. "You can't do that. I've been arrested here. You can't take me back to Texas." His voice rose as the door closed behind him. Barrett grinned at Jack.

"I think your suggestion might have gotten him a bit upset."

Jack, pensive, nodded to the San Francisco police captain. "Yeah, on the one hand, I'd sure like to be taking him back with me. He needs to stretch a rope. However, there are three little girls who can't wait to see their mamas and papas. They're more important than him getting his just punishment."

Barrett sat on the couch, leaned back, and stretched his legs. "Don't worry, if I were a betting man, I'd bet he won't last three months. Though most prisoners are in the lockup for heinous crimes, the majority can't stand anyone who harms a child. I'm thinking the appropriate sentence will be passed on Ainsworth on a dark night or in a crowded room, and no one will know or say who did it."

"A comforting thought." Jack turned to Rodney. "So you need to tell me all about how you saved my life."

The boy blushed and looked down at his feet. "I didn't do that. I just had your horse out front when they dragged you out of the hotel, and I followed them. Then I told Mrs. Wagner and Aunt Doris. Aunt Doris got Captain Barrett, here, and that's it." The boy grinned at the big man. "I think the better story is how those little guys overpowered you."

Barrett threw back his head and roared. "Now that's a story I'd like to hear."

Jack's expression turned hard, and he frowned at Rodney, but he could only hold it for a second. He joined them in laughter. "It's all about ether."

22

It was May in the Texas Hill Country. *A great time to be alive,* Jack thought. He sat on the back of Smokey, gazing across the hills and prairie at the small distinct town of Fredericksburg. *It's funny,* he thought, *how life seems to work everything out.*

The prairie was light green, just beginning to fade to brown under the growing heat of the summer Texas sun. It was covered with a carpet of yellow and reds of Indian blanket, Mexican hat, and brown-eyed Susan, the flowers thick across the landscape. On the rocky slopes and bluffs, browns, yellows, and reds of the rocks complemented the flowers.

Jack was anxious to reach Fredericksburg. From his information, the man who had been responsible for sending the pictures to Ainsworth was there and would be for several days. Jack was more than ready to see this case closed. It was time he was riding on. He was in a good mood. He laughed out loud at the thought. "Riding on, Smokey, it seems like that's all I've been doing for almost this whole year. Maybe I need to stop and relax for a while." The gray horse took that moment to nod his head several times.

Jack laughed again. He bumped the grulla, and they, with Pepper, Thunder, and Stonewall, headed for town, constantly drawing closer as the horses walked through the wildflowers.

He had managed to get a message to Major Wilson of his arrival today, and asked that the Schmidts be in town. *I am very thankful,* he thought, *that Marlene and most of the other girls survived their ordeal, and every single one of the men who committed those heinous acts have been punished or will be before the day is out.*

Jack rode through Fredericksburg toward the rangers' office. He passed the wagon he was looking for and felt his heart leap. It was parked in front of the mercantile, a big sign on both sides. Through the window he could see a line of people inside the store. He was filled with excitement, thrilled to at last capture the last of the monsters who worked for Senator Cowden.

He tied Smokey and the other animals to the hitching rail and walked into the office. Major Wilson and Gabby were standing at the coffeepot, along with Cart and Captain Heath. He grinned. "Looks like a reunion. Any of that coffee left?"

Cart looked him up and down. "Well, sir, I don't rightly know who this tourist is."

The room broke into a roar of laughter as Cart poured and handed him a cup of coffee. He took it and smiled. "It's good to be back. I'm not much for those big cities anymore."

He took a sip of his coffee. "Major, do you know when the Schmidts are arriving?"

Major Wilson pointed his cup to the window. "There they are. Right on time."

Jack took another sip and set it on the table next to the potbellied stove. "Major, would you like to do the honors?"

Major Wilson shook his head. "You originally got recruited for this duty, Jack. Why don't you finish it."

"Thanks. Just so you know, the suspect might get a little bruised, maybe a broken bone."

The major grinned. "As long as it's not me getting bruised, I'm fine with it."

All the rangers laughed as the Schmidts opened the door to the office. Marlene saw Jack and dashed to him. *She looks so much better,* Jack thought. *Happy, like a little girl should be.* He bent and scooped her in his arms.

"Oh, Ranger Sage, you're back. Did you catch all those bad men and save the other girls? Ranger Cartwright came by and told us what you were doing."

He gave her a final squeeze, tossed her in the air once, and set her down. Speaking to her and her parents, he said, "We got them all. The San Francisco police were a big help, but we have one more to scoop up. We thought you'd like to be here to see it." He looked down at Marlene. "This way, you'll know all of them are caught, and none will ever bother you again."

She looked up at him, her blue eyes big and sincere. "Oh, good, Ranger Sage. Sometimes I worry about that."

Her words and her soft tone touched Jack's heart. "Would you like some help to stop worrying?"

She gave a vigorous nod of her head, blonde hair bouncing around her.

"Good, why don't you let us go first, then you and your family follow." He looked over at Major Wilson. "Ready?"

"You want all of us?"

"Oh, yeah. You've all been involved with this. Let's get him together."

He led the entourage of rangers and the Schmidts out the rangers' office door and the short distance down the boardwalk to the mercantile. He opened the door and saw a man sitting at a desk to the side of the heavily stocked room. A family was standing in front of his desk, and he was asking them questions. Jack walked directly to him.

"Mr. Abney?"

The man looked up at the giant standing to the side of his

desk. His eyes took in the man's bulk, then fell to his ranger badge, and then moved to the other four rangers behind Jack. He swallowed. "What can I do for you?"

As Jack looked at the man, he felt the rage building inside him. This was the person who directed all the hell down on the Schmidts and the other families. Without him, Cowden wouldn't have known whom to grab. Sure, he might have found someone else, but this was the man who'd said yes. Jack's voice was hard as stone. "I asked you if you are Mr. Hanson Thwaite Abney."

The man looked around the room. He looked at the Schmidts, his eyes falling on Marlene. He blinked several times and swallowed. "Why, why, yes. Yes, I am. What can I do for you?" he said again.

Jack, seething inside, hid it well. "Mr. Abney, you are under arrest for the abduction of minors for the sale of said minors."

Abney jumped to his feet. "See here. I am conducting business. You can't—"

Jack felt if he waited any longer, he would explode. He doubled up his huge right fist and drove a short punch with every ounce of strength his massive shoulders and arm could generate. The fist struck Abney on the end of his pointy nose, flattening it and his lips. He flew across the room, slamming into the wall shelves behind him. Abney struck the shelves and slid to the floor like a wet dishrag.

Jack eyed the unconscious Abney for only a second, then turned to the Schmidts. "Do you recognize him?"

Both Wilhelm and Deborah nodded. Wilhelm looked as if he'd like to march around the desk and smash Abney a few times himself. Deborah took her husband's arm, looked up at him, and said, "He was the man who took the photograph of Marlene. The one we gave you."

Jack nodded. "I gave it back to you before I left, didn't I?"

Wilhelm had regained some of his composure. "Yes, you did."

Jack pulled one of the copies he'd had made in San Francisco from his inside vest pocket and handed it to Deborah. "Was this the one?"

"Exactly." She looked up, eyes wide, not quite understanding. The owner of the mercantile came running from the back, and other people were gathering around. Jack looked at the major.

Major Wilson stepped to Jack's side. "Why don't you take the Schmidts and use my office. You can explain everything. We'll take care of this." He walked to the prone, still unconscious photographer and nudged him with the toe of his boot. There was no response. "Cart, why don't you and Gabby take this pig to the sheriff's office and throw him in jail. After you get him locked up, you can go get the doc."

Jack led the Schmidts from the mercantile to the rangers' office. He took them inside and seated them in the tiny office of the major. It was tight, but everyone fit. After they were seated, he asked Marlene to take the two other children outside. Marlene asked if they could go to the mercantile. Jack took three dimes from his pocket. He gave Wilhelm and Deborah a questioning look. They nodded, and he placed in each child's hand a dime. Deborah told them they could go, and all three of them ran for the door.

Jack closed the office door and returned to sit behind the desk.

Deborah smiled at him. "You know they can buy so much candy with a dime they'll probably be sick tonight."

Jack grinned. "Ahh, the wages of sin."

They laughed and grew serious as Jack began to tell the story. He first told how Abney fit into the puzzle. How the photographer took pictures of little girls as he traveled through the German communities, and sent them to Ainsworth. The two parents were shocked that the man they knew would treat them so badly.

Jack continued with the story. He was careful about what he

told them. There were parts that no parent needed to know, especially since almost all of the culprits were dead.

Deborah and Wilhelm took turns asking questions. Wilhelm asked, "How long will this Ainsworth be in prison?"

Jack nodded. "Justice has a way of working out. He survived jail because the jailers kept him in isolation, but when he went to prison, he only lasted three days. One morning, on the way to breakfast, someone stabbed him multiple times and left the knife in him. They never found out who did it, but most prisoners aren't at all fond of anyone who harms a child."

Deborah leaned forward. "What happened to Rodney?"

"Rodney found himself in an excess of riches. The newspapers ran many stories. Of course, the senator's story offered lurid headlines for quite a few days. But Rodney turned out to be the hero of everything the newspapers printed. Several people lined up to adopt him, each wealthy and concerned for his welfare. Captain Barrett won out. He was the police captain who saved my bacon. He and Rodney hit it off. He isn't wealthy, financially, but he's like you folks. He has a terrific family, and Rodney will fit right in."

Deborah sighed. "I'm glad there was a touch of good coming out of all this evil and loss. I feel so sorry for those two families who lost their daughters."

Jack leaned forward and placed his forearms on the desk, his gaze holding Deborah's. "So do I, Mrs. Schmidt. I'm almighty sorry I wasn't around for them."

She must have seen the sincerity and sadness in Jack's eyes. "Oh, Ranger Sage, it wasn't your fault. You know that if you hadn't been there, we would have probably all died under those outlaws' guns. You brought these girls home, seven of them, all except the first two. You made seven families very happy and changed what could have been terrible lives." Deborah paused and took a handkerchief from her sleeve and wiped her eyes. "You brought our Marlene home and wreaked righteous judgment on those evil men." She shook her head. "My goodness, I can't imagine how one man, no matter how big he is, could have managed all that." Then she smiled. "But I'm glad you did." She reached out and laid her small, calloused hand across his. "Thank you."

They sat like that for a short time, and then Jack cleared his throat and straightened. "Well, thanks, ma'am. I'm glad I could, but I sure didn't do it by myself."

The children burst into the office, each carrying a large bag of candy in one hand and holding their other hand behind them. Entering the room, they held the candy bags high to show their parents. Deborah placed both of her palms against her cheeks, feigning surprise. "You bought that much candy?"

The three grinned and brought their other hands out from behind them. In each of the little hands were two smaller bags. Marlene's held three. "We didn't want to leave you out."

Dirk added, "That's right. One for each of you."

Elke's smile was less enthusiastic as she looked at the bags. "That's what Marlene said to do. I wanted more." But she held the bags out to her parents along with her brother and sister.

Marlene frowned at her sister. "Elke."

Deborah gave Marlene a stern look, but it didn't last long. She gathered her three children into her arms and gave them a hug. "Thank you. That is so sweet of you."

Marlene giggled at the play on words, then went around the table and handed Jack the third bag. Jack took it, leaned over, and kissed the girl on the cheek. "Thank you, Marlene. I sure am glad I rescued you, because I really like candy."

Everyone laughed and stood. The moment had come. Jack admired the happy family and felt a moment of regret for the loss of his. He smiled at them, his hand resting on Marlene's shoulder. "You folks have any more questions?"

Wilhelm shook his head. "No, Ranger Sage, we know all we need or want to know. Our daughter's back, and we're happy. Thank you again."

They walked from the small room into the office. Deborah turned and stood on tiptoe. Jack bent to receive her kiss on his cheek. "Thank you, Jack. You have saved our family."

Marlene extended her arms, and he picked her up. She gave him a final hug, her arms gripping his neck so tight he felt she might squeeze right through it. Those little arms felt so good. Finally she turned loose, pushing back and looking into his eyes. "Thank you, Ranger Sage. I love you."

He cleared his throat. "I love you too, Marlene."

She gave him one more hug. He set her down, and they walked out the door.

Jack watched them through the wrinkled glass. They seemed to waver and float when they climbed aboard their wagon. They pulled out and disappeared down the road. He cleared his throat again, feeling the thickness in his chest, and thought, *This is a day to be happy, not sad.* He wiped the corner of an eye with the back of his finger. Jack stepped to the coffeepot, poured himself another cup, and took a sip. The door opened, and Major Wilson, with the rest of the rangers, walked in.

Major Wilson picked up his cup and held it out. "I'll take some of that." He looked up at Jack. "How's it taste?"

"Terrible, but I've tasted worse."

Gabby harumphed indignantly, and Cart grabbed his cup. "Fill 'er, boy. I'm a sucker for punishment."

Gabby walked back to his desk and dropped into his chair. "If you poor excuses for rangers—you're excepted there, Major Wilson—think my coffee's so bad, then why don't you fix it yoreself."

Cart took a sip, smacked his lips, and looked into his cup. "I declare, this here is as sweet as the nectar of the gods."

Major Wilson motioned to his office. "Jack, why don't you come in the office and tell me the whole story."

23

Jack followed the major into his office. He started to close the door.

"No, no, the boys deserve to hear the details. Have a seat, and go ahead."

Jack pulled three statements from inside his vest and handed them across the desk. One was the statement of the coroner on the senator's death, the other was Ainsworth's statement implicating Abney, and the third was signed by the judge, certifying the first two and the guilty verdict of Ainsworth.

The major read them through and set them aside. "Now, let me hear it."

Jack began his story. No detail was left out. At the telling of Rodney's spotting O'Rourke and his men dragging Jack from the hotel and his efforts to save Jack, the major shook his head. "That boy saved your life. You would've been a dead man."

Jack nodded. "I know. I owe him a lot. I didn't tell the Schmidts, but I sincerely thought about adopting him myself, but he needs an education and a stable life. He's been living on the street and has plenty of street smarts, which will help him out, but he needs to go to school so he can learn to fit in with others. I did tell him if he ever needed my help or wanted to join me out here, after he gets an education, he was always welcome." Jack went on with the story, ending with Ainsworth being stabbed to death in prison.

The major had kicked back. His feet were on the corner of his desk, and the other rangers had squeezed into the office. There wasn't room for all, so Gabby listened from the doorway.

Cart took a long slurp from his coffee. "I'm surprised that Ainsworth feller lasted that long. It couldn't have happened to a nicer guy."

The major nodded his agreement. "I'd say you've had quite an adventure."

Jack shrugged. "I always wanted to see California, but not like this. I was thinking about pulling up stakes and moving out there."

"And now?" Cart asked.

Jack shook his head and grinned. "I know that's about as far west as you can get without getting on a ship, but this part of the west is for me. Maybe New Mexico or Arizona territory, but California's a little too far west for this soul."

Next, Jack pulled out three hundred twenty-seven dollars and forty-seven cents. He laid it on the desk and slid it across to Major Wilson.

Wilson looked at the money for a moment and turned to the listening rangers. "Boys, would you mind waiting outside, and close the door." The others stepped out and pulled the door closed behind them. Then Wilson tapped the money with his forefinger and looked up at Jack. "What's this?"

Puzzled, Jack's brow wrinkled. "That's what's remaining of the money you gave me for expenses before I left to chase those outlaws."

Wilson slid it back across the table. "I wrote that off when I gave it to you. It's yours."

Jack shook his head. "Major, I don't understand."

Wilson placed his elbows on the desk and steepled his fingers. "Jack, Captain Heath did not have the authority to make you a captain in the rangers."

Jack gave a single laugh. "I knew that. I figured the captain's badge was the only one he had with him. I used the rank in California because, frankly, it helped open doors, but I never thought of myself as a captain in the rangers."

"But that's not all. If it were up to me, you'd definitely get it, but Austin says they're not paying you as a captain, but as a private."

Jack grinned at the major. "I expected that, too. Bureaucracies are all the same. Don't worry about it."

Jack could see the relief in the major's face as he pulled an envelope from the top right drawer and slid it across the desk. "This is your first three months' pay from Austin. It'll amount to seventy-five dollars, a private's pay."

Jack took the envelope and, without opening it, shoved it into his vest. He also picked up the money on the desk, folded the bills, and stuffed them into an inside vest pocket. He dropped the change into an outside pocket and removed the captain badge from his vest. He looked at it for a moment, laid it on the desk, and slid it slowly across to the major. "Don't worry about it, Major. I planned on filling you in on the case and resigning." He stood and extended his hand across the desk.

Major Wilson stood and grasped the hand. The men held the grip for a short time. "You've done exceptional work, Jack. I'd ask you to stay, but I can see it in your face. You're moving on."

Jack stepped to the door. "Yes, sir, I am, and for the first time, I don't have the slightest idea of where I'm going. I've always had a goal of ranching in the Colorado mountains, but I liked the look of the territories, Arizona and New Mexico. Maybe I'll mosey out that way."

They walked into the office, where Gabby, Cart, and Captain Heath were all gathered around Gabby's desk, talking. They looked up when Jack and the major stepped out. Jack could see they immediately spotted the blank space on his vest.

Cart was the first to speak. "Where you headed?"

Jack shook his head. "Danged if I know, west probably."

"Well, you get out around El Paso and west, watch out for them Apaches. You had a taste of 'em with the stage, but don't forget, they're mighty sneaky."

Jack stood around talking for a few more minutes while he finished his coffee. He liked these men. They were the type he had been around most of his life, good hearted and hard fighters when the time came. *I've put it off long enough,* he thought.

"All right, boys, time to hit the trail. Take care of yourselves." It took another couple of minutes for the goodbyes, and Jack stepped outside to a hot, sunny day. White puffy clouds drifted across the blue sky.

Stonewall was watching Jack as if he were chiding him for leaving them out in the sun for so long. He began with the mule. He rubbed the long nose and scratched him behind the ears. "You're about the best mule a man could have." He scratched some more, stepped back, and pulled out some of the new treats he'd had made before leaving San Marcos. He gave Stonewall one, and the big brown eyes followed him. Jack felt the tie he had with this animal. *With all the ups and downs,* he thought, *life is really good.*

He moved to Thunder and then Pepper, talking, scratching, and rubbing both of them and giving them their treat. He came to Smokey. *I hate to say I have a favorite,* he thought, *but if I do, this grulla is it. He's gotten me out of some mighty bad scrapes.* He gave Smokey his treat, scratched his ears, and flipped the stirrup over the saddle to check the cinch.

"Well, if it ain't the big man hisself." Before he straightened, Jack reached down and lifted the leather thongs securing his two Remingtons in their holsters. He raised his head and looked across Smokey's back. There in the middle of the dusty Fredericksburg street stood the man he had expected to never see again, Hud Forester, the young ranger with a chip on his shoulder.

Jack took a deep breath. This was not the way he wanted to leave Fredericksburg. He liked the good feeling he was having only a few moments before, but now that feeling was gone. Chased away by a grudge-holding, liquor-filled young man. *Yeah,* Jack thought, *Hud's so-called friends have probably been egging him on, building him up, telling him how good he is with a gun. They should be out here, but they'll be cowering in some saloon, watching.* Jack shook his head. *He may be good, in fact, he may be good enough, but he won't keep me from putting lead into him, and I don't want to, not today.*

He stepped from behind Smokey, at the same time hearing the door to the ranger office open. "How have you been, Hud?"

The big man was standing in the dusty street, partially crouched, his right arm slightly bowed, his hand hovering over the butt of his revolver. "I ain't here for talking."

"Get out of that street, Forester," Major Wilson commanded. "Jack Sage has done you no harm."

Hud's eyes, narrowed and mean, stayed on Jack. "He insulted me, Wilson. And anyway, you ain't givin' me no orders 'cause I don't work for you no more. That captain standing next to you fired me, or ain't you rememberin'?"

"I remember because I was the one who gave him the order. Now ease up, and get out of the street. You don't want some innocent bystander hurt, do you?"

"Ain't no innocent about to be hurt here. Now you just shut your yap."

Pedestrians had cleared the street. Wagons were pulled over and horses tied, their drivers and riders inside the adjacent buildings. Only Jack and Hud were in the street and no more than thirty feet apart.

"I'm gonna kill you, Sage. Then they'll be writing about Hudson Forester, fast gun, who killed the Texas Ranger hero. My name'll be in all the papers. Shoot, it might even make it to them California papers."

"I'm no hero, Hud, and no one needs to be shot today." Jack's eyes were locked on Hud's, watching, waiting. He had faced men like this before, and very few had he been able to talk down from their fury once they'd called him out. They were usually too worried about what their drinking buddies or the other cowhands or thieves would think of them if they backed down. He hoped, but didn't think, Hud would, but it never hurt to try. "Come on, Hud. Give it up. I'll go in the saloon with you and buy you and your friends a drink, and we can all sit around laughing about this and how brave you were to call it off."

Hud's lips drew back in a hate-filled grimace. "You talk too much." He went for his gun.

The two-letter word blazed across his mind, *No,* but it was yes now. Yes, someone would die, and yes, there was no more time for talking. His right hand flashed to his little Remington.

As had happened each time he was involved in a shoot-out, time appeared to stand still, and he seemed to float outside of his body. He watched Hud, who thought he was so fast, and Jack could see he was too slow. He was faster than Jack thought, for his opponent was a big man. He had supposed, like many people did of him, that because he was big, he'd be slower. Jack felt the warmth of the revolver's butt. His hand closed around it, and his thumb reached for the hammer even as he was lifting the weapon from the holster. Hud's was also lifting from the holster, and the expression on Hud's face was triumphant.

Everything was automatic for Jack. Smooth and automatic. His weapon came level, and Jack watched Hud even as he felt his finger squeezing the trigger. The face that had shown triumph only moments before showed fear, for Hud's Colt, Jack could see it clearly, was still angled at the ground.

The blast of Jack's weapon rocked the street even as Jack, his eyes glued on Hud, thumbed the hammer back on his revolver, even as he saw the smear of blood where Hud's third button had been.

With the shock of the bullet, Hud stepped back, but didn't fall. His face had gone from triumph to fear and now to determination. His Colt had stopped, in its rising arc, with the strike of Jack's bullet, but it hadn't lowered. Now, his jaws locked together, he summoned reserves to assist, and began raising the Colt again.

Jack waited, thinking, *Drop the gun. You may still have a chance to live. Drop the gun,* but he wouldn't. It continued up. Just before it leveled, Jack fired and saw the red bloom of the bullet strike to the right of the first. He immediately thumbed the hammer back and waited.

Hud did not fall, but the gun hung down by his leg. He muttered in a tone of disbelief, "I thought I was faster than you."

Jack started walking in. "We all think we're faster than the other man. Sometimes we're right."

Hud started bringing the Colt up again. Jack speeded his step, hoping to get close enough to grab the gun, but they were too far apart. Hud had placed his left hand under his right forearm and was lifting the revolver with both hands.

Jack yelled, "Drop the gun, Hud."

But he wouldn't do it. He almost had it level.

Jack fired again. The red bloom, this time, was just to the left of the first. Jack heard Hud moan with the strike of the bullet, and the ex-ranger, the bully, the almost gunfighter, dropped to his knees. He still held his weapon, but though his hand gripped it, the Colt lay in the dirt. As Jack neared, the revolver started moving toward him, the barrel leaving a track in the soft dirt like the track of a snake. Jack stopped in front of Hud, bent down, and yanked the Colt from the man's hand. He saw two notches cut in the butt. Hud was on his knees, in the middle of the Fredericksburg street, his head hanging, breaths rasping.

Jack turned away and walked to his horses. Major Wilson and

Cart stepped from the boardwalk. Jack handed the major the revolver he had taken from Hud. "He's dying."

Major Wilson took the weapon. "Jack, you had no choice."

Jack nodded. "I know."

Cart stepped closer. "Hoss, that feller's been lookin' for trouble. He prodded a farmer, just a few days ago, until the sodbuster drew. Hud killed him and then bragged about how fast he was. He was getting meaner and dangerous. This ain't your fault. You gave him what he deserved and saved some other innocent feller."

Jack untied the animals and, with Smokey's reins and the other leads in hand, swung into the saddle.

Major Wilson stepped off the boardwalk and placed his hand on Smokey's shoulder. "The sheriff's out of town, but I'll square it with him. We have plenty of witnesses. You don't have to worry."

"Much obliged." Jack touched his hat and turned Smokey out of town. He rode by Hud now lying on his side in the street. People had gathered round him to stare. They moved out of Jack's way as he passed. Fredericksburg was small, so he was out of town before he really noticed.

When he looked up, a red-tailed hawk circled lazily above him, and three mourning doves flashed by, gray, streamlined bullets. *Water,* he thought, *it's getting late. They'll be heading for water.* The low sun in the west burnished the tops of the Indian blankets, Mexican hats, and brown-eyed Susans, giving the swath of flowers a heavenly glow.

Jack patted Smokey on the neck as the animals walked along. "Heavenly, Smokey. I just killed a man, and I'm thinking heavenly." They continued west for a few more minutes while the sun drifted lower, and Jack pondered what he had said. He spoke to his grulla again. "Heavenly, now that would be nice. Maybe Hud and I will meet up there and shake hands. Yeah, I'd like that. We'll shake hands and laugh about it. Now wouldn't that be a hoot."

He reached up with one hand on the front of his hat brim, the other on the back, and leveled the gray, wide-brimmed, San Francisco hat just the way he liked it. He felt better. Most of the day had been good. Marlene and the other girls were home, and he was on Smokey's back, headed out of town, not lying in the dusty street leaking out his life's blood. All in all, the day had been mighty fine. He nodded to himself a couple of times and took a deep breath. The air smelled fresh and alive. "Head west, boys. That's as good a direction as any."

Follow Jack Sage as he rides into his next adventure.
Book 4:
THE HANGING STAR

AUTHOR'S NOTE

I hope you've enjoyed reading *Return of the Star,* the third book in the Jack Sage Western Series.

Thanks for reading my books. It is a true privilege to be able to share these stories with you.

Many people ask, "Where do you get the ideas for your books."

I usually tell them, "They just come to me." That's mostly true. But they come to me after a lifetime of experience and reading. That doesn't mean that you can't come up with an idea if you're twenty-eight, instead of eighty-two. It means that an author is a reader, and most are intense readers. Sometimes, when I'm deep into a story after two or three weeks, and I've neglected my reading, I will feel deprived. I have no statistics to back it up, but of all the writers I've spoken to, there are none who do not read for information, entertainment, education, or relaxation, most for all four. As you read, ideas will come to you. Jot them down. You never know when you might have the idea that is the seed for the next best seller.

If you have any comments, what you like or what you don't, please let me know. You can email me at: Don@DonaldLRobertson.com, or fill in the contact form on my website.

www.DonaldLRobertson.com

I'm looking forward to hearing from you.

BOOKS

A Jack Sage Western Series
STRANGER WITH A STAR
WITHOUT THE STAR
RETURN OF THE STAR
THE HANGING STAR

Logan Mountain Man Series
(Prequel to Logan Family Series)
SOUL OF A MOUNTAIN MAN
TRIALS OF A MOUNTAIN MAN
METTLE OF A MOUNTAIN MAN

Logan Family Series
LOGAN'S WORD
THE SAVAGE VALLEY
CALLUM'S MISSION
FORGOTTEN SEASON
TROUBLED SEASON
TORTURED SEASON

Clay Barlow - Texas Ranger Justice Series
FORTY-FOUR CALIBER JUSTICE
LAW AND JUSTICE
LONESOME JUSTICE

NOVELLAS AND SHORT STORIES
RUSTLERS IN THE SAGE
BECAUSE OF A DOG
THE OLD RANGER

Printed in Great Britain
by Amazon